DESIGNED FOR

Love

PRAISE FOR DESIGNED FOR LOVE

Designed for Love is charming, with a touch of humor and spunk. Pitts' happily ever after tale is one for your TBR list. Don't miss it.
—**Rachel Hauck**, New York Times Bestselling Author,

Fans of romance will love meeting interior designer Izzie Ketterling and her friends in the panhandle of Florida. You'll find yourself saying over and over, "this should be a Hallmark movie." With an authentic southern voice, an unforgettable setting, and colorful characters, I highly recommend *Designed for Love.*
—**Debra DuPree Williams,** author of *Grave Consequences, A Charlotte Graves Mystery*

Another Sally Jo Pitts story that delivers intrigue, hilarity, and romance intwined in a perfectly paced plot. A satisfying read from beginning to end.
—**Mary A. Felkins**, author of *Call to Love*

REVIEWERS ARE SAYING:

—*Designed for Love* needs to be a Hallmark Channel movie.

—Love, love the characters.

—The author has me wanting to move to small town Hamilton Harbor and mingle with its interesting characters.

—The characters were a delight to spend time with.

DESIGNED FOR

Sally Jo Pitts

Copyright Notice

Designed for Love—Book Three in the Hamilton Harbor Legacy series.

First edition. Copyright © 2020 by Sally Jo Pitts. The information contained in this book is the intellectual property of Sally Jo Pitts and is governed by United States and International copyright laws. All rights reserved. No part of this publication, either text or image, may be used for any purpose other than personal use. Therefore, reproduction, modification, storage in a retrieval system, or retransmission, in any form or by any means, electronic, mechanical, or otherwise, for reasons other than personal use, except for brief quotations for reviews or articles and promotions, is strictly prohibited without prior written permission by the publisher.

This is a work of fiction. Names, characters, businesses, places, events, locales, and incidents are either the products of the author's imagination or used in a fictitious manner. Any resemblance to actual persons, living or dead, or actual events is purely coincidental.

Scripture NIV or marked

Cover and Interior Design: Derinda Babcock

Editor(s): Cristel Phelps, Deb Haggerty

Map Design: Gracie Booth Wursthorn

Author Represented for the Hamilton Harbor Legacy Series by The Seymour Agency

PUBLISHED BY: Elk Lake Publishing, Inc., 35 Dogwood Drive, Plymouth, MA 02360, 2020

Library Cataloging Data

Names: Pitts, Sally Jo (Sally Jo Pitts)

Designed for Love—Book Three in the Hamilton Harbor Legacy series / Sally Jo Pitts

300 p. 23cm × 15cm (9in × 6 in.)

Identifiers: ISBN-13: 978-1-64949-077-3 (paperback) | 978-1-64949-078-0 (trade paperback) | 978-1-64949-079-7 (e-book)

Keywords: Romance, Beach Read, Small Town, Cozy, Christian, Interior Designers, Clean and Wholesome

LCCN: 2020946270 Fiction

🙞 🙞 🙞

Finally, brethren, whatsoever things are honest, whatsoever things are just, whatsoever things are pure, whatsoever things are lovely, whatsoever things are of good report; if there be any virtue and if there be any praise, think on these things. —Philippians 4:8 KJV

ACKNOWLEDGMENTS

First, I want to acknowledge the good Lord who nudges me to portray through fictional characters how prayer and reading His Word give vision, hope, and practical application to our daily lives.

Praise is due those who have poured over these pages to make them sound just right—editors Cristel Phelps and Deb Haggerty, content readers, Jennifer and Tommy Vaughan-Birch, and critique partner, Marcia Lahti.

Sincere thanks go to Susan May Warren and fellow Deep Thinkers for help in initial plotting; my late husband, LaVelle, for his patience and encouragement; and Elk Lake Publishing Inc., who believed in this project.

The Quaint Town of HAMILTON HARBOR

← Harbor Beach

- Harbor Town Bagel Bistro
- Southern Life Realty
- Hope Community Church
- The Pampered Pooch
- The Flower Cottage
- Historical Society
- Library
- City Hall
- Top of the Harbor Apartments
- Violet Feldman House
- Gardner Hamilton House
- Albert Feldman
- Hamilton Harbor Marina
- Pirates' Cove Motel

Davenport Plantation

ALLEY
MAIN STREET
1ST STREET
FLOWER LANE
FELDMAN AVENUE
2ND STREET
Feldman Park
BAY DRIVE
HARBOR LANE
HAMILTON AVENUE
HARBOR BAYOU
HAMILTON BAY
The Cove →

CHAPTER ONE

The urgent call came the night before.

"You've gotta be here tomorrow." Bagel shop owner Elaine Robinson's anxious voice surprised Izzie Ketterling.

After six weeks in Tallahassee helping her mom recuperate from shoulder surgery, Izzie was more than ready to get back home but hadn't expected to be needed at the Hamilton Harbor Commission meeting.

Not that Izzie had any special pull.

What she did have was gumption.

She could be counted on to take a stand. With the windows down on her Suburban, Izzie belted out the words to "Open Up the Heavens" along with the song on the radio. Mulling over downtown redevelopment concerns replaced her worry about passing the National Council for Interior Design Qualification test.

A half hour into the trip, she stopped worrying all together and enjoyed the colors of nature splashed on wild persimmon trees tucked among pine-scented evergreens. Crisp October air, so welcome after a hot summer in North Florida, swirled about her face. She fingered her hair, stiffened with hair gel. Earrings she'd fashioned out of golf tees clunked in the breeze.

On the outskirts of Hamilton Harbor, the bright red Tally-Ho Drive-In sign appeared to hang suspended in the gathering thunderclouds. Somebody must have finally located the bulbs to light up all the letters.

Throughout her high school years, the sign read, Tall O.

Eight years ago, tall zero could have made an appropriate label to hang on her.

If it weren't for her rearview mirror, she might have made it past Hamilton Harbor High School and the conflicting memories the building brought, but she couldn't help looking back.

The school's bigger-than-life wildcat mascot statue stood out front in its mundane tan coat with black stripes. Frozen in a muscular stance, his open mouth brandished sharp teeth to warn all rivals.

She still thought the mascot painted in the school colors of forest green with white spots looked better and made more sense. Principal Johnson and the 1957 alumni, who donated the replica, didn't have the same eye for school spirit. What she called creative, Mr. Johnson deemed vandalism. And then there was prom … another painful recollection she'd just as soon leave in the rearview mirror.

Her tummy grumbled a feed-me signal. Since she had some time to kill before meeting her friends at City Hall, she wheeled into the Tally-Ho parking lot.

"The town has become divided," Elaine had said. "The newspaper labeled the two factions oldies and newbies. We might be headed for a not-so-civil war. We need you to bridge the gap."

Imagine. Her, Izzie Ketterling, bridging a gap. In high school, she was more like a drawbridge stuck open, giving traffic no way to cross to either side. She was neither a student from old aristocracy with all the right connections nor from the new money on the beach side of town.

"I don't know about me, an apartment dweller from the blighted neighborhood on Feldman Park, being a bridge."

"I know. But you work in both worlds."

Izzie opined, "True."

One world lay across the long bridge that linked

Hamilton Harbor to Harbor Beach. There, high-rise condos and sherbet-colored beach houses overlooked pristine white sands and green Gulf waters.

Amidst heavy wallpaper books, paint swatches with exotic names, multi-textured flooring samples, and bolts of crisp fabrics came the call, "Give me something beachy. I want a comfortable place to sit in my second home, away from CEO obligations, and watch the magnificent sunrises and sunsets." Those out-of-state interior design clients didn't know or care about her past, only about what she could do to make their beach dwellings amazing getaways from their own pasts.

Her other world lay on the bay side of the bridge in historic downtown Hamilton Harbor. She lived and worked part-time in the Flower Cottage on Feldman Square, just off Main Street. In this area, she'd developed her own unique melting-pot style as individual as each of the tenants she grew up around. This was the location that sparked her spirit and held her soul. The place she called home.

"Financially. I'm trapped between the two realms, with both tugging in opposite directions. But downtown holds my heart."

"That's why you're perfect to champion the cause for the oldies."

"Just remember, I'm the girl voted most likely to talk herself into and out of trouble."

"I remember. And I'm voting you the girl most likely to plead our case to include historical restoration in the city's redevelopment project."

She still wasn't convinced she was the right spokesperson, but she'd worry about that later. Right now, the smells of Tally-Ho fries and their time-honored grilled burgers beckoned. Besides, she could use a break after the two-hour drive from Tallahassee. As she stepped out of her car, two seagulls screeched and swooped down at her feet, competing for the French fries tossed out of a car parked nearby.

"Hey. Can't you read?" Zelda, the faithful waitress, shouted at the French fry throwers. She balanced a tray of burgers, fries, and drinks in one hand, while pointing to the bold letters painted on the wall underneath the Curb Service sign. "Don't feed the birds means don't feed the birds unless you want poop in your food." Zelda wore a red Tally-Ho T-shirt, jeans, and an apron with pockets on a figure kept slim by carting food orders to cars for as long as Izzie could remember. She strode to the car on Izzie's right and anchored the tray on the car window.

"Hi, Zel. Some things never change, huh?"

Zelda plunked napkins and straws on the customer's tray and waved. "Long time no see."

"Been in Tallahassee. Can you order my usual?" Izzie tossed her request to Zelda on her way to the restroom.

"Fries, crisp like potato chips and a burger heavy on the pickles, light on the mustard, half Coke-half Sprite, heavy on the ice." Zelda hollered Izzie's standard as she scribbled down the order.

"You've got a first-rate memory."

"Shug, some orders, just like people, are unforgettable." Zelda gave her a wink.

In the restroom, Izzie washed her hands and attempted to rub out the grease spot on her yellow capris decorated with orange tassels on the hem. A piece of sausage from her on-the-go breakfast had landed in her lap earlier. Her efforts turned the postage stamp stain into the size of a lunch plate. Great. She'd be sporting an unforgettable look at the commission meeting. She gave up and tossed the wet paper towel in the trash.

Outside, a silver compact car had pulled in beside her, giving her only inches to open her car door. Izzie cracked her door open, turned sideways and tried to wiggle in.

Whoosh.

A seagull dove, hitting her hand. Izzie swatted the bird away. The bird, wings flapping, shot into the silver car's open window.

"Hey ... what ... shoo ..."

The bird screeched, then escaped out the driver's window. Izzie unwedged herself from the door and poked her head through the passenger window of the silver car.

"You okay?"

The guy in the driver's seat sat stunned. He was a study in handsomeness marred only slightly by the straw on his shoulder and drink lid perched atop his head. The spilled drink had created splatter art on his suit pants and shirt.

Wordlessly, he reached for his door handle and stepped out of his car. Ice cubes clattered to the pavement. Izzie closed her door and circled his car. Zelda reached him at the same time she did and handed him some napkins.

"Good thing you ordered water. I'll get you another drink right away."

Izzie grabbed napkins from Zelda's apron before she left. She brushed ice from the driver's seat and tried soaking up the excess water, then turned to face piercing, near-black eyes. The irked driver had slicked back hair and stood a good three inches taller than her five-foot-nine. He looked like he could play at least second string on a decent college football team.

"What were you thinking?"

"Wha ... excuse me?" She stared at his brow knit into a scowl.

"Why did you shove that bird into my car?"

"You think I did it on purpose?"

"You tell me."

This guy might be long on looks, but he was definitely short on civility. "For your information, I was trying to get into my car without touching yours. You didn't exactly leave me much room."

He raised one brow, walked around the rear of his car, and inspected the distance between the cars.

"Plenty of room where I come from."

"And that would be some wee little kingdom in …" she glanced at the license plate, "… Mississippi? I have every confidence your fellow Mississippians would call this too close." She pointed to the space between the cars.

He circled his car and inspected the passenger side. "You scratched my car."

"I most certainly did not."

He stooped down to inspect the passenger door. "There. A scratch that wasn't there before."

"I was squished trying to get in my car without touching yours." Izzie straightened. "Hold up. I've heard of this before—accusing someone of damage already on your car."

If his look had substance, it would have shot arrows, very sharp ones, in her direction. He pulled out his cell phone and punched in three numbers.

"Reed Harrison. I need you to send a police car to work a car damage incident."

Zelda walked up behind him, drink in hand.

He turned, waved the drink she offered away and asked, "What's the name of this place?"

"Tally-Ho."

A horn blew.

He frowned and repeated the restaurant name as if the words tasted bad. "No. No injuries."

Zelda left, carrying the drink. Mr. Reed Harrison

finished his call.

"You have got to be kidding me. You called 911?"

He shrugged and pocketed his phone.

"You might as well take a closer look. Maybe my car door came unhinged and dinged yours somewhere else."

He paused at the back of his car. "Don't go anywhere until the police get here."

Izzie fisted her hands on her hips. "Fine. Just see that you don't move either. I want the police to see just how close you parked." She stomped over to the passenger side of her car, got in and slammed the door.

Zelda brought out Izzie's order, hooked the tray to the passenger window and leaned against her car door.

"Don't worry. Some people are picky. These things happen. It won't be the first time we've had to deal with car door dents."

Izzie crunched a crispy fry and sneaked a look in her foe's direction. "But my door didn't touch his. I defended myself from a bird attack."

Zelda smiled. "You stick to that story."

Izzie's heart cranked up a few beats. "Story? You think I scratched his car and won't own up to it?"

"No. Not me. Some might … maybe more than some might, but—"

"Zel. You know what? You may think you're helping, but you're not."

"Just sayin'." Another horn honked. Zelda shrugged and went to check on her customer. The gray thundercloud overhead decided to release heavy raindrops that hit the tray attached to her window and sprayed her in the face.

"Just sayin'," Izzie muttered.

Even after eight years, she was proof that it's hard for people to forget a checkered past. Would she ever be taken seriously in her own hometown?

DESIGNED FOR *LOVE*

🏠 🏠 🏠 🏠

Reed stood under the overhang at the Tally-Ho Drive-In and watched the second hand on his watch make another round. What possessed him to stop at a place like this to begin with? The short-lived rainstorm had come and gone, leaving steam rising from the hot pavement.

He stole a look at the car parked beside his with the striking girl inside. Striking in more ways than one. He huffed a snort-laugh at the notion. She seemed the type who could be just as comfortable featured on the cover of *Glamour* magazine as she might on the *Hit & Miss Roller Derby Magazine,* he'd seen in the Memphis airport during his layover on the flight from New York.

He had about an hour and a half to resolve this matter. Unfortunately, if he was to get any satisfaction on the damage, he had to go through this process. And if what he understood of the South held any truth, the process would be slow-moving.

The black and white police cruiser pulled in the parking lot, and Reed motioned to him. The policeman parked and got out, adjusting his gun belt.

"What seems to be the trouble here?"

"Damage to my car. I want to file a complaint."

He'd barely started explaining the situation when glamour-roller-derby-girl sprung from her car and strode over on three-inch wedge heeled sandals.

"Jeff," she addressed the officer, then pointed an accusatory finger at Reed. "He started all this when he parked too close to me."

Jeff? She's on a first name basis with this policeman? "I take it, you two know each other."

"He's married to my former college roommate."

Great. Were his chances for a fair hearing doomed?

The officer reached out his hand to Reed. "Jeff Robinson. I've known Izzie here for quite a long time."

Izzie. This outspoken girl, dressed in canary yellow capris with orange tassel trim more suitable for throw pillows, was named Izzie. He'd never met an Izzie.

Officer Robinson reached in his car and pulled out a pen and report form, attaching it to a clipboard. He seemed level-headed. Maybe he could get a fair assessment.

"I'll take down your complaint first. Name?"

"Harrison, Reed Harrison."

Officer Robinson wrote.

"Don't I get a say in this?" Izzie asked and cut eyes filled with venom toward him.

"After I talk to Mr. Harrison, then I'll hear from you."

"Whatever happened to ladies first?" Izzie huffed.

The officer remained stone-faced and walked over to inspect the damage Reed pointed to.

"So," Robinson said, "you believe her car door did the damage when she was getting into her car?"

"I didn't do it. The bird did it." Izzie said.

"After she batted it through my window." Stupid to argue, but the girl seemed to draw out the worst in him.

Officer Robinson raised his hand. "One at a time. Izzie, you stand over here." Robinson pointed to a spot behind her car. "Let me get his statement, then I'll talk to you."

"Fine. That's when you'll get the *real* story." She moved to the spot the officer directed. Reed noticed a "Follow me to Hope Community Church" bumper sticker on her car. She crossed her arms and said, "He. Parked. Too. Close."

This policeman was a master ignorer.

"Your address?"

"1056 G Street, New York, New York."

Izzie interrupted. "New York? But your tag—"

DESIGNED FOR *Love*

Reed didn't have the ignore technique of the officer. "I'm driving a rental car."

After Reed answered a few additional questions, the officer said, "Now tell me what happened."

"I arrived, placed my order, the waitress had just delivered my drink when this girl walks between our cars, starts to get in her car then reaches up and swats a bird flying over and flings him into my lap. Either the startled bird or her car door scratched my car. I don't want to have to pay for something somebody else did."

"I was defending myself from a crazed bird." She added foot tapping to her crossed arm posture.

Don't respond. "The bird wouldn't have been crazed, if you hadn't walloped him." His words made a surprise appearance.

"Please. Hold your comments." Officer Robinson had patience of gold.

A chubby man with a mop of wild dirty-blond curls, dressed in a blue work shirt unable to cover his ample belly, walked up and spoke to Izzie.

Reed checked his watch again. An anxious tingle shot through him. He couldn't be late. Officer Robinson continued filling out his report. If only he hadn't pulled into this wacky place. "I need a record of the accident and—"

Blue shirt spoke up. "Excuse me, Jeff, I don't mean to butt in, but if it's just a scratch like Izzie says, I can buff it out in a jiffy."

"Hi, Rusty," Robinson said. Then to Reed, "He's the best auto-body man around. Mind if he takes a look?"

Did everybody know each other in this town? Not likely there were many auto-body guys to choose from. "I guess not. I have a meeting to attend."

"Sure. I'll get pictures. Then get Izzie's statement."

Reed watched as Rusty—fine name for an auto-body repairman—inspected his passenger door. The slogan imprinted on his shirt read—We Meet by Accident.

"Ain't nothin' to this. Have it rubbed out in no time."

Rusty looked at the water-spattered rental car paperwork Reed lifted from his front seat.

"I know Susan from that rental company. Got her on speed dial. Want to get her approval?"

"I suppose if—"

He punched a number on his flip phone while Officer Robinson snapped shots of the vehicles. Was he in the midst of some kind of small-town insurance scam?

"Susan, me, Rusty, got a nothin' scratch on a silver Honda Accord rental. Yeah. Easy buff out. Uh-huh, right here."

Rusty pressed his phone to Reed's ear. "She wants to talk to you."

Susan was saying, "... talk to him."

"Hello?"

"The silver Accord ... are you Mr. Harrison?"

"Right."

"You purchased the insurance, so if Rusty's there and can take care of it, that's fine. We'd send the Honda to him for repair anyhow."

"Okay, but I have to be at a meeting in—"

"Ask Rusty, I'm sure he can get you there."

Ms. Outspoken straightened from her slouched position against the rear of her car. "What about me having my say? He's not the only one with a meeting." Izzie complained to Officer Robinson while Reed handed the phone back to Rusty.

"I'll get your statement, but we might as well let him drive to Rusty's garage." The officer used his pen as a pointer. "Rusty's shop is just one street over. Will that handle your concerns satisfactorily?"

"As long as I can make it to my meeting."

"No problem," Rusty said. "You can leave your car at the shop and I'll git ya' where you need to go."

Zelda arrived with a food tray. "Here's your order. Want this hooked on your window?" she asked Reed.

"I don't have time now."

"I'd be glad to bag it up for you."

"No. I'm not hungry now. Here, this should cover everything." Reed plunked a twenty-dollar bill on the tray.

"No, siree. No charge."

"Take it as a tip then for your trouble."

"Thanks, but you keep it, doll-face. We want you to come back when you are hungry." Zelda stuffed the bill into his shirt pocket, wiggled her finger in front of his chest, winked, and hurried off to a car with its lights on.

"Follow me," Rusty said. "I'm in the blue truck yonder, with boxes on the back."

Reed followed the direction his finger was pointing. The truck wasn't just blue, it sparkled with a fancy finish that shimmered. The eye-catching shine looked suitable for an evening dress, but a truck?

"I'd like a copy of that report when you're finished," Reed said as he climbed into his car.

"It will be at the police department."

Reed cranked his car and backed out. Rusty waved at him to follow. Was this what was meant by Southern hospitality? Or was this called getting hoodwinked in the South?

CHAPTER TWO

"You know it could have been those earrings that started all this," Zelda said.

Jeff arched a brow.

"What are you talking about?" Izzie asked.

"Those orange golf tee earrings. I bet they looked like French fries to that poor seagull."

"Like I'm out here tempting seagulls, and it's my fault?"

"Just a thought."

Izzie scowled. "Yeah, well, some thoughts don't need to make it to the light of day."

Jeff allowed his cop face to crack a smile. "I'll leave a copy of this report for you at the police station."

Jeff returned to his police car and pulled out.

"How about I put in a fresh order for you?" Zelda asked.

"To make up for accusing me of starting this whole affair?"

"Hey. I take pride in bringing my customers food, fast and hot."

"I'll give you that. You're a master at juggling customers in and out of here." Izzie glanced at her watch. "I'd better get going. I'm supposed to be at City Hall for a commission meeting."

Izzie slid into her car and fished out a ten-dollar bill as Zelda removed the tray from the passenger window. "Here you are, Zel."

"Keep it. No charge for cold food."

"But—"

"No arguments. I hate you had such a tough time." She leaned in and lowered her voice. "But seriously, you might not want to wear those earrings around here again." She winked and hurried off to another customer.

Izzie's stomach grumbled as she pulled from the Tally-Ho parking lot. She popped a salty, limp fry in her mouth and was treated to grease-flavored mush that formed a lump in her throat. She washed it down with a watery soft drink. Her car held the tart smell of the extra pickles that had soaked into the soggy hamburger bun. She closed the wrapper over the burger and pushed the food aside.

"Thank you, Mr. Handsome-but-irritating, Reed Harrison."

What kind of person calls 911 over a scratch? One who wears a suit and tie to a drive-in burger joint? Weird.

It's like he dropped in from another world—which might be accurate of a New Yorker. Hopefully, he completes his business and leaves. It wouldn't be good to have his "don't give anyone a break" attitude rub off on folks here. Anyhow, she had other concerns. Best she stopped stewing over the incident with "doll-face."

She slowed as she came to the five-block section of old downtown Hamilton Harbor, established in 1913. Many of the shops had been abandoned to ride the wave that carried them to the new mall or shopping centers north of town. But Main Street was reawakening as if it had been asleep. She drove past Appleberry's Furniture store where she operated her interior design business from a desk squeezed into Olivia Appleberry's office. A law office, bank, and antique shop had opened in remodeled spaces. Most recent renovations were those of her college roommates—Claudia's Pampered Pooch and Elaine's Harbor Town Bagel Bistro.

Intermixed with these restored buildings were empty

buildings, some closed for years, others reopened a short time and reclosed. There was the old boarded up Regina Hotel that stood as a reminder of five-star lodging and fine dining once offered in town.

At the end of the block, before Main Street yielded to the marina jutting out into the salty bay waters, was her church, Hope Community, housed in the old Ritz movie theater.

City Hall loomed ahead at the end of Main Street, sitting on the site of an old manmade landfill. The two-story building carried all the design attributes of a milk carton. It had been considered a modern building thirty years ago, along with a string of deserted, box-like office units that marched down the center of the marina. Boat slips lined either side of the area, with a sea wall and guard rail at the very end bordering the bay.

The city commission was considering redeveloping the marina area. Elaine said the Downtown Reconstruction Board, an arm of the Hamilton Harbor Historical Society, wanted to be included in any design proposals.

From the looks of the parking lot, there were lots of others interested in the hearing.

Izzie found a place to park and hurried to find Elaine and the others.

"Izzie, over here." Elaine called from near the glass door entry. Claudia and Emme were with her.

"I just had an interesting encounter with your husband," Izzie said.

"In his official capacity as a law enforcement officer?"

"It involves a seagull ..." She threw up her hands. "Never mind ... I'll explain later. I'm just glad to be here." Izzie watched as a steady stream of people entered City Hall. "Gee whiz. From the looks of things, you were right. This meeting is creating quite a stir."

"Yes. And I must warn you, the two factions are solidifying," Elaine said.

"The newbies are advocating 'out with the old and in with the new,'" Claudia said. "According to them, they are forward thinking, and the oldies are clinging to old, outdated, backward thinking."

Izzie stiffened. "I don't call safeguarding our heritage backward. You don't toss out the very foundation that shaped and brought this community into existence."

Emme, owner of The Flower Cottage, smiled and nodded. "Preach it, Izzie."

"It's the truth. The commission has a chance to right a wrong. The tacky stuff built on the marina matches nothing of the town's character."

"Well put." Claudia said. "That's why you're the perfect one to speak for historical preservation as a key to redevelopment."

Izzie pushed her face into a grimace. "I hope someone else will voice our concerns. Remember, I'm not viewed as a real credible source by some."

"You're still uptight about high school stuff?" Elaine said.

"Face it. I'm branded."

Emme wagged an index finger at Izzie. "Would you stop and listen to yourself? You are a sought-after interior designer."

"On the beach, maybe. I have no past with the out-of-towners."

"This is no time to argue." Elaine held out her arms behind the little group and herded them toward the entrance. "Just keep an open mind about standing up for our cause if things start to go south."

Izzie shrugged, sucked in air, and puffed out a prayer. "Lord, I pray we only need to provide an amen corner."

"Amen to that," Elaine said. "Come on. You need to see the preliminary plans to be discussed. They are showcased on screens in the commission meeting room."

Inside, the commission room teemed with people chatting, pointing at the displays on the screens, laughing, and studying agenda sheets.

Ed Blackburn, president of the yacht club, had two commissioners cornered. Loretta Huggins, the Historical Society president, stood on the opposite side of the room speaking to two other commissioners.

"Claudia and Emme, commandeer seats for us in the back." Elaine said.

Izzie zigzagged through the crowd behind Elaine. The sketches on display included a band shell, an outdoor amphitheater, pavilion, and civic center. There was also space allotted for a yacht club, signature restaurant, and lighthouse at the end with proposed future boat storage and a hotel shaded in.

"What's with the lighthouse? Won't it be in the way of fishing?"

"This is a mockup of another Emerson project. It's a sample of the kind of work they do."

"Well lovely, but I think they should be showing us what they propose to do in Hamilton Harbor."

"That's why we wanted you here." Elaine said. "You don't mind speaking up."

"I leave town six weeks, and everything goes nuts?" Izzie teased.

"Oh my gosh, Izzie. I'm so centered on this stuff I didn't think to ask. I'm sorry. How's your mom, and how did you do on your test?"

"That's okay. Mom's doing great, and I don't have the test results yet, but my study review went well. Receiving the National Council for Interior Design certification will be quite an achievement—if I pass."

"Think positive. Will the new classification mean you'll be too busy to continue helping Emme at the Flower Cottage?"

"When she needs me, I'll be there like Batman's Robin … or is it Batgirl? Anyhow, give me a feel for what the newbies are pushing."

"They are excited about several of the Emerson ideas, but want things patterned more after the Oceanside development on Paramount Beach in Palmetto County. That project is state-of-the-art from the ground up. Ed Blackburn is spearheading that crusade."

Elaine pulled out the editorial page from her purse and handed it to Izzie. "And when I say the ground up, they basically propose tearing down all the dilapidated buildings and rebuilding downtown Hamilton Harbor, including the houses bordering the bay side on Feldman Square."

Izzie's eyes widened. "You're kidding."

"It's time to begin. Everyone, please sit down," the mayor announced over the PA system. The commissioners began taking their seats with the mayor seated in the center.

"Some on this commission would just as soon obliterate over ten decades of the town's history as if it never existed," Elaine said as she and Izzie moved behind others taking seats on the pew-type benches. Izzie responded in a hoarse whisper. "That ain't gonna happen."

Mayor Brimstead rapped the desk with his gavel. "We are grateful for the good turnout today. Let's bring this meeting to order."

After the minutes of the prior meeting were read and approved, the mayor moved on with the current day's agenda. The tension in the room hung like a heavy rain cloud.

"Any room on this bench?" Izzie looked up to see Pastor

Creighton.

"Sure." Izzie and the others scooted to squeeze in an extra seat.

Elaine leaned over Izzie to speak to the pastor. "I believe the crowd is heavily weighted on the Blackburn side. We may need some heavenly intervention." Then, nudging Izzie, Elaine added, "And help from Batgirl too."

🏠 🏠 🏠 🏠

"Here ya' go," Rusty said as they arrived in a truck Reed was surprised made it to City Hall. They chugged to a stop. "Worked out just right. You're only ten minutes late."

Reed's neck muscles tightened. "Thanks for the ride."

"Sure thing. I have to tell Harley to check his plugs. Give me a call when you're finished." He thrust a grease-streaked business card into Reed's hand.

Reed stepped out from the Chevy truck with a motley maze of sandblasted sections of brown and green belonging to Harley, Rusty's paint prep man.

"After Harley unloads my truck, I'll git right on that scratch. Wouldn't ya' know my buffing supplies would be on the bottom? Have 'er done in a jiffy."

What was the time range of a "jiffy?"

Reed thrust the business card in his suit pocket, grabbed his briefcase, forced a smile, and pushed the truck door closed. The old truck belched a puff of burnt oil fumes when Rusty pulled away from the curb.

Reed shuddered. Harley's truck proved to need a lot more than a paint job.

If the controlling partners at Emerson, Emerson, and Padgett could see him arriving late for this meeting, his ladder-climbing days in the design section of the company would take a downward spiral. The powers that be might decide the risk was greater than the benefits of allowing him to present a proposal for this or any other redevelopment project.

As he hurried to the glass doors of City Hall, he tamped down the fear of messing up his presentation. But then there was the fear the scratch on the door of his rental car might end up buffed down to the base coat, and he'd be held responsible.

Reed followed the commission meeting directional signs, picked up an agenda, and entered the packed room. A man wearing a priest's collar motioned him to take his seat on the back row.

Reed mouthed his thanks but shook his head.

The minister stood. "Please. I've been sitting too much. I'm ready to stretch my legs."

Religious sorts were interested in redevelopment? Was that a good or bad sign? "Really, I …"

A man turned with a frown.

Reed accepted the seat rather than cause a disturbance.

Squeezing onto the bench, Reed dropped the agenda sheet. When he stooped to pick it up, the color orange caught his eye. Orange tassels, to be exact. On the hem of yellow pants. Couldn't be.

He sat up abruptly and stared into the gray eyes of the subject of his police complaint.

"This was the meeting you had to attend?" she asked.

He creased his brows. "Yes. And I suppose your meeting too?"

"Why would a New Yorker want to attend a Hamilton Harbor commission meeting?"

Her question was a repeat of his when Vance Padgett assigned him to present Emerson's request to conduct a feasibility study for the Hamilton Harbor marina development.

He didn't owe her an explanation but remaining silent didn't seem right. "Business."

She shrugged. "Is the scratch fixed?" Her eyes narrowed. "That I wasn't responsible for, by the way."

Another man seated in front of them turned his head and gave them a "be quiet" scowl.

Reed shook his head and mouthed, *tell you later*.

The straight-back wooden bench hardened as he listened to a request from a garden club woman for matching funds of $250 to put up a billboard for the annual Clean-up, Paint-up, Fix-up campaign. The commission, comprised of four commissioners and the mayor, gave her a favorable vote.

Five hundred-dollar billboards? He pinched the bridge of his nose. If only he could be back behind his desk in his cubicle in New York working on lighting layouts for a hospital cafeteria or a library.

His plan had been to fly into town, rent a car, request the feasibility study, evaluate the pros and cons voiced on the project, fly back, and report. Instead, he sat scrunched on a bench next to a golf-tee-adorned, wild-bird-tossing woman, with his rental car having goodness knows what done to it.

Izzie pointed to the next item, Waste Separation and Disposal, and whispered, "Is that your business?" She wiggled her brows. Was she flirting or making fun of him?

"And if it is?"

"Maybe we'll both learn something."

A short, slight man with a neatly trimmed fringe of black hair decorating his bald head went to the speaker's lectern. Reed listened to an impassioned presentation on the merits of recycling refuse.

The speaker recommended the city move forward on

the purchase of residential recycling bins. A motion passed to investigate pricing. Two approvals. Good. With the commission on a roll, maybe they'd look at his presentation favorably.

"More to garbage than I thought." Izzie whispered to Reed. She tapped the knee of the woman sitting next to her. "Now, what we're here for."

The mayor said, "The commission will now hear from the chairman of the committee for the downtown marina redevelopment. Commissioner Taylor, what do you have to report?"

The commissioner began speaking, and someone in a dark suit hollered, "We can't hear you."

Scooting nearer to his microphone, he continued. "A call for proposals was sent out in January with a deadline for submissions in May. Of the five submitted, three were selected to present detailed plans. They are Hargrave Developers, Atlanta; Bonnevilla and Banks, Jacksonville; and the New York firm of Emerson, Emerson, and Padgett. Their written submissions are posted on the commission website. The New York firm sent preliminary sample sketches, which we had on display before the meeting, and there is supposed to be a representative here to speak before the commission today. If that representative is here," he peered over his glasses into the audience, "would he please come forward?"

Show time. Curious eyes searched the room. Reed straightened his tie and stood. Did that gasp come from Izzie? He brushed damp palms against his slacks and hoped the water spilled in his lap earlier had dried sufficiently. He grabbed his briefcase and approached the lectern.

Click.

The sound of the briefcase lock opening broadcasted over the PA system followed by the rustling of paper. He should have removed the proposal file beforehand.

Reed cleared his dry throat and began reading remarks, once memorized, but now looking foreign to him.

"Our development firm understands the City of Hamilton Harbor's goal is to balance the public's access to its waterfront resources with economic activity to stimulate jobs and investment for your downtown area.

"Since our firm is in the business of meeting needs, we wanted to earn your trust by showing you a similar project on a bay harbor in Maine. We, of course, would need to adapt the concept to your town. Because of this, my firm sent me to gain approval for an in-depth feasibility study. This will be at our expense and does not obligate you to accept our proposal. The study will give us the opportunity, if approved, to produce a detailed plan tailored to your community."

He made it. Reed blew out a short breath and gave a nod to the mayor that he'd finished.

"Thank you, Mr. Harrison. If you would take a seat there by the lectern, we'll open the floor to discussion."

Reed sat down, grateful for the opportunity to rest his wobbly knees.

A tall man, dressed in a knit shirt and slacks perfectly suited for a golf course, stood and walked to the speaker's lectern.

"State your name for the record."

"Ed Blackburn."

"Mayor, commissioners. I would like to encourage you to accept this offer. Even though the sketch they sent was a project in Maine, the marina development process would be similar to ours. I like the idea that they have experience with bulkheads and, of course, the fact they made space for a yacht club."

A titter floated over the room.

DESIGNED FOR *Love*

Blackburn turned to Reed, "I hope your people prioritize a yacht club. We have a strong membership. Nothing against the Clean-Up, Paint-Up, Fix-up group, as its brand new buildings bring a fresh look that will bring beneficial growth to this town. I'm in favor of the commission approving the Emerson study."

Wow. Reed returned a congenial nod to Mr. Blackburn. He should be on E, E, & P's payroll.

A woman stepped slowly to the microphone, her stature straight, confident. She spoke clearly.

"Loretta Huggins," she gave a nod to the girl transcribing the minutes, "for the record, Lucy."

"Yes, ma'am," the girl responded.

"Commissioners, fellow citizens, and …" she turned her head in acknowledgment, "Mr. Harrison. I am a retired history teacher—"

"All Hamilton Harbor High graduates know that," someone called out from the center of the room. There were snickers and nods from the audience.

She raised a brow at the interruption. "—and current president of the historical society. I have grave concerns because this young man," she nodded in his direction, "has made no mention of maintaining the integrity of history in our town. I appreciate the comparison to a harbor town in the sample they have sent us to review, but these sketches and plans give us no hint that they would tap into our heritage. I am concerned that Emerson's delving into our existing situation is premature until the commission compiles unified input from all the developers. Before voting on Mr. Harrison's request, I would like a statement included from the downtown marina redevelopment committee stating they will include a way to honor our downtown history and celebrate its future."

Substantial applause erupted.

Commissioner Robert Hunter responded, "You have a valid point. Gentlemen, I don't want to set the New York firm loose to start a study until they know the consensus of the community."

"Bob," the commissioner whose name plate read John Philmore spoke from the opposite end of the dais, "how's he gonna know the consensus of the community unless we let him do his feasibility study?"

The comment received some "yeah" responses and a smattering of handclaps.

"Mr. Harrison," Commissioner Philmore said, "Am I to understand that your purpose is to explore the community and assess the people's opinions?"

Reed stood. "Yes, sir."

"Please approach the lectern," the mayor said, "to be heard for the record."

Ms. Huggins stepped aside.

Reed leaned forward and spoke into the mic. "That is correct."

To Ms. Huggins still at the lectern, the mayor said, "He's on notice that you want the historical society's input. You had another matter to address?"

"I do. I want to commend the Hamilton sisters for giving the historical society the use of the old private school house on Feldman Square. In addition, they have donated Feldman Park and sections of property behind the restored Feldman and Hamilton houses for a running trail."

"Their vision is to restore the Gardner Hamilton home and the city's first garden club next to it to be used as a maternity home and a pregnancy resource center.

"Since the Feldman Square properties border the city marina and downtown, I propose this project be included in the marina redevelopment plans."

Mr. Blackburn shot up. "Mayor, may I say something?"

"Step to the lectern."

"I concede the generosity of the Hamilton sisters, but frankly, the old schoolhouse is shabby. There's a nice sign out front, but the shrubs are overgrown, and the paint's peeling," He turned to Ms. Huggins who had taken a seat beside Reed. "I think they're hoping you'll fix it up for them. And those vacant houses she's referring to are rundown eyesores with back taxes due. About the only thing those empty houses are good for might be haunted houses for Halloween."

"Hold up." Reed turned, along with everyone else, toward the back of the room. Izzie. "I'd like to say something."

"Step to the lectern. State your name."

Izzie walked in long strides to the lectern. Her spiky black hair matched her spry spirit.

"Mr. Blackburn may have something. We won't have time to set up haunted houses, but with the fall festival only days away, we could clean up around the old schoolhouse, add a museum tour and charge admission. We already have publicity that will bring people out for the pumpkin carving and pumpkin walk fundraisers. It would be a snap to add a historical tour. Money raised could be designated for the Save the Square fund and should take care of the back taxes." Izzie shot a determined look straight at Blackburn.

"Why not get with Ms. Huggins on the idea," the mayor said. Ms. Huggins nodded.

"No problem." Izzie turned to Reed, "Mr. Harrison, mark this down. Feldman Square is a major part of Hamilton Harbor's history and should be included in your project plans."

Blackburn poked himself back in front of the lectern, "This chit chat is all lovely, but may I make one more point before you vote?"

"One," the mayor said.

"For purposes of redevelopment as I'm sure this young man will agree," he pointed a finger in Reed's direction, "the property will be worth a lot more if those old abandoned houses are torn down and removed."

Reed didn't miss the glare Izzie sent to Blackburn's back. This meeting was turning into a cauldron of near boiling water, and he was feeling the heat.

"Mayor, I move we approve the feasibility study by Emerson, Emerson, and Padgett," commissioner Philmore said, "with the understanding that City Attorney Brewster draw up an agreement that spells out the fact we are not obligated to award the redevelopment project to them and that their study will be at no cost to the city.

"Second."

"Discussion?"

Loretta raised her hand and returned to the lectern. She pointed a bony index finger, powered with the authority of a former teacher, at Reed. He adjusted his collar.

"Make no mistake, young man. We may be a small town, but we understand you're in business to make money and will make up these study costs." She turned to the commission. "Say what you will, allowing any one company to do a study before the submission deadline seems to give unfair advantage to the others still working on their proposals. I don't like it."

"If they are working to make a plan that meets our interests and concerns, what's not to like?" Blackburn said.

Reed stood and moved to the lectern. "If I might speak? Ma'am, Mr. Blackburn is correct. You will benefit from our ideas even if we aren't chosen to do the redevelopment, and you pay nothing. If you award us the contract, the study's cost will simply be a part of the project cost, which any developer would charge. We just offer to do it up front, so we can do a better job for you."

With two opposing views rapidly taking shape, the commission voted for Emerson, Emerson, and Padgett to conduct the feasibility study. But what had looked like a dream project was turning into a nightmare.

CHAPTER THREE

"He's the one." Izzie, the center of attention, had Elaine, Emme, and Claudia grouped around her.

"Who's the one?" Emme asked.

"The one who called 911 on me."

"You mean the seagull incident Jeff worked?" Elaine asked.

"Seagull?" Emme's brow wrinkled.

Izzie folded her arms and nodded. "Yep, the same."

"Hey, Claudia and I are in the dark here," Emme said.

"Mr. Harrison." Izzie dipped her head toward Reed amid a huddle formed by Blackburn and some of his cronies. "He accused me of scratching his car at the Tally-Ho and called 911. Jeff took an incident report."

Elaine chuckled. "Poor Jeff. How did my super-cop husband handle the situation?"

"Rusty, the auto-body guy, happened to be there. Jeff negotiated the issue by having Rusty fix the scratch."

"That's my man."

"At least Jeff's reasonable. I'm still steamed this guy called the cops on me."

"Well, put it behind you. Livelihoods are on the line. We can't have Blackburn influencing him," Emme said.

Izzie rolled her eyes and puffed out air. "I'm afraid you're counting on the wrong person for help."

"Hey. Give it the old college try and all that good stuff." Claudia said.

"Ah, for the good old days when all we had to worry

about was going to class and figuring out what the teacher thought was important enough to put on a test."

"Speaking of tests, you need to fill me in on your interior design test," Emme said. "But right now, I'm off to the flower shop. Mellie has a hair appointment."

"Will do."

The others patted Izzie on the back as they made their exits too.

Now what? Like it or not, she had to mend fences with Mr. Reed Harrison. Should she be bold and interrupt the men's party?

Ms. Huggins beat her to it. She approached the men's conclave, her voice easily heard.

"Young man, I thank you for coming and want to reiterate the importance of our town's history. Mr. Blackburn, you keep comparing us to that Oceanside development in neighboring Palmetto County."

Blackburn's eyes widened, and he took a step back.

She didn't give him a chance to speak. "I'd like to point out they are building on virgin land. Hamilton Harbor is an established town with a dramatic history."

Reed spoke up. "I'll see that the study team interviews you at the historical society. Your input is important."

"Fine. Here's my card."

Ms. Huggins left him and headed toward Izzie. She could teach lessons on working a room.

"Izzie Ketterling."

"Yes, ma'am." Izzie straightened her shoulders, then relaxed. She wasn't being called out for talking in class.

"You surprised me. I'm very pleased with your taking a stand, and your suggestion for fundraising at the fall festival. I look forward to working with you."

"Thanks." Affirmation from Ms. Huggins? She needed to mark this day down. "I'll meet with you tomorrow?"

Ms. Huggins agreed and left, while Blackburn and his cohorts persisted in talking to Reed. Calling the police on her or not, Reed sat on the cusp of determining the direction for her beloved downtown. Her friends were counting on her. She'd best swallow her indignation and show a little southern hospitality.

She walked across the room and plunged in. "Your car should be ready." Izzie pointed to the clock on the wall. "Can I drive you to the body shop?"

Glancing at his watch, Reed said, "Yes. You're right. Thank you for reminding me."

"Gentlemen," he said and shook all hands. "It's been a pleasure, and our team will want to evaluate your ideas and concerns. If you'll excuse me."

Reed joined her. "You'd help me out after—"

Izzie held up a hand. "Forgive, forget."

He squeezed his brows together, like he wasn't sure he could trust her. "Do you really think the car is ready?" Reed pulled a business card with a grease smudge from his pocket. "I'm supposed to call Rusty. He told me he would have my car fixed in a jiffy. I wasn't sure how to calculate that."

Izzie laughed. "Jiffy is southern for 'it will take less time than it takes to skin a rabbit.'"

"Oh, that clears it up." His sideways look revealed a dimple hidden in his cheek.

"Look, I owe you an apology."

"You? After I called the police?"

"Well ... you are in unfamiliar territory."

"True. In New York, cars park as close together as possible to allow for more cars."

"Not so necessary in Hamilton Harbor. And I suspect you wouldn't know about the erratic behavior of French fry-loving seagulls."

Reed sucked in air and released it. "Listen, I'm sorry for the rough start we had. Who would ever imagine we were headed to the same place? How about a do-over? Make this our first meeting."

Izzie grinned and stuck out her hand. "Hi, I'm Izzie Ketterling. I see you're new to our town."

Reed clasped her hand and added a warm and friendly pat that surprised her. "Reed Harrison. Nice to meet you and visit in your town."

"May I address you as Reed, Mr. Harrison?"

"Please. And may I call you Izzie?"

"Why, I'd be delighted." Izzie exaggerated her southern drawl and attempted a curtsy.

"Izzie." Mayor Brimstead hailed from across the room. He turned off the projector showcasing the marina sketches, then picked up his cane and hobble-walked to join them.

"I like your new fundraiser idea. Let me know if you need anything."

"You know I will."

"I have another meeting," the mayor said. "Thank you for your presentation, Mr. Harrison, and I look forward to working with you and your team."

"Likewise, we'll start right away."

"Glad you're taking time to meet the locals," he said and winked at Izzie with an eye void of lashes due to a burn injury.

When the mayor exited, Reed asked, "How did Mayor Brimstead get so badly burned?"

"Napalm. Viet Nam War. He's undergone several surgeries and is a beloved figure in our town."

"Quite a testimony to rising above your circumstances."

"He is."

"Thank you for the rescuing me from Mr. Blackburn,

by the way … if that's what it was."

"You found me out. You are welcome, but I do have a proposition."

"Oh?"

"Since the mayor wants you to meet locals, there is no better place than the Harbor Town Bagel Bistro downtown."

"Sounds good. My flight doesn't leave until seven-thirty tonight, but I must check on the rental car and report to my firm on the meeting."

"How about I call Rusty and tell him we'll be by in an hour or so, while you report in?"

"Fine." His upbeat answer produced another glimpse of dimple as he handed her Rusty's business card.

Izzie stepped outside the commission meeting room to give Reed privacy for his business call.

"Rusty's Auto Body, Rusty speaking."

"Rusty, is that rental car ready for Mr. Harrison?"

"It is. Looks brand spankin' new. Is this Izzie?"

"Yes."

"You two make amends? I thought he was none too pleased with you, callin' the law and all."

"Long story. We're off to the Bagel Bistro, and then, we'll pick up Harrison's rental car."

"Be here 'til five-thirty."

"Perfect. See you later."

Reed emerged from the meeting room, all smiles.

"Your firm is happy I presume?"

"I don't know about the firm, but my boss is."

"Good. And your car is ready. Looks brand spankin' new, according to Rusty."

"I assume that means you can no longer see the scratch?"

Izzie clasped Reed's arm. "Stick with me. I'll be your interpreter."

From the aroma Izzie inhaled when she walked into the bistro—cinnamon, pumpkin pie spice and cloves—she guessed Elaine had introduced her fall line-up of season specialties, including pumpkin bagels and pumpkin spice lattes. The bistro was humming with chatter from the afternoon faithful who were also the morning faithful. Men at one table and ladies at another. All were sixtyish-seventy somethings and lovingly known as the hens and the roosters.

"Well, looky here. Our latest neighbor."

Reed looked behind him.

"That's Dave Burbank, and he means you," Izzie said.

"Neighbor?"

"Sure." Dave, a retired Florida Marine Patrol officer, had dark, weathered skin, a slight build, wore his silver hair in a crew cut and peered over black-rimmed glasses. "You're going to be a part of us. I live in The Top of the Harbor apartments at the end of Main Street."

"Everyone," Izzie announced. "This is Reed Harrison. His firm was just given the go-ahead to run a feasibility study for the marina and downtown redevelopment project."

Dave stood, shook Reed's hand, and made introductions around his table. "I'm Dave Burbank, this is Lake Spencer, Ralph Ensley, and Grady Miller. We're retired law enforcement—also known as The Old Geezers."

Chortling came from the ladies' table.

Dave turned. "And I might as well name the ladies while I have the floor, or they'll pitch a hissy. You've got Francine Waterman, Margaret Meadows, and the infamous Hamilton sisters, Marigold and Petunia."

All the ladies drank from fine china teacups and saucers. The men drank from mugs with their names on them.

Marigold, gray hair pulled in a tight bun at the nape of

her neck, stiffened. "Dave, you can stop with that infamous stuff."

"Hamilton sisters," Reed said. "You're the two Ms. Huggins spoke of at the meeting?"

Petunia rested plump arms on the table, her mass of silvery curls bouncing as she nodded her answer, "We are."

"Emerson will definitely want to listen to your plans and projections for the maternity home," Reed said.

"You will." Marigold's response carried an edge of fair warning.

"See?" Dave muttered. "Infamous, famous. Pick one."

Oh, yeah. Izzie had Reed in the right place to give Blackburn's agenda a counterpunch.

When the two tables lapsed into conversation, Izzie steered Reed to the order counter. "Meet Elaine Robinson, my former college roommate and owner of the bistro."

Elaine, her face pink from the heat of the expresso machines, held a coffee.

"I saw your presentation today. Good to meet you."

"I recommend Elaine's pumpkin bagels, but what would you like? My treat," Izzie said.

"Oh, no. I couldn't allow you to pay for me."

"Forget who pays," Elaine said. "This is on the house."

They placed orders for pumpkin bagels and Izzie ordered a chai tea latte. Reed opted for a vitamin water.

"I see the bistro has its own library." Reed slid from his stool, walked to the book shelving that covered one wall, and ran his fingers over the routed shelving edges. "Nice, very effective against the old brick walls, especially with the mahogany wainscoting."

"You're interested in interiors?"

"I am. My specialty is interior design."

"Really? I'm an interior designer. In fact, I'm waiting results from the practicum for NCIDQ certification."

"I've taken all three sections, and I'm glad it's behind me."

"You're certified?"

He nodded. Who would guess he was a New York interior designer? Maybe if he were slight-built, in pencil-thin tapered slacks, and Italian lace-up shoes. But he had more the look of a banker or stockbroker. The guy was disgustingly perfect—perfect credentials, perfect slicked back hair, perfect dark brown eyes … and a perfect dimple.

"All right, everybody, straighten up, the police are here," Dave said.

Izzie turned to see Jeff's tall, imposing figure in his black police uniform coming in the door.

He raised his hand to the customers.

"You guys run Elaine off?" he asked as Elaine pushed through the kitchen door.

"Hi, hon. I haven't been run off yet. Just boiling a pot of hot water for the ladies' tea. Izzie, your order is ready."

Jeff turned and gaped. "I didn't think I'd see you two within shouting distance of each other."

"I may have overreacted," Reed said. "Sorry to put you to the trouble."

"No problem, if you've worked things out." He turned his attention to Elaine while Izzie and Reed took seats at the counter.

Izzie bit into her bagel. "Mmm … fall is not official until Elaine bakes pumpkin bagels."

"These are good," Reed said.

"You seem surprised."

"New York prides itself on bagel-making."

"Nothing compared to southern pride. I bet you've never even eaten a fried pickle."

His forehead wrinkled. "Fried? Pickle? You're talking about those green things made from cucumbers?"

"Yes. Tell you what. For a New York city slicker to touch the heart of the South, knowing the food is essential. When you return, promise you'll go with me to eat some real southern cooking."

"Agreed."

"Pinky swear?" She held up her hand and crooked her little finger.

He frowned, then smiled, held up his hand and wrapped his little finger on hers. The touch of his hand sent a shock of warmth straight to her southern heart.

"Is a pinky swear more binding than a handshake in the South?"

"You are a quick learner."

Reed wheeled into a rental parking space at the airport. Rusty didn't disappoint. With the scratch gone and the car washed and shined down to the tires, Rusty was certain to get repeat business from the rental company.

He grabbed his computer bag, hitched it over his shoulder and headed to the terminal.

Five-thirty. Plenty of time to get through security and update his meeting notes. Then he'd kick back and dream of the solitude of his apartment. He'd take a nice hot shower, mix a thick chocolate malt like his grandma used to make, and settle into his soft leather recliner to watch a recorded episode of NCIS.

He entered the terminal. The public address system blared. "All passengers on Delta flight 2588 to Atlanta, check in at the desk."

When he pulled his ticket from his inside suit pocket, Izzie Ketterling's business card flipped onto the floor. He stooped to pick it up. Izzie's winsome smile, accented with orange golf tee earrings, brought a sweet nudge to this heart. She was one baffling bright spot in a tiring trip.

His grandmother had said it takes all kinds to make up this world. But seeing this world in the South gave his grandmother's statement a whole new meaning. Growing up in New York City, 'all kinds' meant people worked with their muscle or their brains—dock laborers to suited executives in the high-rise office buildings.

By the time Reed was sixteen, his grandfather, a construction foreman, had put Reed to work digging foundations and learning construction from the ground up—literally. In college, his interest went to interior design, so he figured he had seen all kinds.

Now, he'd just met a fresh variety. From the car hop who seemed to know all her customers, to the skilled auto-body guy who talked like someone out of the backwoods, to the feisty girl whose clothing style would fit better in the art district of New York City than north Florida.

He scanned his ticket for the flight number. Delta 2588. "Great." He hurried to the Delta ticket desk. "You called for passengers on flight 2588?"

"Yes, sir. Flight 2588 to Atlanta is delayed. We'll keep you posted."

"But I have a short window for my connecting flight in Atlanta."

"I'm sorry, sir. If the delay interferes with that flight, we will work with you on alternatives."

Reed's phone sounded. Vance Padgett. He stepped away from the ticket desk to take the call.

"Reed. Glad I reached you. I just came out of a meeting on the Hamilton Harbor project. Everyone is delighted you got our foot in the door. Impressive. We've selected a team for the study who will join you, ASAP."

"Join me?"

"Right. You're staying."

"But my flight leaves in a couple of hours. At least I hope it does."

"Susan's already canceled your flight and extended the time on your rental car."

"But I don't have any clothes. This was supposed to be a one-day deal. What happened? Why the rush?"

"Hargrave happened. It's a good thing we got a jump on them."

"The commission made it clear our study would give us no favored treatment."

"I understand, but we've learned over the years it's the little things that secure a project whether or not they acknowledge it. This is where you and the rest of the team come in. You need to work your way into the community right away, keep your ear to the ground. Bottom line. Please the people. And if there are things we need to do that don't please them, make them think they are pleased. Got it?"

"I think. Except for the part about making them pleased when they're not pleased."

"Trust me. You'll learn. You worked construction before getting into interiors. That's why you're down there. Artful deal-making will make you a well-rounded asset for the firm. Nothing like on-the-job training that I could never teach you up here in a million years."

"Susan has handled lodging arrangements. I'll connect you."

Susan, Mr. Padgett's secretary, picked up. "Hi, Reed. How's the South?"

"Making me homesick."

"Longing for break-neck taxi rides and heartburn-producing vendor sausages?"

"And my comfy apartment with my own comfy bed."

"Speaking of bed. I guess you'd like to know where

yours will be tonight."

"Indeed."

"Mr. Padgett asked me to look for something as close to downtown and the marina as possible. I only found one place—Pirates' Cove Motel. I'll text you the address. Did you turn in your rental car keys?"

"Not yet."

"Stop by the car rental place and pick up your new paperwork. I scheduled one week, which can be extended if necessary."

"Thanks, Susan. You covered everything, even from afar."

"Anything else you need?"

"Just clothes and food."

"You have a charge card for expenses. Mr. Padgett okayed purchasing clothes since we left you stranded."

"You really do think of everything."

The call ended, and the lady at the ticket counter motioned to him.

"Sir?"

"Yes?"

"Good news. Your flight will not be delayed—they're sending another plane."

"Thank you, but it looks like I won't be needing the flight after all."

"You want to cancel?"

"My company already canceled."

He plodded down the tiled corridor that led to the rental cars. The company also canceled a hot soak in his tub, remote in hand to change channels on his wall-mounted television. His legs felt like he'd added exercise weights from the gym. Another activity he would miss in the morning.

With the car inspected, Reed pulled out of the airport

surrounded by nothing but acres of pine trees. There was potential for growth galore in Florida. A state he'd resented. His mother had been lured to Orlando, and his father was somewhere in north Florida.

But resentment aside, there were literally miles of untouched property ripe for urban planning and the need for interior designs. To launch this golden opportunity for his company, all he had to do was head back to Hamilton Harbor. He gripped the steering wheel and raised his shoulders to release the tension in his neck. It didn't work. All he had to do was head back AND please the newbies headed by Blackburn and oldies championed by Izzie AND get some clothes and toiletries.

"Call me if you need anything," she had said. He pulled Izzie's card from his pocket.

He needed clothes, but was it safe to get clothing suggestions from a woman who had such unusual taste in clothing?

He'd take his chances. Turning onto Highway 77, he drove south toward the small town whose development, and a certain intriguing girl, just might hold his future.

CHAPTER FOUR

The setting sun washed the houses on Feldman Square with a rosy glow. Izzie drew in a deep breath. Someone in the early 1900s had experienced this view. A kinship with the past empowered her—almost as if she was part of a divine purpose and plan.

Izzie parked her Suburban in front of the yellow and green Flower Cottage. Since her friend and sometimes boss, Emme, married and moved to Davenport Plantation a couple of years ago, the upstairs cottage apartment had become Izzie's home. Actually, it was her second home on the square, but all of Feldman Square felt like home to her.

She stepped from her car and pushed the door shut. The sign hanging over the front gate creaked in the bay breeze. The same light gentle wind immersed her in the sweet scent of the pink and purple petunias growing in pots hooked on the iron fencing. Circling her car, she leaned against the passenger door. The cool nip in the air sent a shiver about her shoulders and brought a smile to her face. This would be perfect weather for the fall festival on the square.

What was it about this little portion of town that made her want to fight for its existence?

The city's spruce-up with a running trail, edged flower beds, a splashing fountain in the center, and a gazebo for special events was a nice improvement. But more likely her attraction came from the oak trees draped in lacy moss. She used to love to sit on a park bench and watch the treetops waltz lazily in the breeze. The cozy homes hugging the square, though some were bedraggled as Blackburn pointed out, held memories close to her heart.

From behind the Victorian Feldman house that was undergoing renovation, Claudia emerged alongside an elegant Afghan hound. His silky brown hair swirled about him like a model in a chiffon dress on a fashion runway. They both trotted on the brick path that meandered from the park behind the Feldman house, along the bayside and into the neighboring residential cove area. Joining Izzie beside her car, Claudia slowed and then lunged into alternating leg stretches.

"Whew, I need a cool down." she said, breathing heavily.

"You have Mister T looking sleek and smelling sweet."

"The scent is Hawaiian Delight." She paused to take a couple of deep breaths. "I thought the fragrance fitting since he's staying with me while the Presnells are vacationing in Hawaii. Anything exciting happen after I left the commission meeting?"

"Does introducing Reed to the afternoon crew at Elaine's bistro count for exciting?"

"I'll say. And you're on a first name basis?"

"Yup. All for the good of the square."

"Oh yeah." She addressed her smug remark to Mister T. "Handsome New York guy. We appreciate the sacrifice, don't we?"

The dog tilted his head and blinked.

"He's thinking about it." She winked at Izzie and tugged on the dog's lead. "Gotta go. Francine is picking up Toby. And Pete, bless him, said he had a romantic dinner planned." She jogged the short distance to the back door of her grooming shop.

The word romantic stuck. Izzie hugged her arms to her body and admired the newly restored Hamilton house where Claudia had found love with Pete. At the flower shop, Emme and Clifton found a second chance on love. Izzie was still searching for her first chance.

Opposite the florist shop were the two houses brought into question at the commission meeting. She couldn't let Blackburn nullify the park revitalization or nix the renovations of the remaining houses on the square.

But who was she to champion this cause? She was a minor player. A struggling interior designer, whose debatable claim to fame was spray painting the ceiling of the high school gymnasium.

The Gardner house had closed shortly after she graduated from high school and left for college. It troubled her heart to see how the appearance had deteriorated in those eight years. The white paint was peeling, and vines that had overtaken the porch railing were beginning to entwine the porch swing. To bring these houses back to life would take time and money. The Hamilton sisters had the will. They just needed help with the way.

Izzie took one last look and passed under the rose-covered arbor to enter the Flower Cottage.

"Hi, Mellie. Any new gossip from the beauty parlor?"

Mellie waved at Izzie with a piece of greenery filler she was using in an arrangement. "Emme's making a hospital and nursing home delivery on her way home. She needs you to make two funeral deliveries tomorrow."

"Will do. I have to meet a client in the morning, but I can make the deliveries beforehand."

"I hear you took on a new fall festival fundraising project."

"I suppose. You know how it goes. You suggest something, and then, you're expected to make it happen." Izzie deflated onto a stool. "Something about this whole marina-downtown redevelopment has me concerned.

DESIGNED FOR *LOVE*

The firm the commission is allowing to evaluate the project presented an awesome preliminary sketch, but the example was of a development in Maine. It had a yacht club and reworked boat slips. Blackburn loved their design and rode that idea to promote his all-new resort vision, like the one at Paramount Beach in Palmetto County. He even suggested the Gardner house and old garden club be torn down. That's when I opened my mouth."

"Thank goodness. You're the perfect one to speak. I ran this flower shop during the square's golden years when Feldman Park was the hub of Hamilton Harbor activity. But the square declined when the houses were made into apartments." Mellie jabbed a notecard holder into the mixed plant arrangement. "That is, until you moved in with your mother. You brought a brightness of hope where things had grown dull. Speaking at the commission meeting will lend a young person's perspective, not just pleas from us seniors." She set the finished arrangement in the refrigerated flower case and dusted her hands together. "Besides, I've always thought of you as ... a kind of mascot for the square. A force to rally around."

"Me? Who snuck flowers from the Flower Cottage garden?"

"When I saw you give the flowers you swiped to the WWII veteran who always sat alone in the park, I decided to consider your picking, pruning. You've always had a good heart. Maybe this brewing battle between the old and new will be a blessing to get people interested in downtown again and pitch in to help."

"I hope. But have you ever had a good and bad feeling about someone, all at the same time?"

"Hmm. Maybe ... Santa Claus."

"Santa. Really?"

"Oh yes. I thought he was fearsome looking as a

youngster, but I also knew he was supposed to be a good guy that brought toys."

"Well, this New York guy looks dreamy, but I don't know if what he's bringing to town is really good for the home team."

"Make sure they hear our concerns, and pray the firm brings good things to the town."

"Pray. Of course. This project is going on the top of my prayer list." A lightness tickled Izzie's chest, and she popped up to help Mellie clean up the worktable littered with cut stems, leaves, florist wire, and ribbon.

The phone in her pocket jingled. She didn't recognize the number. "Hello?"

"Izzie? Reed Harrison."

"Reed. Hello." The lightness in her chest turned into tingling. "Did you make it to the airport all right?"

"I did. But the firm asked me to stay. Did you mean it when you said if I needed anything to call?"

"Of course, how can I help you?"

"I didn't plan on staying. I need clothes and a … uh … drug store.

"Well, sure you do. Where are you now?"

"On the highway leaving the airport."

"Tell you what. Turn right when you reach Highway 77 and head back to town. Go probably ten miles, and you'll see the mall. That will be your best bet for clothes at this time of night. I'll meet you there."

"I don't want to put you out. I can manage once I get there."

"You're not putting me out, and I can direct you to the hot spots."

"Hot … spots. Not sure that's what I need."

Izzie smiled into the phone. "Just meet me at the mall main entrance. You can't miss it."

Izzie sat on a bench beside the entrance to the mall—the mall that was the beginning of the end of Hamilton Harbor's old business district. Shopping under one roof had drained the lifeblood from downtown. But getting the surprise call from Mr. New Yorker gave her a boost. She recognized the silver sedan right away and directed Reed to park near her car.

"Are we destined to meet in parking lots?" Izzie said.

"Could be. Thank you for meeting me."

"Absolutely. I'll give you an official tour, and you can count this as part of your fact-finding."

Inside, easy-listening music and children's laughter from the play area greeted them. Izzie steered Reed to the mall directory.

"The mall has three wings, each anchored with a mainstream department store. They all carry men's clothing. But here," she pointed, "and here, and here, you'll find some local styles with a kick." She couldn't resist raising her eyebrows.

Reed went pale but remained gorgeous. Dark eyes, long lashes, thick brows.

"A rule-following suit man?"

He shrugged and nodded.

"Okay. Follow me." She put on her confident voice, but underneath wondered if a nix on local style would mean a nix on local preservation too.

CHAPTER FIVE

"You don't have to stay with me." Reed clutched a pack of undershirts. The plastic crinkled in his hand. "You've done enough already."

"Oh, but I do. Pinky swear. Remember?"

At a nearby sale table, a lady customer held up a package of briefs to the man with her. "Why don't you try these? Your boxers are wore slam out."

Call him old-fashioned, but he didn't feel comfortable picking out underwear with a girl he just met. "We didn't expect to see each other so soon."

"Life's full of surprises." She flashed a grin.

"Right—a surprise lesson. In business travel, you better always pack an overnight bag."

"And a second lesson is that in the South you keep your word. I promised, the next time we were together, to take you for a real southern meal. Besides, you missed lunch, and I know you've only had a bagel and water. You have to be getting hungry."

His stomach gurgled.

"See? Your stomach agrees."

He loosened the grip on the undershirt package and allowed himself to laugh.

"Well, well. Fancy meeting you here." Ed Blackburn materialized from nowhere. "Fraternizing with the enemy?"

He spoke in a joking manner, but his words carried a note of sarcasm.

"Why am I the enemy?" Izzie asked.

"Maybe that word is a little strong, but we disagree on redevelopment emphasis."

Izzie's smile had disappeared. "On that, I do agree."

Reed's stomach forgot about being hungry. "I wasn't planning to stay. My firm wanted me to start the study right away, so I needed clothes. He held up the undershirts." Was he a kid with his hand caught in the cookie jar?

Blackburn's eyes shifted from Izzie to Reed. "Ah ... I see." He made it sound like he saw more than the eye could see. "Then be my guest for lunch tomorrow at the yacht club. Since a new club building was in the plan you presented, you must include our chef in your study. He turns out something magnificent every day of the week."

"Remember, that sketch was just an example," Reed said.

"And remarkably suitable for our marina here. If you're in the market for clothes, let me show you some shirts on sale over here."

Blackburn tapped his arm and motioned him to follow. "Excuse me, will you Izzie?"

"Sure, I need to check on a fabric order a few stores down." She pointed. "I'll meet you at that exit in a few."

Reed grabbed a pack of boxers and made his way down the aisle to Mr. Blackburn's sale. Not surprisingly, it was a rack of knit sporting shirts, like the one Blackburn and his friends wore.

Thirty minutes later, Reed thanked Blackburn for his assistance in selecting some clothes to hold him over, promised to meet him for lunch the next day, and went to find Izzie.

He heard squalling as he entered the heart of the mall. A helium balloon had escaped and bounced along the high ceiling. Izzie, in her elevated platform sandals, balanced precariously on a bench, reaching for the tip of the string that inched from her grasp.

Reed plunked down his bags and climbed on the bench with her.

"Better let me get that before you take a tumble."

Reed had a few inches of height on Izzie and managed to grab the string attached to the balloon. He helped Izzie down and handed the balloon to the child with a tear-streaked face.

"Thank you so much. You saved me from a miserable evening of crying. Nathan," the boy's mom said as she wrapped the string around his wrist, "thank the nice man."

The youngster sniffled a thank you.

Izzie crooked her arm inside Reed's. "Sir, you are a hero."

"Hardly. I just know what it's like to lose something treasured and feel so helpless that all you can do is cry. Besides, if you fell and cracked your head, I'd be out a dinner."

He received an elbow to the ribs.

"My dinner place will give you a better feel for our town than Blackburn's stuffy yacht club." Now he felt like a kid being wooed by divorced parents.

Leaving Reed's car at the mall, the two traveled in Izzie's car toward the downtown area. Turning onto Main, they found the street essentially deserted. They passed a gas station converted to a used car lot and The Flamingo Motel, the color of medicine his grandmother used to give him for an upset stomach.

"I've heard of towns rolling up their sidewalks at night, but from the looks of the many empty buildings, Hamilton Harbor's sidewalks are rolled up during the day too."

Reaching the heart of the old downtown, he took note of two-story brick buildings that featured classic decorative facades of the early 1900s lining the sidewalks on either side of the street. Some with tattered awnings. "I'll bet these storefront windows haven't seen a cleaning cloth in years."

"I can remember when downtown was the center of activity for Hamilton Harbor. I was around ten when the mall made the scene, and the town gradually folded. Sad. But that's where the Downtown Reconstruction Board comes in. You'll need to include them in your research."

"In New York City, these empty, neglected structures would be teeming with restaurants and businesses downstairs, and high-rent living quarters upstairs."

"See? Potential. That's what I like to hear."

"Where is the bagel shop you took me to today?"

"It's closer to the marina, just past my church."

"There's a church downtown?"

"In the old Ritz Theater. My pastor is the one who gave you his seat at the commission meeting."

"I haven't heard of a church in a theater. Is that normal in the South?"

"I don't know, but it works here."

"Besides Elaine, my two other college roommates are doing their part to rebuild downtown. On the left is the Pampered Pooch. Claudia, who you met at the meeting, owns the business. Emme Davenport owns The Flower Cottage behind Main Street."

Izzie slowed in the next block. "There's Elaine's Harbor Town Bagel Bistro you asked about, and ..." she gestured toward a high rise at the end of the street, "... that is The Top of the Harbor apartments where most of the oldsters live who gather at Elaine's in the morning and afternoon. Growth potential to include in your report."

The rows of buildings stopped, yielding to a scene that took Reed's breath. The moon hung low, huge and golden, reflecting its light along the rippling bay waters.

Izzie fell silent a moment. "When I want to be alone ... and just dream," Izzie said, "this is where I come."

"You live near here?"

"I do. You'll see in a minute, but first, the marina—which is actually a landfill added onto Main Street back in the 1930s." She drove at a crawl. "In the 1960s, the city added these little flat-roofed boxes they call office space down the middle. Like the rest of downtown, these businesses left little by little. There is one hang-on barber shop."

A faded traditional red, white, and blue barber pole stood alone by a glass-fronted store. A two-story square nondescript structure came next.

"This building used to house a popular restaurant until the health department shut it down, and they gave up their lease. The city owns the property. There's City Hall to the right where you were today. The public library next to it has to put out buckets and toss tarps over book racks whenever it rains." They continued past boat slips, most filled with bobbing boats of various types and sizes. "At least this part of the marina is well-used," Izzie said.

"I imagine the boat use helps the city stay afloat financially," Reed said. "But the property definitely needs a new plan." The marina ended with a T-dock seawall. The firm's Maine development could fit in this setting amazingly well. Blackburn's interest in the project was a big positive he'd better court, while keeping the downtowners appeased.

Izzie made a U-turn, traveling back toward Main Street. "Now look at town from this angle. As a designer, you should appreciate the incongruity here."

"If you mean tacking on modern, now tired and worn, motif to old historic on a bay waterfront of indescribable value and potential, I do."

Izzie brightened. "Agreed. Now for the important part of your tour." Coming off the marina, she turned right. Then took an immediate left behind Main Street and came to a hidden cluster of homes nestled on a park with giant oak trees draped in mossy robes. "This is Feldman Park, donated to the city by the Hamilton sisters, and the hot topic at the commission meeting today."

Streetlight filtered through the trees. Dark and light shadows cast over the park emitted a cozy warmth. Here, nature created the emotion he tried to produce in some of his interiors. Surrounding the park were homes, replicas of styles he was familiar with in his design experience. "In their day, these houses must have been quite stylish."

Izzie stopped in front of a quaint 1930s Craftsman. A wrought-iron fence with pointed posts and intricate scrolled ironwork outlined the property. A climbing red rose decorated the arbored gate.

"This is the Flower Cottage. I live upstairs."

"No wonder you're interested in preservation."

"Yup. This house was built in 1936 and has been in operation as a flower shop since the early 1970s. I can tell you more about it later." Izzie stopped in front of the house next to the florist shop. It was another Craftsman two-story with three dormers, end chimneys, and broad central steps leading to a deep porch with railings. Impressive, but begged for paint and yard work.

"Here is the old schoolhouse the Hamilton sisters donated to the historical society. The members have done a lot of cleanup inside, but as you can see, it could use more TLC."

She turned right, revealing a classic two-and-a-half story American farmhouse. The gleaming white home surrounded by trimmed shrubs and a giant oak tree had a porch that wrapped around the left side.

"The Hamilton house," Izzie said.

"Is this where the Hamilton sisters live?"

"No. They moved away, but returned a couple of years ago, determined to restore these homes. Claudia lives here with Pete, her handyman husband who restored the house. The home originally belonged to the sisters' grandparents. Pete is also restoring the Feldman house next door belonging to the sisters' other grandparents. These are the homes of our city's founders—important to know for your study."

"I'm not sure I'm following all this. The sisters wound up with all these houses?"

"Long story, but they are the heirs."

As they rolled closer to the house under restoration, with scaffolding reaching up to the second story, Reed had a fluttery feeling in his stomach. The house was a Victorian, complete with a turret.

"Can you stop a minute? I'd like a closer look."

He stepped out of the car onto the sidewalk. A dusk-to-dawn light was just easing on, illuminating the decorative trim along the eaves. Uncanny. This house was almost an exact replica of a house in Manhattan he had traveled past many times. He had always wondered about the people who lived there and what it looked like inside.

"Grand isn't it?" Izzie said.

"It looks a lot like one near my old neighborhood in New York City."

"Really? Then you're going to love the old garden club house you'll see in a minute—it's the mirror image of this house. The sisters plan to sell the Feldman house and use the money toward restoration of the ones Blackburn complained about. It's a slow process," she puffed her cheeks into a pout, "but the square is worth saving."

She took another right turn. "Here's what Blackburn

calls eyesores."

The first house was a two-story modified Victorian with an interesting combination gable and mansard style roof. The front featured a roomy front porch in desperate need of repair.

"This is the Gardner house I grew up in."

"You do have your roots here."

"When I lived here in the 90s, all these houses, except the Flower Cottage, were rentals. This one," she pulled in front of the next house, "was the city's first garden club but was originally built for Feldman's daughter, Violet."

Reed did a double take. "It is literally the mirror image of the Feldman house." A doubly delightful discovery. However, the houses *could* be classified as eyesores. "These two places need a lot of work ... and then housing a maternity home and pregnancy center. I can see why Blackburn might think they'd be a detraction. Especially since they border the marina area."

"Bite your tongue. These homes are a part of Hamilton Harbor history. We have to save them. It would be like throwing a diamond ring out and keeping the box it came in. These are treasures."

Better watch his words with her. "They ... are interesting structures and have a ... certain charm?"

"The sisters are philanthropic and have given the city a lot already. They're just short on cash and deserve our support. Besides, removing these two houses would be like ripping a page out of a history book."

She pointed to the Gardner house, "Right on that front porch. Arnie Blauser, one of the renters, used me as his audience to practice his Elvis impersonations. He could sing 'You Ain't Nothin' but a Hound Dog' and 'Blue Suede Shoes' that would make Elvis proud. He won second place in a Nashville look-a-like contest."

His brows shot up. "You had an interesting upbringing."

"I did. These homes housed a diverse group of renters that formed a large extended family for me. After I went to college and Mom moved her cleaning business to Tallahassee, the sisters closed the houses. The cost of upkeep outgrew the rent coming in. It's sad to see what eight years of going unattended can do."

"Nature tries to reclaim its space."

"I suppose, but nature would be covering up a history of intrigue that should never be forgotten."

"Intrigue?"

Izzie cut him a sideways glance. "A hint. It's part of the history at the motel you're staying in."

"Pirates?"

She shot him a I-hope-I've-got-you-hooked-grin. "How about we talk more over dinner?"

And she did have him hooked. If he had made his flight back to New York, he would be settling down for a frozen dinner and TV. But here, he not only had the promise of dinner with a flamboyant guide but the possibility of hearing tales of pirates and allure. This feasibility study mission was way more involved—and fascinating—than he'd ever imagined.

Izzie and Reed pulled into Calico Jack's in a small cove just one block off Feldman Square. When Izzie turned the ignition off, a cloud of dust settled onto the car from the dry gravel lot.

"I doubt this looks like a place someone like you would ever consider going, but—"

"Someone like me?" Reed asked. "What's that supposed to mean?"

Izzie, watch your choice of words. A rerun of her mother's frequent caution jabbed her. "Just that you look like a person who might prefer the tried and true—a franchise, maybe."

He angled a glance toward her. "I tried the Tally-Ho."

"You did." Izzie grinned. "Trust me, you need to know about this place and include it in your overview. Blackburn would like to have you think their new chef is the be all, end all. Wait till you try Calico's southern fare."

Passing under a lopsided sign hanging from a rusty frame that appeared to be salvaged from some old bed springs, they walked down a dirt path lined with odd pieces of painted driftwood interspersed with ground accent lights.

A frown creased Reed's forehead, but Izzy was banking on him warming to the place.

"It looks ramshackle, but don't let that fool you."

"Hmm."

The path joined a covered wooden dock jutting out over the water, with a variety of fishing boats rocking on the rippling water along either side. Izzie inhaled the salty aroma of the wharf highlighted by fish cooking. Exhilarating for her. Reed wrinkled his nose. Maybe not so much for Mr. High-rise.

They walked toward a flat-roofed structure, a patchwork of different colored wood from old road signs. "That's where all the good smells are created."

He muttered something unintelligible, then asked, "Do they have steak?"

"Not sure. Fried maybe."

"Fried steak?"

"In the South, if it's edible, it's able to be fried. Here the specialty is fried fish." Izzie pointed to the wooden walkway. "Watch your step. These deck boards are uneven."

They reached Calico Jack's, which had outside seating at dock's end. Spicy smells seasoned the surroundings. Several customers were already enjoying food and the view. Two squeaky seagulls glided by while extras stood on pilings waiting for food offerings.

"I see the seagulls know about this place too."

Izzie chuckled. "Around here, if you eat outdoors, those birds will find out."

They settled into plastic chairs beside the water. A waitress dressed in ragged jeans and a Calico Jack's T-shirt brought menus and took their drink orders.

"This is pleasant." Reed scanned the interior.

Interspersed with portraits of bearded pirates, fish netting decorated the walls along with plaques of mounted fish. His purview came back to her. "Lots of character. So, who is Calico Jack?"

Pleased with his interest, Izzie leaned in, resting her forearms on the table. "His real name was John Rackham. He was a famous pirate in Florida's history and had two famous but menacing female crew members— his lover, Anne Bonny, and Mary Read."

Reed lifted his menu. "And they started developing recipes and cooking when their pirating days were over? I see Mary's hearty stew and Bonny biscuits are on the menu."

Izzie appreciated his dry wit. "I guess they did trade swords for chef's knives. They even have Rackham's rack of ribs."

"What do you recommend?"

"You can't go wrong with Calico's blackened scamp or grouper."

"There's really a fish called scamp? Sounds more like a puppy."

"Cute. But, yes. It's a nice white meat fish. Tell you

what. Why not let me order?"

"Fine. Thanks."

The waitress brought their drinks, and Izzie placed the order. The sound of lapping seawater against the pilings beneath them cozied their extemporaneous dinner. Swirling a drinking straw in her sweet tea to mix in the lemon, she caught Reed's gaze. This man had a cautious reserve that needed loosening up. She leaned back in her chair and said, "Can I check my instincts regarding you?"

"Like personality analysis?"

Izzie nodded.

"Go for it."

"I'd say Mr. Reed Harrison is an only child. He kept his toys orderly, his shoes in matched sets in his closet, and he obeyed his parents by always eating dessert last."

A grin spread over his face, showing off his one-sided dimple—adorable.

"I was orderly and grew up as an only child, but it was my grandparents who raised me."

"Ah."

He looked down at his paper placemat.

Had she stepped where she shouldn't? After a pause, he continued.

"My parents married young, divorced, and moved on with their lives … without me."

"Left you with a giant question mark in your life?"

"That's one way to put it."

An urge washed over Izzie to know all about this good-looking guy with a chiseled jaw line and bold brow. His hairline came to a point centered in his forward—so perfectly centered and combed she wanted to reach up and muss his hair a bit.

He ran his finger around the rim of his water glass. "And, doesn't everyone eat dessert last?"

"I knew it. You *are* a rule-follower. If there's a big chunk of chocolate cake calling my name, dinner eaten or not, it's a goner."

"What's a goner?"

"You know, gobbled up, eaten, no longer there, gone—a goner."

"I see." He smirked, flashing his dimple. "My turn for analysis. I'd say you grew up with lots of youngsters all vying for attention, so you developed your own individual dress to stand out in the crowd?"

"Um … interesting analysis and kind of right. I grew up with lots of people from all walks of life, not youngsters. I told you about Arnie the Elvis impersonator. There was Ms. Easton, the artist who specialized in painting sunrises." Izzie giggled. "If she saw an especially glorious morning, you'd hear her 'hallelujah' all over the square. She taught me a lot about the use of color."

Reed's brow wrinkled. "I bet."

"I accumulated all kinds of hand-me-downs from the people who lived on the square. Making interesting outfits out of what I had, I suppose, did make me stand out in the crowd. I was labeled weird by students and unconventional by teachers."

An approaching boat caught Izzie's attention. "Speaking of unconventional, look behind you."

Reed turned. "Am I seeing things? A pirate ship?"

Izzie chuckled. "It's Tuesday evening. Jack Rudman's night to roam the cove. He owns this restaurant and the motel across the bayou where you'll be staying."

The boat, crafted with plank-like sides and portholes, pulled dockside. The tall mast bore a flag with a pirate's hat atop a smiley face in place of skull and crossbones. Dressed in a black waistcoat, breeches, a linen shirt, knit cap, and eye patch, Jack stepped from the boat into the restaurant.

"Yo-ho, mates, and a happy Tuesday. Time for Calico to make his rounds."

Izzie leaned toward Reed and whispered, "It's kind of like the ice cream truck for kids, he sails his pirate galleon around the cove, rings the ship's bell and hands out gold coins of chocolate to the kids with coupons for ice cream treats at his restaurant."

"Smart marketing."

"Well, if it isn't Izzie. Nice to see you out. Here's a bit of gold for ye." He tossed gold foil-wrapped chocolate coins on the table. "Who's this bloke with you?"

"Capt. Jack, meet Reed Harrison."

Reed stood.

"He works for the development firm the commission voted to do a feasibility study on the marina and downtown project. He will be staying at your motel."

Jack grabbed and pumped Reed's hand. "Welcome, mate. I told the secretary who called to make your reservation that we'd treat you so many ways, you'd be sure to like some."

"Thank you. Izzie tells me I must include your restaurant in my research as an area landmark."

"Absolutely." He motioned to the waitress. "Cindy, bring this table a special Calico appetizer. On the house." He turned his attention back to Reed. "If you're smart, stick with her to acquire the heartbeat of Hamilton Harbor. That's when your study will pay off, not only for you but also for us, if we receive a good redevelopment plan. Izzie, I heard about you speaking on behalf of Feldman Square at the commission meeting. Proud of you." He gave her shoulder a pat.

"Mr. Harrison," he slapped his hand on the table and fell back into character, "be seein' you around, mate. You need to board my ship, so you can see the harbor from the water."

"I'd appreciate that. Three others will join me for the study. May they come along?"

"Of course, more the merrier. Bye, matey."

"I promised intrigue. Legend has it that pirates left buried treasure somewhere in this cove that joins the bay. Jack likes to play good pirate and give out gold instead of taking it."

"He's quite a character. I'll have a lot of notes to take down tonight." He took a sip of water as the waitress arrived with the appetizer Jack ordered for them.

"Here's your gator and swamp cabbage." The waitress set a plate in front of Reed.

Reed choked, spraying water on Izzie.

Izzie jumped up and whacked him on the back.

Reed sucked in a breath of air.

"You okay?"

Maybe the charm of Hamilton Harbor was coming at this New York preppy, rule-follower too fast.

"Move."

Reed felt a prod at his back. His sweaty hands bound to his sides. He tried to comply with the pushing, edging his foot forward on the plank. The wood creaked underfoot. Knees weak, his legs refused to move him. He felt another poke to his back. Below him, wind-whipped bay waters lashed out. To his right, Izzie struggled in the rising swells to steady her rowboat and beckoned him to join her. Blackburn in a yacht on his left, hollered, "Over here," motioning for him to come in his direction.

Reed stood, toes curled on the edge of the plank.

Powerful jaws with sharp, jagged teeth snapped below him. Which way should he go? Through a cloudy blanket of fog, he blinked his eyes, attempting to see more clearly. Gradually, the murkiness lifted.

He had wrapped his toes over the edge of the footboard on his bed. The fan overhead whirred, blowing against his face and clunking with each rotation. The red numbers on the digital bedside clock read 7:00. He pulled at the hard object pressing into his back—a pen. He'd fallen asleep while writing his report.

Willing his legs to slide over the edge of the bed, his feet hit the coarse red and black carpeted floor of the Pirates' Cove Motel. He made his way to the bathroom to put cool water on his face and splash away the frenzied dreams that plagued a mostly sleepless night. The water smelled of sulfur, and left rust stains in the sink.

The mirror, trapped between old light fixtures that cast yellow light from the heavy glass globes, had a dark corner that needed re-silvering. The bathroom, with its white and black inch-square tiles underfoot, spoke of a good three decades of wear and accented the decor of red, white, and black in the rest of his room. But the motel was, if nothing else, a quiet reprieve from yesterday's troublesome introduction to Hamilton Harbor.

Although, being in the middle of controversy was not new to him. Izzie's attempt at personality analysis had flushed out thoughts he'd long kept suppressed.

He stared at his bare feet the way he had the night his parents were last together.

"You can't let a child go outside and play without shoes on," his mother had complained to his father. "What's wrong with you?"

"Wrong with me? At least I take him outside, or else he'd be shut up in this stuffy old house watching you draw.

This is no life for a little boy. No life for me. No life for any of us living with your parents."

"I know. But we have Reed, no money, and that's that."

And the "that's that" philosophy turned into the catalyst for ripping the life out of his world at his Grandma's house. With a paper sack of clothes in his father's hand and the slam of the front door, his dad left to live life elsewhere. Later, his mom sat him on the edge of his bed and explained about a big school far away where she would live and study. She went out the same door as his dad, and that was that. She never came back. He never went outside barefoot again.

He yearned for the warmth of his gray office cubicle. He'd be glad to turn the information he'd gathered about history, preservation, and Blackburn's vision, and return to the routine at the office.

Reed showered, put on his newly purchased underwear, and used his new shaving gear. He took advantage of the Danish and coffee set out in the motel's tiny office. Back in his room, he re-read his report and emailed it.

Drawing back the heavy, red room-darkening curtains, he gazed at a massive oak tree covering a wooden walk bordered by tiny pink flowers. The walk led to a short dock where Capt. Jack was working on his pirate ship. Across the water stood Calico Jack's, where he'd had dinner with Izzie.

The sun streamed in, lighting up his makeshift desk on a side table and highlighted Izzie's business card. He picked it up, running his fingers over the card. He gave the room a once over. With his eye for decorating, he couldn't help imagining what he might do to give the room an uplift.

Considering the rust-stained sink and old fixtures. Would it be easier to take the Blackburn approach—level this tired building on this gorgeous property and start over? Or would it be better to apply a clever retro look within the structure, affirming the merits of saving and rejuvenating—the Izzie approach. One thing for sure, this waterfront area had tremendous potential.

He tugged the sliding glass doors open and stepped out onto the patio with his coffee. The soft breeze played against his skin. Reed sipped his coffee and watched Jack work on the boat motor—smart to have a gas powered back up on a sailboat. This sailing vessel was complete with a cabin, raised step platform with a railing in back, porthole windows on the sides, and a main sail flying his smiling pirate flag. A second flag, inscribed with "Pride of Hamilton Harbor," flew beneath the first. "Captain Jack" was emblazoned across the back in black letters outlined in red.

Reed strode down the walkway toward the pirate ship.

Jack looked up. "Morning. You ready for the tour of the bay, I promised?"

"I don't want to interrupt your work. I'm doing some sightseeing. It's beautiful out here."

"You haven't seen anything until you've cruised the bay at sunset."

"We're on the bay?"

"Under the drawbridge," Jack indicated with a nod of his head. "This is Harbor Bayou. Its waters wind through the cove—the original residential area of town. The draw bridge joins the cove to downtown. When you go under the bridge, you're in the bay. Hang a right, you'll be at the marina where your firm is involved. If you continue southwest, you enter the Gulf of Mexico, and from there anywhere in the world."

"Our project stands at the gateway to the world?"

"You've got it. Even from this humble dock, if you want to be technical. But before seeing the world, I have to help set up the Pumpkin Watch. Another sight you won't want to miss."

"Do you watch people chunk pumpkins?"

"Oh, no. It's not like those catapult events. The Downtown Reconstruction Board started the watch about five years ago as a fundraiser. We have a pumpkin walk by land and a pumpkin watch by water. It's a community effort. People bring a pumpkin and carve them at the park on Friday. Then the pumpkins, with candles inside, are placed along the waterfront trail that weaves along the bayou into the cove for viewing."

"Sounds charming."

"People from all over come out and either walk the trail or watch from a boat. The funds raised support downtown improvement efforts. I'm prepping the boat to take spectators around."

Jack walked to his truck, parked near the dock, lowered the tailgate, and started pulling out a bench seat.

Reed set down his coffee to lend him a hand.

"I add these benches that hook into the floor for extra seating."

Reed helped unload and with the last seat was attached, his phone sounded. Mr. Padgett. He excused himself, tossed his coffee cup in an outside bin, and returned to his room.

Padgett was upbeat. "I read your report. Sounds like you've made some key contacts to help pave the way for the team when they arrive on Saturday."

"Three more days? I only bought a couple of changes of clothes."

"Ever heard of a laundry and dry cleaners? They have those in the South, don't they?"

"That and a lot of other stuff," he muttered.

"Well, use them. You can return to New York after the rest of the team arrives and acclimates. I see on your report you're to meet with Mr. Blackburn, the yacht club president, at noon?"

"I am. He's picking me up shortly."

"He brought up the Oceanside Development designed by Hargrave?"

"Right."

"We have good information from an associate in the neighboring county that Hargrave Developers pulled the specs on the Hamilton Harbor request for a proposal. They would like nothing better than to expand their influence along the coast. But what they don't have is our ace in the hole. You—on the ground gathering inside information on the desires of the people."

This ace had found not just a hole but a gorge with the likes of Zelda, Rusty, Officer Robinson, the factions gathered at City Hall, the hens and roosters at Harbor Town Bagel Bistro, not to mention the intrigue of pirates, treasure, and a girl with gray eyes.

"Find out what interests Blackburn about that development and what his reservations are about working with historical downtown. Oh, and that fall festival fundraiser, I want you to volunteer to help."

"Interior design school never prepared me for all this."

"Welcome to the real world of development. That's why I wanted you on the ground floor of the project to see how it all comes together."

Reed ended the call, assuring Mr. Padgett that he'd keep his nose and ear to the ground.

How had he moved from procuring permission for a feasibility study to landing smack in the middle of controversy—the very thing he worked hard to avoid?

CHAPTER SIX

"That wallpaper doesn't look straight." Ms. Huggins said.

Izzie stood on a ladder in the historical society building smoothing a dampened roll of wallpaper onto the kitchen wall. She drew in a breath that carried the musty smell of paste and released it before speaking. "I aligned it with a plumb line."

"Maybe, but old houses are bound to be crooked. You shouldn't have picked out a vertical pattern."

Izzie tightened her grip on the wallpaper brush. Wasn't this fitting? In this old schoolhouse, like in high school, she was under Ms. Huggins's critical eye.

"Izzie, how do expect me to read this when you write so small?" Ms. Huggins had asked for a one-page paper, and she had a lot to say. When she wore a pair of earrings she'd fashioned from shards of a broken mirror, Ms. Huggins hadn't appreciated her creativity. "Izzie, take off those ridiculous earrings, they're blinding me."

Izzie stepped down from the ladder. "Wallpaper Depot was kind enough to donate these rolls, and they had the right amount on hand."

"Probably stuff they couldn't sell."

Restraining a heavy sigh, Izzie said, "This style paper gives the look I was hoping for. I assure you, when the papering is complete it will all come together. You'll see."

"I certainly hope so. I'm not so sure it was a good idea to start this decorating project when festivities start tomorrow."

"If we charge admission, things should be spruced up."

"I suppose you're right, but I can't arrange these old kitchen utensils for display until you're finished." She gave a half snort. "I guess I can work on historical inscriptions for the latest items brought in. We received a complete set of copper kitchen molds and an old food chopper this morning."

"Good." Izzie placed another wallpaper strip on her makeshift table made of plywood-covered sawhorses. Had she been too ambitious wallpapering with such a tight deadline? When she suggested the extra fundraiser in front of a packed house at the commission meeting, she should have guessed she'd be appointed to carry it out. Now her reputation was on the line, she couldn't mess this up.

Izzie peered out the old sash window in the corner of the kitchen where she could just see a bit of the Gardner house. If the back taxes were not paid, no doubt Blackburn would snap up the tax deed and have the house removed. How could anyone want to destroy that house? It would be like cutting the feet out from under a soldier while standing guard over a town. That house—the entire square—was a part of Hamilton Harbor's heritage and needed to be safeguarded. Along with this kitchen. Even if it had to be under Ms. Huggins's watchful eye.

Besides, this wasn't her first challenging wallpaper project. She'd make it work. Climbing the stepladder with the pasted strip folded over her arm, she positioned the paper under the ceiling, gradually smoothing and aligning it with the piece next to it.

"Could you use a hand?"

Izzie jumped. The pasted paper flopped over her head, and Reed rushed over to steady the ladder.

Izzie's pulse rate jumped again when she lifted the

paper from her head and took in Reed. He looked dashing in a blue knit shirt Blackburn undoubtedly had a hand in recommending.

"Reed, hi."

"Sorry, I didn't mean to startle you. Ms. Huggins said I could find you back here." Reed took in the room. "You plan to paper this room all by yourself?"

"I've done solo papering many a time." The upper part of the paper pasted, she let the lower part loose. "But if you're game, I'm not refusing the help."

"At your service. I owe you for helping me out last night."

Izzie stepped down from the ladder and gazed straight into his dark eyes that shone like high-gloss black tile. Amazing.

He cocked his head.

Oops, she was staring. "You don't owe me anything. That's known as southern hospitality. You're just supposed to accept gracefully."

He made a quick bow from the waist. "Then I humbly appreciate the kindness you've shown and would sincerely like to help if I may."

"Mr. Harrison, you may. There's an extra brush. Can you smooth this section while I prep the next one?"

He nodded and picked up the smoothing brush. "Nice pattern. The tan and muted grays fit the 1930s look."

Ms. Huggins walked in. "You're familiar with historical interiors?"

"I am. I grew up in a 1930s-built neighborhood in Brooklyn. This pattern is very close to the one in my grandma's kitchen."

"Well, well, an expert to help you, Izzie."

She scrunched her face at the wall. What was she—chopped liver? She had a bachelor's degree in Interior

Design with six years' experience in the field. She sucked in air. Perhaps counting to ten was in order. Old reputations were hard to shake. "Yes, we are fortunate."

Izzie moved the ladder in front of the sink. "Hand me the next section, please."

Reed complied.

She couldn't quite get leverage with the sink in the way to hang the next piece. "This is hard to ..." She turned one hand loose to reposition. The wallpaper turned loose and plopped on top of her head again.

"Hang on. Don't move. Let me ..." Reed joined Izzie on the ladder. He reached around her and lifted the wallpaper off her head. "Excuse me ..."

"Upsy ... there." Izzie patted the wall.

"Watch out." Reed lunged and pressed his body against hers. "It's coming down again. Sorry to crowd. Let me squeeze against ... you ... there. I think it will stay fixed now."

He need not excuse himself. This was one time being crowded didn't bother her. Well, maybe a little. He was so close the smell of bath soap and fragrant aftershave managed to overpower the starchy odor of the paper paste.

"Here ... let me help you down." Reed held her hand while she stepped down. A task she was perfectly capable of executing, but feeling like a pampered lady, she accepted the assistance. Was it glue fumes or his hand on hers that made her a bit heady?

He touched her hair, removing a glob of wallpaper paste. "This may start a new extra-hold trend in hair products."

Izzie ran her hand over her hair, already heavily moussed. "A little extra won't hurt." She brushed some paste off his shirt. "A new means of putting heavy starch in your shirts?" She gave his arm a playful nudge. This New

York guy was surprisingly fun to work with.

"One more wall needs paper. If these are the only rolls left, you will be short."

He made his declaration just as Ms. Huggins walked back into the kitchen. "Not enough wallpaper? Did you measure wrong, Izzie?" Ms. Huggins honed in on Izzie's expected shortcomings.

"No. I intend to add boards to this wall and paint it gray." She pointed to the paint can by the door. "Since you want to feature old-fashioned kitchen utensils, I planned a backdrop for the display. Reed, can I borrow your pen?"

He unclipped the pen in his shirt pocket and handed it to her. Izzie drew in the margin of a newspaper. "I asked Pete to save any leftover boards from his restoration work at the Feldman house." She sketched a tall rectangle to represent the wall and drew in boards running horizontally on the wall. "This will simulate an old country kitchen and give a secure place to hang and display all the utensils you've been collecting."

"Hmm. But what will fill in between the boards?" Ms. Huggins asked.

"Space the boards to let the gray paint show through. That will give the appearance of mortar."

"With only a little extra effort and expense, I can pick up a sack of mortar mix and fill in between the boards," Reed said.

Ms. Huggins brightened. "Excellent idea."

Izzie had never seen such enthusiasm displayed in her former teacher's eyes.

Ms. Huggins tapped her index finger against her lips. "We have a bit of mortar mix in the supply shed left after chimney repairs."

"If mortar and boards cover the wall, I guess we won't need to paint the wall gray," Reed said.

"Mr. Harrison, I like your thinking. You are saving us time and helping with authenticity. Now Izzie, where are the boards you were talking about?"

"Pete promised to bring them over when we were ready."

"Don't you think you should let him know we're ready? No time to waste."

"We just …" Izzie shrugged and pulled her phone from her back pocket and punched in Pete's number.

Ms. Huggins grabbed Reed's arm, "Young man, come with me. I'll show you where the mortar mix is."

Reed looked back at Izzie and gave her a sheepish grin.

Izzie rolled her eyes behind Ms. Huggins, who was marching out the back door, motioning for Reed to follow.

Ms. Huggins fulfilled the Old Testament scripture about no prophet—in her case, interior decorator—is accepted in her own hometown.

The afternoon air was crisp and cool coming off the bay. Downtown Reconstruction Board volunteers were outlining the oaks and fountain in Feldman Park with strings of orange and white lights. A banner announcing, Hamilton Harbor Fall Festival, rippled in the breeze between two oak trees at the corner of the park.

With the mortar drying on the kitchen project, Reed stood in the back of a farm truck unloading pumpkins. "Are enough people going to come out to carve this truckload of pumpkins?" He handed a pumpkin down to Emme, who had come out of the florist shop to help. "Tomorrow night, you will be amazed … I hope." Emme said.

"Last year, people brought their own pumpkins, but we should have even more people take part with pumpkins being sold here," Izzie said.

"I hope so. I'd hate to load these back up."

"We'd never impose on you like that," Izzie said.

"Why not? I've already helped load a pirate ship, wallpapered, and mixed mortar." A little chuckle accompanied his deadpan words.

Izzie laughed. "We do have a mixed bag of needs around here."

"We appreciate how you've stepped in to help," Emme said.

"Glad to. I can pass along how everyone bands together to raise funds for this square to my firm."

"That's good for our team." Izzie held her arms out for another pumpkin.

"Your team?" His brows drew down.

"You know, for those of us who support downtown and preservation of this square," Izzie said. "How did your meeting go with Blackburn at the yacht club?"

"Outstanding food. They're outgrowing their facility, and everyone I met liked the idea of a new club on the marina."

"I'll bet." Pouting, she set down a large lopsided pumpkin. "To me, if all things are shiny and new like Blackburn promotes, you lose the flavor of the town."

Reed let her comment sink in a moment while she hauled the pumpkin to line up with the others. Padgett had instructed him to keep both factions happy, but how could he keep two opposing forces all smiles?

A pickup truck pulled in behind them.

Pete Cullen, who had delivered the lumber for the historical society project, stepped out, rubbing his hands together. "The shirts are here." He went to the back of his truck, lowered the gate and pulled an orange t-shirt from a box, tossing it to Izzie. "The results of your labor."

Izzie held the shirt up for the others to see. The front had a smiling jack-o'-lantern with "Hamilton Harbor Fall Festival" printed underneath. The back was inscribed with "Save the Square" and beneath it, "Hamilton Beach Printers."

"I promised publicity for the donation of these shirts."

Emme peeked in the back of Pete's truck. "You got four cases of shirts donated?"

"Yup. Plus, we're helping Beach Printers get these shirts out of their warehouse. A supplier messed up an order, sent the wrong color, and told them to keep their error."

"We're lucky the wrong shipment was orange," Emme said.

Izzie pulled the shirt over her head. Her spiky hair bent, then popped straight up again. She twirled about, sent her giant orange hoop earrings swaying, threw up her hands, and let out something on the order of a Comanche whoop. What on earth?

Emme and Pete laughed, taking the spectacle in stride.

Izzie trotted to the boxes in Pete's truck and pulled out more shirts. "Put these on." She handed one each to Pete and Emme. She pulled out another, rolled the shirt into a ball and pitched it to Reed, hitting him square in the chest.

"Pete," Izzie said, "can you help Reed unload the rest of the pumpkins? Emme, let's take shirts to the volunteers stringing the lights."

Pete slipped on his shirt and joined Reed, still holding his shirt and staring after Izzie.

Pete looked up at him. "Ready to unload the rest of these?"

"Huh? Oh. Sure." Reed draped the shirt on the truck side and started to hand down a pumpkin. "Is that screaming a norm around here? I don't think I've ever heard anything like it."

"It's the norm for Izzie." Pete took the pumpkin and nodded at the shirt Izzie had thrown to him. "Might as well put it on. If you rile her, she's liable to howl at the moon," Pete's grin spread to his eyes.

"Ah. Thanks for the warning."

"You don't want to be on her bad side."

"Sounds ominous."

"Just kidding, sort of."

Sort of? "I take it life is easier around here if you're a Save the Square fan."

"Saving the square is a unifier. And you seem to fit right in."

But he wasn't supposed to fit in or take sides. His mandate was to please the people, and that was *all* the people involved in the redevelopment project. "Thanks, I think."

Reed pulled the orange shirt over his blue oxford, one of two shirts he owned right now. He could use a work shirt. Ms. Huggins had been kind enough to let him use an old paint smock to protect his clothing. He worked steadily with Pete and finished the rest of the unloading project.

"That shirt looks great on you, Reed," Izzie said when she returned. "Your limited wardrobe is expanding."

"Uh ... yes." The shirt was not exactly a wardrobe addition he would have ever selected, even if handed to him free. But to keep a woman from howling at the moon ... probably something he wouldn't put in his report to Emerson. "You ladies have the honor of taking the last two pumpkins."

"Good. I'd better get back to the flower shop before Mellie thinks I've turned into a pumpkin," Emme said.

Pete grabbed the pumpkin from Emme. "You go ahead. I'll handle this for you, then I'm off."

Reed climbed down from the truck and joined Izzie in

a sea of orange.

"Okay, Reed, pick your favorite pumpkin, 'cause I'm challenging you to a carving duel."

"Is there a contest?" Reed asked.

"You bet. Pastor Creighton has agreed to judge. We discourage spooky and scary, although you will see some. The main thing is attracting families to participate. Sunday school classes from Hope Community Church are making five hundred *luminarias*."

"I've seen pictures of luminarias, but I don't know how they're made."

"Such a sheltered life you lead. I guess there's no demand for luminarias in a city that never sleeps. A tea-light candle is nestled in white sand poured into a small brown paper sack. When the candles are lit, they give off a soft glow along the pumpkin walk trail. With the lighted carved pumpkins, it's beautiful."

"The Sunday school classes make five hundred, free of charge?"

"Why ... sure."

"But why?"

She stared at him, wrinkling her forehead. "Seriously?"

He nodded.

"To help their fellow man, the community ... it's the Christian thing to do." She pointed at him. "You're helping and not charging for services ... are you?"

"No, I'm volunteering ... but ... well, as part of the study, my boss expects me to help."

"I see, totally non-altruistic?"

"Well, maybe a smidgen of my help is selfless."

"Okay, then. How about we tap your altruistic side, because I could use help setting out the pumpkins and luminarias tomorrow."

"With this shirt, how can I refuse?"

"You are absolutely right."

"And … I heard I shouldn't cross you."

Izzie stopped examining pumpkins. "What do you mean?"

Reed lifted his shoulders. "Just that it wasn't good to irritate you."

She harrumphed at that remark. "Oh … well … only with things I hold firm convictions on."

"Like Saving the Square?"

"Yes … just like that," her gray eyes expressive. "You look good in orange by the way."

He smiled at her quick change of topic. "Thanks. I can't recall ever wearing orange."

"Never worn orange? Stick with me. I'll entice you out of your shell and introduce you to all kinds of new—"

Reed's phone jangled. "Excuse me."

"No problem, I'll be on a search for the very best pumpkin for my creation."

He answered his phone.

"Reed, Blackburn here. I'd like you to join me on my yacht Saturday for dinner and a cruise around the bay."

"May I take a rain check on that, Mr. Blackburn? I'm committed to helping with the pumpkin walk."

"Ah … I see. You're spending a lot of time with that Save the Square group, aren't you?"

"I … I'm just trying to learn all I can about your community."

"Of course." The inflection in his voice seemed skeptical. "Maybe we can look at what the Hargrave developers did with their Oceanside venture and get some ideas."

"Yes. Please. Make arrangements and let me know when." Reed ended the call and looked for Izzie.

Was he living in a shell as Izzie put it? If it was not wanting to choose sides in an argument—his mother pitted against his grandmother—she had him there. But he was a designer. He had to be open to varying ideas. Eventually, choosing sides would be a hot topic. And right now, he was beginning to feel like he'd been dropped in a pot of water with the heat turned on high.

He scrutinized Izzie as she wandered among the three hundred pumpkins.

If he stayed in his shell and minded his own business, he'd be out of controversy. However, Padgett had made this civil war, of sorts, his business. If only he could find the neutral zone.

Izzie motioned to him. "Here's the perfect pumpkin for me. Which one is yours?"

Keep both sides happy, win them over. He pointed to a pumpkin that was more oblong than round. "That's mine."

"Reminds me of Mr. Potato Head."

"Shucks, you spoiled my surprise."

"You know who Mr. Potato Head is?"

"I'm not that sheltered."

"We'll see," Izzie said. "I'm betting you won't be able to guess my pumpkin's identity."

"You're on. What's the bet?"

"Dinner. Winner's choice."

Reed stuck out his hand and clasped hers. "Deal."

Those clear gray eyes and the grasp of her hand were beginning to draw him out of his shell, as Izzie put it, but he doubted this fit the description of neutral zone.

CHAPTER SEVEN

Even with the scent of fresh fall air on the Flower Cottage porch, Izzie's morning devotion drifted into worry time. She could not add one more thing to her mental to-do list. Nor did she have any extra minutes today to do one more activity. The possibility of her not passing the interior design test loomed heavy and championing the Save the Square cause verged on overwhelming. Then there was Mr. Reed Harrison.

A sparrow perched on the edge of a pot of burgundy mums.

Birds. Worry. She flipped her NIV Bible open and scanned a section she'd highlighted and read many times. "Look at the birds of the air," she read aloud. "They do not sow or reap or store away in barns, and yet your heavenly Father feeds them. Are you not much more valuable than they? Who of you by worrying can add a single hour to his life? Therefore, do not worry about tomorrow, for tomorrow will worry about itself. Each day has enough trouble of its own."

Like P-day. Pumpkin carving day. She just needed to focus on getting through this day.

A car pulled up in front of the historical society house. Reed. Right on time. The bird flitted away. She closed her Bible. *Thank you, Lord, for the little bird directing me to your Word.*

Reed stepped out of his car. Bless him, he wore the orange Save the Square T-shirt. His black hair and black slacks made a striking contrast.

"You're a study in Halloween colors." Izzie strode over to join him. "Very fitting."

"Same to you."

Izzie looked down at her orange shirt with her black wrap skirt and shoes. "Oh yeah. I guess we're twins today."

"Uh … fraternal maybe." Reed touched one of Izzie's earrings. "You're one up on me with these black cat earrings with orange eyes."

Izzie grinned. "Ready to see how our rustic wall creation turned out?"

"Sure. It looks like the outside has been spruced up."

"I found some willing volunteers from another Sunday school class at church."

"Really? Impressive."

"You seem surprised again that church people pitch in to help."

"Don't mind me. It's just … I've not seen that kind of giving spirit where I come from."

"I'm sorry to hear that. For me, my Christian friends are my stronghold, along with Scripture. You should come to church with me while you're here."

"We'll see."

His "we'll see" sounded more like "no way."

They climbed the steps to the porch at the historical society. "The table for admissions is set up. It's a relief to see things are coming together."

The porch screen door screeched their arrival. Ms. Huggins was at her desk, just to the left of the entry, and stood when she saw them.

"Glad you're here. Mr. Harrison, your wall made the perfect backdrop for the old kitchen utensils display."

"Please call me Reed. And it's not just my—"

"Reed. Okay. Come and see." They dutifully fell in behind Ms. Huggins and marched down the hall, footsteps thudding on the wooden floor.

"Izzie," Ms. Huggins tossed her name over her shoulder, "I hope you didn't over-do that order of three hundred pumpkins. That's a big chunk of money out of our festival funds."

"After the enthusiasm of last year, we should do fine and make a sizable profit. We're getting the pumpkins for three dollars and selling for ten."

"Well … still … three hundred. Over there by the sink are some carving instruments someone donated for tonight."

"Wow," Izzie said. "You have the utensils displayed and labeled." Izzie ran her finger over the rough mortar. "The wall looks better than I'd hoped."

Ms. Huggins sighed. "The mortar gives the wall just the right old-fashioned feel. Great suggestion, Reed."

"Don't forget, it was Izzie's idea for the contrasting wall."

"Like I told the mayor, Izzie's not having enough wallpaper turned into a good thing." Ms. Huggins folded her arms in front of her and gave the wall a satisfied look.

Izzie pressed her lips together. *Let it go.* She held her hand over an identifying label. "What do you think this gadget is?" she asked Reed.

Reed stepped up and examined the strange-looking metal utensil.

"I'd say … it's a cherry pitter."

"Hold on." Izzie checked the label. "Did you peek?"

"No. My grandmother had one that looked like that. I used to pit cherries for her. She made outstanding cherry turnovers."

"Young man, you don't cease to amaze."

Ms. Huggins had a new teacher's pet.

"Knock, knock. Anybody here?"

"Sounds like Emme." Izzie called to her. "Back here in the kitchen."

"The yard and the front display look great." Emme came in dressed in a smock with The Flower Cottage logo. "New wallpaper. The kitchen looks wonderful, especially this display wall. It will be worth an admission fee, Ms. Huggins."

"Thanks to them." She patted Reed's shoulder and, at least, gave Izzie a nod. "Church volunteers worked hard pruning and mowing yesterday."

"And don't forget Appleberry's Furniture was kind enough to donate some 1950s retro furnishings to use in the front room," Izzie said.

"Yes. But my aim was to keep the display historically correct. This structure was built in 1919 as a schoolhouse."

"I haven't seen the display room. Okay to look?" Reed asked.

"Absolutely."

Ms. Huggins beamed—something Izzie had never witnessed before. She led the way to the large room across from her office that held exhibits highlighting Hamilton Harbor's history.

"Per the Hamilton sister's wishes, we removed some walls that were added when the house was made into a home for Edgar Feldman and later, into apartments. Our goal is to restore the original school room that held grades 1-8." Ms. Huggins crossed the room to the brick fireplace. "Here's a picture of the Hamilton Harbor Community School's student body standing beside this fireplace that's been refurbished—all twelve of them. This school operated in the 1920s, so 1950s furniture didn't fit. I put Appleberry's furnishings in a storeroom for now."

"I thought this room could show the evolving history of Hamilton Harbor, which certainly includes the 1950's,"

Izzie said.

"But if we're representing the old school as historically correct—"

Reed interrupted, "With these refinished floors, fireplace, and the inkwell school desks, you've made the perfect backdrop to show the history of the building. What if you made this into a rotating display with totally different exhibits periodically, like one from the 50s? Then you can draw new and repeat customers. Continue to charge admission, and this building could become self-sustaining."

Ms. Huggins drew her brows in tight. "An excellent point."

"For economy, keep the schoolroom decor as the backdrop and just change out displays in the room. That way you'll be staying true to the old school theme." Reed said.

"I like your ideas." Ms. Huggins said.

Izzie thought Reed's idea sounded a lot like hers but nodded her agreement.

Emme shot Izzie an understanding glance. "All the suggestions sound good to me. I almost forgot. I came to see if you will cover the shop, Izzie, while Mellie makes deliveries. I have a wedding consult in thirty minutes."

"I'll be right over. Reed, the shop has a worktable that will be perfect for our great pumpkin challenge. I set aside the two we selected by the admissions table in the park."

"I'll bring them over." Reed said.

"You're helping with the pumpkin carving activity tonight?" Emme asked Reed.

He threw his hands out and displayed his cute little dimple. "When you volunteer around here, it seems you're enlisted for the duration."

"We are pleased you are so willing to help." Ms. Huggins flashed pearly teeth.

Reed crossed the street carrying the big pumpkin Izzie had selected.

Izzie hurried to hold the Flower Cottage gate open.

"These pumpkins will require two trips."

"I'll take this one and meet you inside. Oh, and would you mind bringing the carving tools Ms. Huggins mentioned?"

"Yes, ma'am." He tipped his fingers to his forehead in a mock salute. "I shall return."

Izzie gave him a lopsided grin.

The aroma of pumpkin-pie-spice-scented candles bathed the inside of the shop.

"Your relief has arrived."

Mellie poked a plastic cardholder into a floral arrangement of mixed green plants with yellow mum accents. "Spicy smells, autumn color—a lovely time of year. Emme already left for her appointment, and I'll make deliveries as quick as I can."

"Don't rush on my account." Izzie hoisted her big pumpkin onto the worktable. "Watching the shop will give me time to work on my pumpkin carving entry. Reed Harrison is coming to carve one too."

"Oh?" Mellie's eyes widened. "Reed? Isn't that the dreamy guy from New York you were worried about?"

"What's with the smirk? He is. I'm just doing my part to introduce him to our traditions."

"Good. He and the redevelopment project are on my prayer list."

"Minc too, and you might add a prayer for the festival. I hope everything is ready for tonight. The pumpkins are unloaded. We've gathered carving tools for those who don't bring their own. We have set up concession tables for sandwiches and drinks donated by Elaine from the bistro and cookies baked by ladies from the church. But the actual festival on Saturday might be a different story. Lots more going on, so lots more to go wrong."

"I've learned in my seventy years, it's best not to speak negative."

The flower shop door opened. Reed, holding his pumpkin and a sack, stepped in, making the buzzer under the mat sound.

"Smells delightful in here."

"Mellie, this is Reed Harrison from the New York firm doing the feasibility study for the downtown marina."

Reed crossed the room, set his armload on the worktable, and extended his hand to Mellie.

"Nice to meet you. I've heard lots about you."

"And me about you." Mellie smirked.

"Really?" Reed said.

Izzie mouthed, "Lay off," and tried to hide the gesture from Reed.

Mellie glanced at Izzie and spoke to Reed. "So, you like pumpkin pie scents?"

"Reminds me of my grandma's kitchen at Thanksgiving."

"Yes, siree. Makes me want to bake pies, which I promised for tomorrow's All Things Pumpkin bake sale. Izzie, I just received a pick-up order for a new baby boy arrangement. Could you take care of it, please?"

Mellie turned to Reed. "The population is growing. You can put that in your feasibility study." She lifted the arrangement she'd just finished. "I'm off to make deliveries."

"Do you need help carrying anything?" Reed asked.

"Thank you, no. The van's already loaded with my other deliveries. Nice meeting you, Reed." Mellie retrieved her purse. "You'll have to try a slice of my pumpkin pie tomorrow and see if it's as good as your grandma's."

"I look forward to that."

Mellie left, all smiles.

"So, you work here part-time?" Reed asked.

"I used to, but I'm more of an as-needed fill-in since I'm trying to build my interior design business. Fortunately, I'm waiting on a curtain order which gave me some extra time to devote to the festival."

Izzie pulled out a blue vase in the shape of a puppy and cut a piece of foam to fit.

Reed picked up a terracotta-colored candle and sniffed. "The look and smell of fall is my favorite time of year."

"Mine too. When I lived at the Gardner house, at the first hint of autumn, the renters built a fire, and we roasted marshmallows."

"Closest thing I came to a campfire was the barbeque grill on our back porch."

"You were so deprived."

"But I did learn how to carve a pumpkin from my grandpa. He always used his pocketknife, which was handed down to me." Reed pulled the brown and white-handled knife from his pocket and held it in his palm.

"How special. You grew up with your grandparents?"

"Until I was nine, when Grandpa died. Then it was just my grandmother and me."

Izzie finished the arrangement and placed it in the cooler. "Lord, watch over this new baby boy. Give his parents special wisdom, so he may grow to fulfill his God-given potential."

"Do you pray over all your arrangements?"

"I do. The flowers might not last, but the prayer with it will. Did you go to church growing up?"

Reed's black-brown eyes clouded. "I did … for a time."

He stared at the pocketknife.

She'd touched a sensitive subject. Best not go there. "Shall we commence with the pumpkin challenge?"

He brightened. "You're on."

Izzie clasped his offered hand, his grip warm, and firm. She liked his touch—a lot.

She set a tall trash can on the worktable that put a barrier between them. "For your scraps, and no peeking 'til we're done?"

"Agreed."

Izzie made her cuts and then searched through a separate trash container for discarded greenery she might use.

"Do you have some paper I can put under my pumpkin, so I don't make a mess?"

Izzie tore brown paper from a roll and handed it to Reed. She smelled the strong chemical odor of paint. What was he making?

"Is that paint from our wall project?"

"It is. I sweet-talked Ms. Huggins into sharing a brush and some paint."

"We are talking major teacher's pet developing here."

"Not sure why."

"You have no history with her like I do. It's too hard for her to fathom that Izzie Ketterling, school detention queen, could be responsible and produce anything worthwhile."

"Detention queen? How did you earn that reputation?"

"Good question. Long answer."

"My study team doesn't arrive from New York 'til tomorrow. Spill."

"Ah. Well, in middle school, an ancient oak tree had to be cut down to make room for portable classrooms. I received my first detention when I drew a giant replacement oak on the band room roll-up door."

"They didn't appreciate your creativity?"

"Defacing school property is what the powers that be called it."

"Bummer." Reed peered over the trash can with amazing, sympathetic eyes.

Heart be still. "In high school, my favorite subject was art. My art teacher encouraged me to develop my talent. But Ms. Huggins used to say, 'If you spent as much time on your essay questions as you do drawing pictures on the back of your test paper, you'd make better grades.' She also said she never should have taught me about Michelangelo and his work on the Sistine Chapel."

"Why's that?"

"I spray-painted an enlarged head of our school mascot on the gym ceiling."

"How could you possibly reach the ceiling?"

"Workmen left scaffolding after installing new lighting. It was too tempting."

"Did they make you paint over it?"

"Nope, the student body loved it. I received detention. The incident went before the school board. The art teacher spoke for me, and the wildcat is actually still on the gym ceiling."

"Mischief-maker makes good?"

"My artistic vandalism didn't turn out so well my senior year. One thing for sure, my detention reputation stuck, and still does for Ms. Huggins."

"What happened your senior year?"

Izzie let her breath out slowly. Would she have any secrets left? "Long story. Short version. Circumstantial evidence surrounding ruined prom decorations pointed to me as the culprit. Two years later, the truth came out. But by then it was too late to salvage my reputation." Izzie snipped at a discarded flower stem and blinked back tears that still threatened after all this time. False accusations were much worse than earned ones.

Izzie plugged stems and some green leaves on the top of her carving. "Are you ready to unveil your gray ghost over there?"

"Is that your guess?" Reed asked. The crinkle of a paper bag sounded on Reed's side of the table.

"Not until I eyeball what you designed. Ready to change places?" Izzie asked.

"I am." Reed said.

Izzie stepped around the table and peeked at Reed's pumpkin and grinned.

Reed blurted, "You've fashioned Cinderella's coach."

"Man. You're quick. I was banking on your disadvantaged childhood."

"Never underestimate a New Yorker. Do you still think mine is a ghost?"

Izzie admired his gray pumpkin topped with an inverted aluminum funnel, no doubt on loan from Ms. Huggins. "How about Tin Man from the *Wizard of Oz*?"

Reed circled back to stand beside her. His after-shave tickled her senses.

"Right." His gaze held on her. His face seemed to inch closer. Or was it her imagination? Her heart fluttered. Had the romance of Cinderella's coach rubbed off on her? The back door burst open.

Reed stepped back.

Emme held up three envelopes. "Izzie, these were returned for insufficient postage. Your information for the fall festival never made it to the radio and TV stations."

Ice-cold fingers gripped Izzie's insides. A vision of three hundred rotten pumpkins with Ms. Huggins saying, "I told you so," blanketed her mind. She folded her arms over her stomach and rocked. "No wonder I haven't heard any public service announcements."

Emme touched Izzie's Cinderella creation. "We need the fairy godmother that goes with this coach to help sell all those pumpkins."

Each day did have its own trouble.

"More than that," Izzie said, "we need prayer."

CHAPTER EIGHT

Izzie sagged against the table for the kettle corn concession in Feldman Park. "Without the golf cart and two volunteers who can't come, we're on an extreme time-crunch getting the jack-o'-lanterns moved to the trail."

Emme patted her shoulder. "We still have three carts operating. Look at the bright side. Our prayers were answered. You sold all three hundred pumpkins and have plenty for the trail."

Izzie straightened. "You're right. It's like good news, bad news. Add the pumpkins people brought to the carving last night, we have close to six hundred to place. She pushed up the sleeves of the black sweater she wore under her orange festival shirt. "I'll rework the schedule. We'll just make more trips. Pull up a cart and we'll start loading."

Returning Emme's salute, Izzie noticed Reed's rental car pull up. She hurried to meet him.

"I promised to help and brought these guys to see Feldman Square." Three men emerged from his car.

"Hallelujah, we can use the help."

"Meet the feasibility team." Reed made introductions while Izzie studied them. There was an architect, Mandeville Smithson, tall and lanky; an engineer, Greg Dickson, with light brown curly hair and round wire-rim glasses; and a marketing specialist, Dan Croley, who had a wide smile and straight teeth accented by a cleft chin.

"Pleased to meet you," Izzie said. "Follow me and see what your teammate accomplished." She took them to a display board propped against the admissions table.

"Look!"

Reed's brow furrowed. "What am I supposed to be looking at?"

The board listed the carved pumpkin winners with pictures. "Notice anything familiar?"

She stepped out of the way and motioned for Dan, Greg, and Mandeville to join Reed. "The pumpkin carving last night was judged, and you won first place in the famous character category."

"Me? A winner?"

"Well, well, congratulations." Dan gave Reed a pat on the back. "Hidden talent. You've been holding out at the office."

"Or they're just hurting for entries in the famous character category."

"Come on. You did a very nice job." Izzie said. "And you get a very nice blue ribbon and bragging rights."

Dan pulled out his phone. "Stand beside him, Izzie. Smile." He snapped a shot. "It's recorded for posterity and texted to you, Reed."

"Thanks, I think. Now we're at your service," Reed said to Izzie.

"Terrific."

They walked to the cart where Francine helped Emme and introductions were made. "Ten pumpkins can be loaded on a cart with as many luminarias packed in as possible," Francine said. "I'd stay longer but I need to check on the bake sale."

"Thank you for helping," Izzie said. "I'm cooling cookies in the flower shop that I'll bring over later."

Izzie looked at the New York contingent. "Mary Ann and Carla are already out on section one. Could one of you take Francine's place with Emme on this cart and put out pumpkins in section two?"

"I'll do it," Mandeville said.

"We're off." Mandeville and Emme waved and headed for the beginning of the trail that ran alongside the Feldman house.

"Greg and I can take the other cart." Dan said.

"Good. We'll load you up. Take section three. Look for numbers on markers like this one at the beginning and end of each section." Izzie held up a sample plastic cardholder donated from the Flower Cottage. "Place the luminarias along the edge of the trail and position the pumpkins among the trees for easy viewing. Emme will be in the section next to you if you have questions."

"You have things well-organized. I'm impressed," Reed said after Greg and Dan left with a load of grinning jack-o'-lanterns.

"Praise may be premature. I should have made an alternate plan for no shows. I'm down a cart and two volunteers. Come look at the trail map."

Spread on the admissions table was a hand-drawn map.

"This is a sketch of the trail where the pumpkins and luminaries are being placed. I have marked thirty sections along the trail to place the near six hundred pumpkins and seven hundred fifty luminarias." Wringing her hands, she glanced at her watch. "That's sixty trips. Then everything has to be lit before dark. The admissions table opens at six o'clock. It's going to be close."

"We can use my car if I can get close enough to the trail."

Izzie ran her finger along the trail map. "Most of the path runs behind residences on the water. But there are a few dead-end streets," she pointed, "that will make sections fifteen and eighteen accessible by car."

"Load me up and point me in the right direction."

"You are a blessing."

"I'm not sure I rate that status, but I need some activity after our big lunch. We went to Calico Jack's."

"I'm proud of you. You're giving your crew the full indoctrination."

"Complete with a pirate ship tour before lunch. They even got to see Mr. Blackburn and some man with bright red hair."

"Oh? What did Mr. Blackburn have to say?"

"We just waved. He was headed toward the Gulf on his yacht. Too bad, he's missing out on this pumpkin walk set-up."

Izzie snickered. "I'm sure he'll be disappointed."

Later, Reed returned to the park. "Ready for more."

"Would you believe I sent the last shipment out?" She handed Reed a fist bump. Dan and Greg wheeled in on their cart.

"All that's left is to place these luminarias around the park before we start lighting everything."

"Load them up on the floorboard. There's room for you two on the back."

Greg drove. Dan handed out the sacks, while Izzie and Reed placed the luminarias next to the sidewalk encircling the park. They wound up across from the rundown houses on the square.

"Is the entire square to be a part of the marina redevelopment project?" Dan asked.

"This is part of historical downtown that I put in my report." Reed said.

"What's the story on those two eyesores?" Greg pointed.

"Eyesores?" Izzie slid off the back seat of the cart, hands on hips. "Those houses are treasures. Part of the festival funds will pay off back taxes and the owners plan to renovate. That one," Izzie pointed to the Gardner house, "is to be a maternity home."

"Hmm."

Izzie wasn't sure if Greg's "hmm" was a positive or not.

"Now to light everything. I know Mary Ann and Carla have to leave."

The last cart with Emme and Mandeville emerged from the trail.

"You people have earned extra stars in your crowns," Izzie said.

"What crowns?" Reed asked.

"It's a Bible saying. You know, doing good deeds that gain favor."

"Placing pumpkins is Kingdom work?"

"Could be. It is all for a good cause."

"Emme, do you have time to help light?"

"Count on me. Mellie is watching the shop, Richie is playing with a friend, and Clifton will meet me here for the festival."

She scanned the eyes of Reed's coworkers. They gave assuring nods. "We are at your service," Reed said.

Ms. Huggins and Francine crossed the park from the historical society. "All the pumpkins and luminarias are out?" Ms. Huggins asked.

"Yes, ma'am."

"I have to tell you I had my doubts. Are these the only people you have to handle lighting?"

Izzie nodded. "Yes, ma'am."

"You'll still be lighting when spectators arrive."

"I can help," Francine said. "I have everything set for people to drop off items for the bake sale."

"Give us lighters and a section and we're gone," Greg said.

"I'll light the luminarias around the park, then I'd like to make some sketches," Mandeville said.

Izzie handed out lighters to the volunteers and assigned sections.

Ms. Huggins turned to leave. "I'm going to check on my helpers. You should have recruited more help."

Izzie pressed her mouth into a straight line and closed her eyes.

"Ms. Huggins seems to feel the need to criticize you." Reed said.

Izzie bobbed her head, sending her tiered, autumn leaf earrings swaying. "Some people have a hard time seeing people can change." Izzie slid into the cart driver's seat, and Reed sat next to her. "We'd better get going. I'd hate to prove her right."

The breeze splashing against her face cooled her emotion.

"Is your motivation to prove her wrong?"

Izzie maneuvered a few turns along the trail before responding. "I never thought of what I wanted as having any connection to Ms. Huggins ... but you may have something. I might not be so determined to save this square if it weren't for her waving her hanky of doubts. Of course, her watchful eye ... is not without reason."

"All because of you painting on the gym ceiling?"

Izzie sniffed. "Well ... a little more than that."

"Only a little?" Reed asked with an amused inflection.

"You're enjoying entirely too much amusement at my expense. We'll start at the beginning of the trail and work over to section twenty." She handed a lighter to Reed. "I'll take the left, you the right."

They worked quickly, moving from one section to the next. The evening shadows turned a deeper gray, and the lighted pumpkins and luminaries created soft, comforting light. "Section twenty complete and the time is four-fifty. We did it."

"I like the cozy glow of candlelight on the trail. So, what was the little more you did in high school?"

"Hey. You tell me why you find it so hard to believe Christian folks do things with no ulterior motives."

Reed hesitated. His expression switched from playful to somber. "A so-called Christian rooked my grandmother out of insurance, and my parents profess to be Christian but left me for my grandmother to raise … so … my experience with Christians has been different."

"Oh. I'm so sorry. I shouldn't have—"

"No need for you to be sorry. It's just the way it is." He raised a brow and looked down on her. "I'd much rather talk about your indiscretions. What is the little more you did?"

"I painted the big plaster wildcat in front of the school our school colors, green and white."

"That doesn't sound so bad."

"Well," she kicked at a tree root, "I painted him green with white polka-dots … that glowed in the dark. The alumni took exception and insisted the statue be repainted tan and black, like a real wildcat."

"Did you have to do the repainting?"

She heaved a sigh. "I did. And it added to my reputation. One that led to a big-time false accusation that I paid for and don't want to talk about right now. By the time high school was over, I had plenty of experience in painting and design—the inspiration for my career."

Izzie leaned against a large oak. Reed's arm pressed next to hers, the touch a soothing balm. The cool night air encircled them.

"You did it," he said. "Proved Ms. Huggins wrong."

"If it hadn't been for you and your team … like I said, you were a blessing."

Under the oak canopy, the sun hung low in the sky

and cast a golden sheen on the bay waters. "A magnificent view," Reed said.

"I used to love to walk down here to watch the sunset in the evening. Sometimes, fireflies would dart about the grassy bank like tiny neon flashing lights."

"All by yourself?"

"Just me."

"I'm happy to share this with you now." Reed patted her hand. "Your hand is cold."

"I left my sweater at the park."

Reed slipped his arm around her shoulders. His warmth flowed over her like the golden glow of the carved pumpkins. The sweet fragrance of scented luminarias mixed with the earthy smell of oak leaves enveloped them. Something—his closeness, the silence—made her lift her gaze. Her eyes met his, and she felt she would drown in their dark depths.

She tilted her face to his. He touched the curve of her mouth, and she closed her eyes as his lips found hers, sending tingles all over. Leaning into his embrace, her hand moved to his arm in a gentle caress. Tension lifted as event pressures floated away. She'd have been content to stay wrapped in his arms 'til the last candle burned down.

An indistinct voice came from a thicket of palmettos nearby. It was Emme. Then, more clearly, she heard Francine. "I think that's the last of our pumpkins to light."

"Only a few more luminarias to light over here."

"Aren't these pumpkins amazing? All so different."

"I'll say. I was a judge, and it was hard to select winners. Except the first-place prize for Reed Harrison that Izzie wanted. The pumpkin was good, but we needed him to win a ribbon."

"Smart. It should leave him with a favorable view of our Save the Square efforts."

Francine chuckled. "Nothing like a little blue-ribbon bribery."

Reed stiffened, dropped his arm, and stepped back.

"And leaving your sweater at the park, was that part of the set-up?"

"What? You think—"

"I think we should go. It looks like your mission is complete."

Reed grabbed the lighters they'd left sitting on a low hanging oak limb. His hasty movement stirred the flickering candlelight in a jack-o'-lantern, distorting its expression from whimsical to disgust.

"Where's your young man?" Ms. Huggins asked Izzie when she walked into the kitchen at the historical society carrying a tray of homemade pumpkin spice cookies. The festival's "Everything Pumpkin" theme filled the old schoolhouse with the sweet smells of cinnamon, ginger, nutmeg, and allspice from the homemade baked goods.

"If you mean Reed Harrison, he's not my young man. And I don't know where he is."

Ms. Huggins raised an eyebrow. "You needn't snap. It's most unbecoming."

Izzie pushed out a short breath. "Sorry. I'm bummed. I burned a batch of cookies this morning. I'm only bringing two dozen instead of the four I promised."

But more than that, Reed's accusation still stung. And worse, *had* she tried to manipulate him? Having him awarded a ribbon, she'd thought, would be kind of like southern hospitality, doing a good turn, making him feel welcome.

Why did she promise to bake cookies on top of

overseeing this festival? Another stupid idea. But a promise was a promise. This afternoon's fiasco with Reed had spilled into her attitude.

"Setbacks. Life's full of them." Ms. Huggins said.

"You're right, per usual." Izzie attempted to hang a smile on her face and set the cookies on the table with the cookie placard. Several varieties were already packaged and marked for sale. "The feasibility team members said they'd drop by for the bake sale and to see the historical exhibits. But I don't know if that's still in their plans." The vision of Reed leaving in a huff filled her mind.

"I hope Reed makes it here for the pumpkin awards."

Izzie flinched at Francine's voice. Her words were just as clear as they had been earlier. She came out of the pantry with an armload of napkins and plastic utensils. Bless her. Francine had no clue Reed overheard her earlier comment and had taken offense. And Izzie didn't want her to know.

"We've been working Reed pretty hard and his team just arrived from New York this morning. I wouldn't be surprised if they didn't crash at the motel."

"I don't want him to miss out. This year, first place is not only awarded a blue ribbon but also a pumpkin pie. Mellie outdid herself and baked ten pies." She held up one of the pies. "I'm setting aside five of them for our five category winners in the pumpkin carving contest. It might generate more enthusiasm about entering next year. What do you think?"

Not if they knew it was fixed. Izzie forced a smile. "I think I picked the perfect person to oversee the bake sale. From the looks of these tables and the yummy aroma coming from this kitchen, 'Everything Pumpkin' will be a success."

Francine's eyes warmed. "I appreciate your confidence."

Izzie heard footsteps in the hall leading to the kitchen. Reed? Her shoulders drooped at the sight of Ms. Nettie

Livingsworth carrying a pumpkin chiffon pie. She'd willed herself to believe that once Reed thought over the remarks made about his first-place win; he'd realize there was no ill intent. Surely, he wouldn't miss the carnival. He'd said the event was perfect for fact-gathering and experiencing the pulse of the community.

"Nettie, pies over here." Francine pointed to the pie table.

In addition to spaces for pies and cookies, tables brimmed with appetizers, soups and stews, and breads and cakes. Something to please every pallet. If not, there were stands around the park with cotton candy, popcorn, pretzels, and hot dogs along with plenty of games for kids.

Izzie turned again at the clicking sound of hard sole shoes.

Not Reed. Dan Croley, followed by Greg and Mandeville, entered the kitchen. Surely, Reed was not far behind.

Izzie grinned. "Here's our pumpkin walk lifesaver recruits."

"We bought tickets for the exhibits, but these smells lured us back here," Mandeville said.

"Please, start your tour right here with kitchen items from the good old days." Ms. Huggins ushered them to the kitchen utensil wall and enlightened them on the origin and use of the different items.

Where was Reed?

"My grandma had these old metal ice cube trays. They were tough to deal with," Greg said.

"My granddaddy said a rolling pin like this one was tough to deal with when Granny chased him." Dan snickered. "He might laugh at the good old days label."

"Just keep in mind that we want history and the good old days remembered in the plans you submit." Ms. Huggins used her no-nonsense teacher's tone.

"Of course. We'll take your concerns under advisement," Dan said.

Oh boy. "How about some pumpkin spice cookies? I made them myself."

"Homemade cookies, reminds me of my granny's kitchen." Dan picked up a pack.

"When she wasn't beaming your grandfather over the head?"

He grinned and nodded. "I'll take a dozen."

Mandeville looked at his watch, "We better check out the exhibits up front. We're to meet Capt. Jack for the pumpkin watch shortly."

"I'll escort you up front where Marigold and Petunia Hamilton will be your tour guides," Ms. Huggins said. She stepped aside as several people filed in. "Francine, you have some new arrivals."

"My stomach is begging me to come back later," Mandeville told Izzie.

"Please do. Uh … where's your other team member?"

"He's at the yacht club. Said he needed to give that part of the project more attention. But he might make it over here later. I'll make sure he knows about all the goodies—the big city offers a lot, but we can't duplicate hometown friendly like this. Excuse me, I'd better not hold up the tour."

"Sure." Izzie willed a smile. She had a festival that needed more attention too.

The Feldman fall festival was in full swing. Twilight had succumbed to dark, bringing a growing crowd of miniature-sized Batmen, Spidermen, princesses and lady bugs accompanied by parents. The evening air brightened with the smells of kettle corn popping, hot dogs roasting, with shrieks and splashing coming from the dunking booth.

"Izzie, I've been looking for you," Claudia said. "The pretzel vendor needs an extension cord."

"I stored extras in the golf cart. I'll get one."

She retrieved the cord and waved at her policeman friend, Tony Duncan, who'd agreed to work the festival. Having him around was comforting, but seeing Reed arrive would do more to soothe her frazzled nerves. She'd stewed over the words he took the wrong way and had rehearsed all kinds of things to say. If only she had the chance to talk to him. Delivering the cord and making her way back to the admissions table, she searched the crowd for his slicked back hair. No Reed.

Olivia Appleberry manned the admissions table and made a perfect, plump Mother Goose with her pointy hat and striped leggings.

"You will have such a good time on the pumpkin walk, Cinderella," she told a little girl in a shimmery blue dress of taffeta with puffy netting. "I've seen some other princesses here that you'll probably see on the trail. Mom and Dad, don't forget to visit the historical society exhibit. It's educational, and admission is for a good cause."

"You are a terrific Save the Square ambassador."

"Thanks. I've even put Corky and Fritz to work advertising the festival in The Pampered Pooch window."

"How so?"

"Corky is dressed as a pea and Fritz a carrot. They go together like peas and carrots. Isn't that the cutest? They sit under Claudia's big sign promoting the festival. And speaking of going together, where is your cute guy from New York?"

"He's hardly *my* cute guy, and I'm not privy to his schedule."

Olivia raised a brow. "Well. He should be here. I want him to see how our downtown efforts are drawing people in."

"I agree." Izzie scanned those returning from the pumpkin trail. Maybe Reed met up with his team to go on the pumpkin watch. He wouldn't ignore the festival altogether. Would he? Had he been so disturbed about his award ... the kiss they'd shared?

On the other side of the park, a crowd had formed.

"It must be time for the mayor to announce the winners of the pumpkin carving," Olivia said.

"I need to make certain things go smoothly."

Mayor Brimstead called out other winners, then said, "The first-place winner in the famous character category—Reed Harrison—for his depiction of the tin man in the Wizard of Oz. Is Reed here?"

There was applause, with people looking for the winner. But, still no Reed.

"Folks, he is on the feasibility team for the marina and downtown redevelopment project." The mayor placed Reed's award on the podium. "We'll see that he receives his ribbon and pie. That wraps things up for the pumpkin contest, but the excitement is just starting. Don't miss dunking our favorite downtown preacher. He chuckled. "Of course, he's our *only* downtown preacher. See you back here in an hour for the costume judging, and it looks like we have some creative dressers this year."

The crowd dispersed, and Izzie spoke to the mayor.

"I'll see that Reed gets the ribbon and pie."

"Good. I needed to tell you about another fabulous fundraiser for the square." The mayor's face, a layered mass of scar tissue, didn't detract from the sparkle in his blue eyes.

"I talked to another mayor at a conference in central

Florida, whose downtown, like ours, had dried up and had some rundown Victorian houses. One was restored. They had an interior design contest to decorate the interior and then charged admission. The contest generated unbelievable interest in downtown, and now their historical section is thriving—attracting tourists, businesses, and new residents. I'm telling you, with the resources we have here, there is no reason we can't do the same thing."

"It sounds fantastic, but—"

"Wait, I'm not finished. The best part is headed our way right now." The mayor leaned on his cane and waved over Lake Spencer and his wife, each brandishing giant pink puffs of cotton candy.

"This stuff is sticky but oh so good," Lake said.

"I was just filling Izzie in on the promotion we talked about. Tell her your plans."

"Mallory and I decided to purchase the Feldman house."

"Fantastic," Izzie said.

"And after talking to the mayor, we are making the house available for the interior design contest," Mallory said.

"But isn't that risky?" Izzie said. "What if you don't like what decorators do?"

"I think it will be fun to see what designers come up with. If I don't like a color they use, I can always repaint. I'm excited for the opportunity."

"In the central Florida contest," the mayor said, "the winning decorator was awarded a TV decorating show. I'm going to check on that idea with our local TV station."

"I'm all over that incentive. I know some other decorators who will probably want to participate. I'll start talking it up," Izzie said.

A contest for decorators might be just the ticket to help

save the square and take her mind off one no-show Mr. Reed Harrison.

🏠 🏠 🏠 🏠

Izzie sat in her car in front of the Pirates' Cove Motel. She glanced at the clock. Was eight-thirty too early to drop in on Reed? His rental car was there.

She couldn't take another miserable night of worrying. The town's people weren't scurrilous and underhanded. Francine meant no harm. Would the pie and ribbon make a good peace offering? If he'd seen the runner-up in the famous person category, Reed would have known he was the best choice for first place anyhow. She took a deep breath, willing herself to move.

Slipping out of the driver's seat, she marched to his door, knocked, and waited.

Nothing.

She knocked again.

The door next to his opened.

"Dan. Good morning. I didn't see Reed at the carnival and wanted to be sure he received his award for winning first place in the pumpkin carving."

"Too modest, I guess. Us guys will be glad to take his pie award and tell him what he missed when he calls from New York."

CHAPTER NINE

Reed tugged at his tie and willed the prickly beads of sweat to stop erupting on his brow. He leaned forward in his desk chair, arched his back, then propped his elbows on his desk. He stared at the reminder pinned to the corkboard behind his computer. "If you don't do it, it won't get done."

Among all the things he didn't know, he knew those words were true. But the thoughts he needed to write in his report to Vance Padgett wouldn't come.

A tingle crept up his back. What was wrong with him? He was home. Back to the familiar. Back to his orderly life. Arise at 5:00. Work out with weights. Shower, shave, and drink coffee with a plain whole-wheat bagel. A brisk walk to the office, and he was in his chair at 7:00.

To keep from wasting time, he practiced a responsible work routine by leaving the next step for work in progress on his desk. But today, that next step eluded him.

Being responsible was one legacy he could claim from his mother, even if it *was* an overheard conversation nearly twenty-five years ago …

"Why waste time taking classes and chasing after college dreams that you won't be using?"

"Why wouldn't I use my college course work?" his mother had asked his grandmother.

Four-year-old Reed had come in unnoticed from the backyard during the argument.

"Eugenia, what about Reed?"

"What about him?" His mother's voice, angry and

determined. "He'll go with me."

"Don't be ridiculous. He can't live in a dorm room, now can he?"

"I'll get a place off campus for us."

"And what kind of neighborhood would that be—likely a bunch of drunken college students? Since you and Randall divorced … he's safe here and should stay here."

"But he's my responsibility."

"Sometimes being responsible is making hard choices. The boy needs a stable home environment."

His mother had made the choice to give him what his grandmother called a stable environment. But it depended on whose lens you looked through as to whether her decision was responsible. She left him behind and went on to chase her dreams.

Reed pulled out his phone and stared at the picture of him with Izzie that Dan had texted. Seeing Izzie's bright face bumped his heart. If only he could be a heartless tin man, void of the emotions that were strangling his thought processes.

He rested his head on his folded arms and allowed the piece of his brain he had tried to close, to push forward. Izzie, in her orange Save the Square shirt with giant pumpkin earrings and her dark spiky hair, refreshing as rays of sunshine, was his source of discontent. He had to own it and move on.

He straightened his back and set his jaw. Think, Harrison. Focus, man. He shook his head to clear the jumble. Look at your notes, concentrate. Pirates. The theme he'd discussed with Blackburn was fitting. Pirates lie, cheat, and take what they want for personal gain. He sniffed. Not unlike the disingenuous award given to him in Hamilton Harbor.

The phone buzzed in his gray cubicle. "Yes?"

"Padgett wants to see you in his office."

A twinge of fear swept over him. What possessed him to return early, without consulting Padgett? Maybe he wasn't cut out for the task at hand. The Save the Square people had him turned upside down.

"I'll be right there."

Moments later, shoulders tight, he sat across from Padgett.

Physically imposing in a gray suit and red power tie, his boss glared at him.

"Why aren't you with the team?"

"I came back to produce sample boards for the project."

"Isn't your timing a little off?"

"Yes, sir, but we're looking at a pirate theme to tap into the history of the town as well as the ships, boating, and marina harbor life. I wanted to get started and all the materials I need are here."

His frown deepened. Padgett drummed his fingers against his desk. "Dan told Susan you were disturbed about some award at a festival event."

A heat flushed Reed's face. "It was more like a bribe to get special consideration for their interests."

Padgett's brows shot up. "Who cares? This is exactly the kind of thing you need to do to gain their favor. Stay involved. That's how you play the game."

"I wasn't aware this was a game."

"It is a game." Padgett banged his clenched fist on the desk. "A high-stakes game. And in any game you hope to win, you better learn the rules." He extended his index finger. "First rule, find out what your client wants." A second finger popped up. "Rule two, focus on that job and deliver. And rule three," his volume increased, "involve yourself, but don't let emotions override your good sense."

Reed dropped his gaze, "I guess I need to learn the

rules of the game. I just ... let their manipulation get to me."

Padgett used both fists to push himself up from his desk. "Then that is the group *we* need to manipulate. Give a little, take a little, make a lot—it's the way to win the bidding game. I need to show you something." Padgett went to his conference table, lifted a brochure, and plunked it down in front of Reed.

His fingers trembled as he opened the impressive display piece.

"Fairland Hotels is joining this northwest Florida coastal development opportunity. If we get this job, you could become the interior designer for any hotel partnerships that come out of the proposition."

A big break for him. How idiotic could he be letting his personal feelings interfere with the confidence Padgett had placed in him?

Padgett returned to his seat. He pressed his elbows on the desk, steepling his fingers.

"That's fantastic. I ... I'm sorry for not consulting with you—"

"Get your act together," Padgett said, his brows pushed together. "To have the pieces of a project all come together, I'm telling you, find out what pleases the client. Give them what you can. The things you can't give, you make them okay with. That may not make sense now, but it will. So, for now, let me be clear. Don't let personal concerns drive you. I don't have to remind you I went out on a limb for you. I like your work ethic and your technique, and I thought you would add the right mix to the team. But I also have to justify using an interior designer with my partners at this stage of the project. Don't let me down."

Izzie, Claudia, and Emme had taken their usual 7:00 a.m. seats at the coffee bar in the Harbor Town Bagel Bistro. The espresso machine gurgled and wheezed, producing sweet-spiced coffee smells that blended with the aroma of fresh-baked bagels. The store sizzled with excitement over the fall festival's success.

"No offense, Elaine," Izzie said. "but after the 'Everything Pumpkin' bake sale, I don't think I can take a pumpkin latte for at least another week. Make mine plain with extra froth."

"No problem," Elaine said, and slid a freshly made flavored coffee in front of Claudia. "What's your pleasure Emme?"

"I'm with Izzie this morning. After so much pumpkin, I'll take a mocha latte."

"Cooks brought in an amazing variety of food," Izzie said.

"Not only did they put pumpkin in pies, but soups, pasta, and chili." Claudia lifted the lid and blew on her coffee.

"New to me," Emme said, "was putting pumpkin in pizza, burgers, and even grilled cheese."

"If it's edible, you can apparently stick pumpkin in it." Izzie said.

Elaine grinned, "Like bagels. I sold a bunch at the festival. You're in luck if you want something different." She set Emme's coffee in front of her and uncovered a tray of bagels on the counter. "Fresh apple spice."

Emme and Claudia helped themselves and slid the tray down to Izzie.

Palm outward, Izzie shook her head. "None for me, thanks."

"All right, what gives?" Emme asked. "The Izzie I know doesn't turn down food."

Izzie let out an impatient snort. "It's just … I guess I'm bummed that Reed left. He didn't get his award. Say sayonara. Nothing. He just left. I wonder what that means for the study—is he going to be hard to work with and unsympathetic to the Save the Square cause?"

"Jeff said he saw the other team members poking around the marina yesterday. So, they're still working. Maybe Reed was called back to New York," Elaine said.

"Maybe, but I doubt it. Reed overheard Francine talking to you, Emme, when we were lighting the luminarias. When he learned he was awarded a blue ribbon to help gain his favor, he was crazy upset. It's like—shazam—his whole personality changed."

"Must be an ethics issue for him," Claudia said. "I can relate."

"I suppose."

"We all have our pet peeves and things that bother us," Emme said.

The bell over the bistro entry jangled.

Izzie checked the clock. "The roosters and hens are here, right on time."

Dave held the door open for the ladies who retrieved their china teacups hanging at the end of the counter and selected tea bags from a basket Elaine had set out for them. The roosters grabbed their regular seats.

"Izzie," Dave said, "I hear your fall festival was a big success."

"It was a success money-wise, thanks to all you guys for pitching in."

"And we are forever grateful," Marigold said.

"We certainly are." Petunia patted Francine's hand. "The bake sale and the historical society admissions, alone, raised enough to pay the taxes on our two closed houses."

"What did our New York friend think of winning a blue

ribbon for pumpkin carving?" Francine asked.

Izzie's heart sank. How could she tell Francine, looking all sweet in her pink polyester pantsuit, the truth? She'd be crushed to know that he was offended at the thought of being manipulated. "Uh … he had to leave for New York before the mayor handed out the prizes. I left his ribbon and pie with his team members. I can tell you, they were excited about the pie."

Elaine came from behind the counter with a tray of the men's personal ceramic mugs filled with their usual coffee orders and a pot of hot water for the ladies.

Lake picked up a coffee and stood. "Speaking of fundraising for the square, has everyone heard about the design contest idea?"

Some had, some had not.

"To bring everyone up to date, Mallory and I are going to purchase the Feldman house."

The announcement brought pleased applause to the bistro.

"Grandddaddy would be delighted," Petunia said.

"I hope so. Mallory and I plan to open the home to a decorating contest fundraiser that we anticipate will raise money to restore the last two houses on the square. The mayor heard about the idea at a conference in central Florida, and their organizers have agreed to give us pointers."

Francine asked, "How will it work?"

Mallory, seated with the ladies' group, pulled a clipping from her purse, holding it for all to see. "Listen to this. Interior Design Contest Yields a Win-Win," she read. "The 1890 House is new inside and out and giving back to the community through a unique contest. After interior designers submitted plan boards for the restored Victorian in historic downtown, five contestants were selected.

Starting on the upper floor of the house, they competed in elimination decorating rounds until a final winner was declared. Funds raised will go toward restoration of another old home to be used for the Cerebral Palsy clinic. The contest brought positive publicity to the historical district and the participating designers. The judges found new talent, and the homeowners of the 1890 House benefited from the free decorating advice and discounted prices on home furnishings."

"Doesn't this sound like the perfect fundraiser to help restore the houses for the maternity home and resource center?"

"Oh my. How wonderful." Petunia pressed her hands to her cheeks.

"Will you enter the contest, Izzie?" Lake asked.

"Absolutely. I'll talk to Cecelia, the decorator I work with on the beach. I know she'll help spread the word."

Dave put on his reading glasses and peered at the news clip. "I'm not sure how it all works."

"Basically, it's like one of those reality shows on TV," Lake said. "Rooms are decorated, there are professional judges and local voting of favorites in elimination rounds until a winner is reached. Proceeds come from admissions to view the competition. I talked to Mattie Mason, who hosts the local television noon show. She said she'd work out a monthly home decorating time slot for the winner. So, whoever wins will have great publicity."

"Izzie, it sounds like a chance to show off your skills," Emme said.

"We're already impressed with your festival organizing skill," Petunia said.

This was her chance to be recognized as a serious professional. A credible designer. Not just the local girl remembered for high school antics and now dabbling in decorating. "I feel rewarded already with your encouragement."

Another rooster spoke up. "You need to educate more people about the Save the Square interests, and this contest might help. I hear the Hargrave Group has representatives in town and plan to present a proposal for the marina redevelopment project."

Dave stood and took his coffee cup to Elaine for a refill. "That Hargrave bunch took a lonely strip of inlet beach and palmetto bushes and turned it into a year-round haven for family getaways. I'd be interested to see what they propose."

"The more competition and choices the better, don't you think?" Francine said.

"Only if they include our historic downtown in their plans," Marigold said.

The other ladies agreed.

"Hopefully, competitive bidders will work harder to accommodate our community needs." Lake said. "At least it should work that way."

"Working, that's what we three need to be doing," Izzie said. "I have to stop by Appleberry's, then I'll come to the flower shop, Emme."

The three paid and started for the door, coffees in hand. Izzie told Elaine, "We leave you with the hens and roosters, to solve world problems or at least the task of preserving our little town."

In Appleberry's, Izzie headed toward her office, a small desk in the corner of Olivia Appleberry's office, which also housed her bichons, Corky and Fritz.

She raised her hand in greeting to Frank Appleberry, chatting with a customer by the mattresses. Corky and Fritz stood and wagged their fuzzy tails, peering through the pet gate in the door to Olivia's office. Olivia emerged from the basement balancing two bins of Christmas decorations. Her brown eyes sparkled.

"Aren't you pushing the season?" Izzie grabbed a box.

"You know I love Christmas and all the smells." She pulled out a can of evergreen spray and spritzed the air. Fritz sneezed. "A customer wants to schedule you for a consultation."

"Good. I'll take care of it. Where do you want this box?"

"Set it by the water cooler for now. Oh, I put a letter you received from the Interior Design Council on your desk. It may be the test results you've been waiting for. I'm unpacking this box by the window with the fake fireplace."

"I'll be right there and give you a hand." Izzie's knees felt weak. It had taken her two tries to pass the first NCIDQ exam. She passed the second test on the first try, but by passing the third and final test she'd become an authentic, real deal, certified interior designer.

"Hi, boys." She unlatched the gate to the office and went in. Corky and Fritz rushed her for attention. She tried to give them equal pats on the head, while her stomach did a flip at the sight of the NCIDQ envelope. With trembling fingers, she pulled at the glued edge.

Four black eyes in a cloud of white studied her.

She slipped out the enclosed paper, and with the word "although" she knew—she hadn't passed.

CHAPTER TEN

Reed woke with a start. He lifted his head from the hard desk surface. His head ached, eyes watered, and he had a pasty taste in his mouth. What time was it?

He tapped the computer mouse. The monitor screen came to life. It was 4:34 in the morning. He stood and brushed cracker crumbs into the wastebasket already brimming with discarded Hamilton Harbor sketches and proposal notes.

Had he finished the project narration? He peered at the computer screen, struggling to bring the words into focus. His last entry was a paragraph full of Ns.

The last thing he remembered was conferring with Mandeville on his idea for an interactive children's pirate ship museum on the marina. Deleting the Ns, he went back to his last intelligible sentence. He reread it and made sure there was enough information for him to hand to Padgett.

In all his planning, he'd failed to allow for rest and dinner. Show time was 7:00 a.m., and it was on him to present the team's findings, ideas, and recommendations from their feasibility study to Vance Padgett. He would be the person to give a thumbs-up to proceed with their final presentation for next week's commission meeting in Hamilton Harbor, or to send them back to the drawing board.

Images of pirates and pirate ships littered his desk. They helped to inspire him with his interior designs for Mandeville's buildings that followed Greg's engineering work. But the real inspiration, truth be known, was Izzie.

The image of her on the first day they met, in her sunny outfit with orange fringe, took center stage. It was Izzie, with her bright smile, perky hair, and enormous earrings, who introduced him to Calico Jack and his pirate ship. She brought a smile to his heart.

Two hours later, Reed was back in his office, showered, and with a bagel, juice, and coffee under his belt. He made a hard copy of the PowerPoint Dan had sent. Gathering his notes and computer, he walked from the minor league players in the office pool of sectioned off spaces to the administrative section of coveted offices with windows. Emerson, Emerson, and Padgett occupied one entire floor of a high-rise tucked three blocks away from Wall Street in the business district.

He entered Vance Padgett's reception area. "Good morning, Susan."

She hooked a long strand of shiny black hair behind her ear and scanned him. "Long night, prepping for the boss?" She always knew what was going on.

"You could say that."

"Padgett said to go on in when you arrived. He's on the phone now with Emerson number two. He shouldn't be long. I'll bring coffee."

She always knew what people needed. A jewel.

Entering through the polished wood door, the double expanse of windows in the corner office surrounded his boss with bright natural lighting. Padgett, ear to his phone, motioned Reed to the round table beside an expanse of shelves holding books, sample boards, and construction models.

"All right. Sounds interesting. I'll fill you in on the Florida project when you return."

Concluding his call, Padgett crossed the room to where Reed arranged materials for review. "Jonathan Emerson is exploring some Texas Gulf properties. Let's see what your team has come up with."

He read the front page of Reed's presentation with Dan's marketing tag. Deep wrinkles furrowed into his forehead.

Reed held his breath.

"Hamilton Harbor—a hidden treasure in Florida's Panhandle?"

The wrinkles relaxed. "I like it."

Reed exhaled.

"Coffee, gentlemen." Susan set a tray on the credenza beside their worktable and left.

Reed pulled up the PowerPoint on his computer and angled the screen for Padgett's review.

"The concept is to tap into the history of the area by highlighting the pirates that once roamed the Gulf waters. Greg studied the marina's condition and capacity, and Mandeville and I have worked on building design concepts following the swashbuckling theme."

"Currently, the marina is an extension at the end of Main Street that ends on the bay. City Hall and the public library are on the right, and a line of old vacant nondescript buildings run down the middle with boat slips on either side, including a fishing pier at the end."

Reed scrolled through current photos, then pulled up sketches he and Mandeville completed.

"We've drawn plans for a civic center, children's museum in the shape of a pirate ship, space for small businesses, boutiques, eating establishments, new and improved boat slips, and a large restaurant with outdoor bayside seating.

At the end of the pier, mock pirate ships can dock, have guests walk the plank to board their ships, and go on treasure hunting adventures around the bay. Of course, these would be family-friendly pirates.

"Hmm. It seems interesting." Mr. Padgett pointed to the buildings marching down the center of the current marina. "The town people are okay with these buildings being torn down?"

"I believe so." He drew on Izzie's assessment. "They were built in the sixties and don't hold the historical value of the original town."

"Good, because we've found in many instances it is much cheaper and less of a headache to tear down and start new."

"Yes, sir, but here is where we may have a problem." Reed pointed to the overhead view of Main Street with Feldman Square and its six houses to the side. "This is the area that the Downtown Reconstruction Board and historical society are staunch on preserving."

"Dan and Mandeville think we can offer them enough of a historical theme to satisfy history buffs and preserve some old buildings. But Ed Blackburn, who spearheads the newbie group, wants to start fresh and new. He's a great fan of what Hargrave Associates have done in the neighboring county and would like to see all the old buildings gone."

"Okay, so the oldies are probably going to be toughest to please."

"In fairness, the original downtown does have character." Reed pointed out the Main Street businesses and those on Feldman Square that had been refurbished and reopened. "It's these houses," Reed said, pointing to the vacant houses on the square, "that are currently rundown and empty."

"These empty houses back up to the property we want

Fairland to consider?" Padgett asked.

"Yes, sir. Mr. Blackburn calls them eyesores, but the owners want to restore and use them as a maternity home and pregnancy resource center. The festival I was pulled into was a fundraiser to save the houses."

"I see." Padgett pushed up from his seat, walked to the window, and stared at the New York landscape for a long moment. He pivoted and returned.

"I'm concerned about the Hargrave influence. They will offer up-to-date designs with proven statistics for bringing in tourists. Developing the historical component in this project is where we can have an edge."

"Right." Mr. Padgett's ability to read the situation amazed Reed.

"As long as we walk a thin line," Padgett sat back down, "these plans for new construction should please the likes of Blackburn. But for Emerson to get the contract, we need to court the oldies." He leaned forward in his chair and tapped the papers in front of him.

"Here's what I want from you. Polish this presentation. Since you are a familiar face, I want you to present the proposal at next week's commission meeting. Leave the eyesores. Only refer to the bayside section that borders Feldman Square as a possible future hotel. If those rundown houses have to go for us to contract with Fairland, that will give you time to lovingly convince the oldies that it's for the best."

Reed's jaw muscles tightened. Izzie's gray eyes flashed before him.

"You follow?"

He gave Padgett a curt nod.

Would he have to become an opportunist—the very thing he disliked—to make it in the property development world? Maybe he was lucky to have parents that taught him to look out for self.

Izzie stood in the atrium of City Hall. Footsteps and chatter echoed across the open area where tables were set up with three-dimensional displays from the Emerson and Hargrave firms.

"Hi." Emme, still in her florist shop smock, hurried to her and held up the agenda sheet. "You're number two on the agenda."

"Not sure I'm the right person to report on the fall fundraiser." Izzie dug through her purse to locate a mint for her dry mouth and offered one to Emme.

"Nonsense. You are *the* right person especially in those fall colors."

Izzie had decided on a layered look of brown slacks, tan knit top with a print scarf in bright orange, red and yellows she'd made using a remnant left over from a design board. A pair of maple leaf earrings made from copper wire, also her design, dangled from her ears.

Emme turned her attention to the displays. "Looks like these are the only two firms to follow through with proposals."

Seeing the professional exhibits and interior sketches made Izzie feel like a wannabe designer. Reed's resentment and failing the NCIDQ weighed heavy on her spirit.

Although your percentage of correct responses show great promise, you did not receive a passing score.

Izzie pointed to the sketches of interiors with RH initials and pushed out a long, low sigh. "Speaking of impressive, look at Reed's interiors."

"Nice. I like the little pirate ship. These exhibits represent a lot of work."

"One of these companies will be bummed when their proposal is not chosen."

"A big crowd is expected," Emme said. "Clifton is going to try to come, and Elaine and Claudia should be here shortly."

"Good. I may need the moral support to press for preservation."

Inside the meeting room, factions were gathering. The newbies on the left of the center aisle, the oldies on the right. The atmosphere was electric. Izzie took a seat near the lectern for speakers. Her mouth cottony, she left her folder and went in search of a water fountain. When she returned, the first thing she noticed were the black dress shoes with the spit-shined glow. Reed.

"You're back," Izzie said.

Dressed in a light gray suit, blue dress shirt and tie, his dark eyes captured hers and threatened to suck her in.

"Izzie. Hello."

He stood. The guy had become devastatingly more handsome since he left. No fair.

"Is this seat saved?"

"It is—for those who pop in and out of town without notice, so you certainly qualify."

The smell of his after-shave swamped her with the memory of grinning pumpkins, flickering luminarias and the light touch of his lips against hers. The whole scene dizzied her already nervous state. Knees weak, she sat down.

He sat. "Guess I deserve that."

Hurt and attraction drew combat lines inside her. Izzie brushed at her slacks. "Listen, I know you were disturbed by what Francine said. But we meant no harm, believe me."

"I had to go back to New York and found a quick

turnaround on a flight."

"I went by the motel … did you get your prizes?"

"The pie, no." He hesitated a moment then that dimple on his left cheek showed up. "The team said they didn't want it to go to waste. The ribbon, though undeserved, yes."

"Oh, but it was—"

He held up his hand. "No matter."

"Right. We have bigger fish to fry."

"Excuse me?" He looked at her, his black brows squeezed together. "Fish fry?"

"Oh. That just means we have other important matters to attend to. I have to report on Save the Square fundraising. And you. You have your proposal to present to the commission. Are you the presenter?"

"Duly appointed and primed full of information."

"Your three-dimensional display looks impressive."

"I agree. That was largely Mandeville's handiwork. I did the sample interior sketches."

"I saw those. Jack will love how you hooked into the pirate theme."

"I have you to thank. The inspiration came from you taking me to Calico Jack's."

"So … is all forgiven?"

He nodded. "As long as you forgive me for leaving without saying good-bye."

The tension released in her neck, then snapped to attention again when Mayor Brimstead rapped his gavel.

"Folks. It is five o'clock. Please, find a seat. Looks like we will be standing room only."

Izzie looked behind her. The room had filled. Claudia, Pete, Emme, Clifton, and Elaine lined the back wall. Jeff walked in and joined them. The Hamilton sisters were seated on the last row of the oldie side. Elaine sent her a thumbs-up. The room quieted.

After an opening prayer, and reading of the previous meeting's minutes, the mayor said, "First on the agenda, Lake Spencer, chairman of the Downtown Reconstruction Board.

Lake, usually in slacks and a sport shirt, wore a suit, and made his way to the lectern. "Mayor, council, and community members. I'd like to bring you up to date on the progress downtown. Since this board's inception, two new businesses have been started—Hamilton Harbor Antiques and Harbor Town Bagel Bistro, two have been refurbished—Appleberry's Furniture and The Pampered Pooch, and the historical society has opened on Feldman Square. Our Save the Square committee worked in conjunction with the town's fall festival this year, and Izzie Ketterling will report those results in a moment."

"Today, I'm announcing a new Save the Square fundraiser. My wife and I decided to purchase the recently restored Feldman house as our home and private investigations business. For the benefit of those who might not know," Lake nodded toward the out-of-town development presenters, "the historic square is in the process of restoration like Main Street. Two other houses are already restored—The Flower Cottage and the Hamilton house. The new fundraiser will be an interior design contest inside the Feldman house."

Lake explained how the competition would work, then said, "In closing, I encourage you to support this new fundraiser to help with our community's preservation and I, like you, look forward to hearing the marina and downtown redevelopment proposals presented here today."

Izzie checked for reaction from Reed. He remained stoic, his hand clutching a folder. She wasn't sure who the Hargrave representative was. There was more than one unfamiliar suited exec-type sitting near the front.

Her stomach swirled as she approached the speaker's lectern. Seated behind nameplates on the raised commission platform were Mayor Brimstead in the center with Harry Brinkman, owner of an air conditioning business; John Kilgore, owner of a flooring outlet store; Celia Tibbs, a banking V-P; and Billy Wills, the retired band director from Hamilton Harbor High. Mr. Wills sent her a quirky smile. Was he remembering her polka-dot mascot makeover?

Izzie adjusted the microphone to her height, six feet when she wore her four-inch Espadrilles. Her voice came out in a squeak she didn't recognize as her own. "The fall—" she cleared her throat and started again. "The fall festi—sorry." She felt a nudge to her elbow.

Reed handed her a small bottled water and whispered, "Here, try this."

Izzie took a swallow of water. Reed had come a long way since calling the police on her. She tried again.

"The fall festival, pumpkin trail, and historical museum fundraisers," the words were coming now, "netted enough to pay off the taxes on the two vacant houses on Feldman square."

Applause broke out from the rear of the room and spread.

She mouthed to Reed, "Thank you."

"In addition, there was enough left over to paint the exterior of the historical society and start up restoration of the Gardner house, which the Hamilton sisters have designated as a maternity home to serve the community."

"What hotel is gonna want to have a bunch of pregnant women behind it?" a man behind her blurted.

Mayor Brimstead rapped his gavel. "Please let her finish. This is just a report. There will be time for discussion later."

Izzie took another swig of water. The man's comments ignited her courage.

"Feldman Square must be an integral part of the waterfront development. If it weren't for the vision, will, and wealth of the Hamiltons and Feldmans who built the homes on the square, there would be no marina to develop, historical downtown to preserve, or community for you to enjoy."

"Hear, hear." A voice that sounded a lot like Jeff's came from the back of the room.

"We are fortunate to have the current heirs with us today. And keep in mind what they have contributed. They donated the park to the city, the old schoolhouse to the historical society, and now plan another community service by providing a safe place and means of support for pregnant women." Izzie turned to the mayor. "I think we should recognize them."

"Yes." Mayor Brimstead stood. "Please. Marigold and Petunia stand," he said in his gravelly voice.

Marigold stood erect, head held high. Beside her, Petunia, standing a good six inches shorter than her sister, gave a nod of appreciation. Her permed curls bobbed like miniature bed springs. The crowd acknowledged them with enthusiastic applause.

"One more thing." Izzie directed her comment to the balding man behind her. "Pregnancy is not some communicable disease like you make it sound." Titters of laughter rippled over the assembly.

With that, Izzie returned to her seat.

Applause erupted again with a few whistles from the oldies side of the room.

Reed leaned in, his arm brushing her shoulder. "You will be a hard act to follow."

"That was no act."

His smile faded. "I stand corrected."

CHAPTER ELEVEN

Reed's stomach lurched. He'd seen the tall man with the red hair striding to the lectern before.

"Thank you, mayor. I'm Harper Billings with Hargrave and Associates Development."

Blackburn's yacht. This was the redhead he'd seen with Blackburn when he and his coworkers were on Capt. Jack's pirate ship.

With each new slide Billings presented, the hard bench seat under Reed produced more discomfort and doubts. What made Padgett ever think he, a twenty-nine-year-old interior designer who'd been working from a cubicle since he was hired, was the one to present this proposal? A pitch which meant so much to the firm. He shifted in his seat and wiped his hands down his suit pants, leaving faint streaks of moisture.

The Hargrave development dubbed their impressive scheme as Oceanside at Hamilton Harbor. Billings, full of knowledge, polish, and charisma, displayed striking photos of exquisitely designed housing. The furnishings complemented the green waters and silky white sands of the area's beautiful beaches. He gave statistics of Hargrave's business success in Palmetto County and assured his audience that they could do the same for Hamilton Harbor. Billings's presentation even made him want to sign up.

He had visited the Hargrave Oceanside development at Paramount Beach and could see why Blackburn was so impressed. No question they put together a beautiful resort

DESIGNED FOR *Love*

town complete with biking trails, green spaces, water-view residences, and condos woven among unique shops and restaurants.

But they had built on virgin property, as Ms. Huggins had pointed out to him earlier.

They weren't dealing with an established community and historical town and people like Izzie, whose presence next to him sent unsettling sparks up his spine. His team had worked hard on the historical pirate theme she'd introduced him to. But would it seem juvenile, unpolished, and inelegant compared to the Hargrave slides?

Reed eyed a red exit sign over Billings's head. His, "I'm sorry, but we were outclassed," and "you picked the wrong spokesman" speech for Vance Padgett formulated in his mind. Hopefully, he'd be allowed to retain his cubicle.

Billings completed his masterful production.

"Thank you, Mr. Billings," Mayor Brimstead said. "We'll move to our next proposal, then take questions and have discussion before voting. Mr. Harrison of Emerson, Emerson, and Padgett is next."

Reed felt a trickle of sweat make its way down his side.

A sweep of emotion struck as he stood to approach the lectern. Like the time his mother came to visit when he was six. He had secretly packed his little brown plaid suitcase in case his mother asked him to go with her. He heard angry voices—a door slammed. When he went downstairs, his mother was gone. She hadn't even said goodbye.

But why was that same feeling washing over him now? He'd quashed the I-wish-I-had-nurturing-parents desire long ago. This was business. His opportunity. His chance to make something of the life his parents gave him, but didn't stick around to develop, support, or encourage. He straightened his shoulders, forced a smile and began with the words he'd rehearsed in front of the motel mirror.

"Mayor, commissioners, and interested citizens, it is my pleasure to be back with you to report the findings of the feasibility study and present the proposal we have named, "Hamilton Harbor—a hidden treasure in Florida's Panhandle." As he went through the slides on his PowerPoint, he emphasized Hamilton Harbor's assets and potential.

"Our plan pays tribute to your history in this area with a pirate-themed playground, interactive museum, and a specially designed docking area for pirate ship dinner cruises and tourist boating excursions around the bay. Reed used a sketch of Capt. Jack's pirate ship to illustrate."

"Our engineer found that most of the old vacant buildings on Main Street were structurally sound. Marketing believes this will be a valuable promotion feature. Many times, new businesses, like your Harbor Town Bagel Bistro, prefer old buildings for restaurants, bookstores, antique shops and neighborhood pubs. This offers the advantage of a unique atmosphere plus helps limit start-up costs for small businesses."

Reed displayed sample sketches of interiors. "Here you see how both old and new settings add contrast and complementary appeal. A civic auditorium to bring in big name shows and a band shell for summer concerts will replace the unoccupied structures built in the 60s. We have proposed a lighthouse and yacht club at the end of the marina with lots of green space in between for picnics and relaxation.

"Again, I thank you for the opportunity to share with you today and welcome any questions."

Reed gathered his materials. His entire body felt drained of every ounce of energy.

Mayor Brimstead rose.

"Thank you for the presentations. Mr. Billings, please

join Mr. Harrison to answer questions. The floor is open for discussion." He motioned to a man with a microphone. "Jim Rutherford will bring a microphone to you, so you can be heard. Remember to state your name for the record."

Loretta Huggins wasted no time standing and introducing herself. "The pirate theme is okay but only a small part of our history. Feldman Square is merely noted on the Emerson model plan, and a blank spot on the Hargrave display. Both plans show the adjacent property as a future hotel site. The square and its houses should be an integral part of the redevelopment project."

Blackburn stood. The man with the mic hurried to him.

"Ed Blackburn. I understand your wanting to keep the restored houses, but the two rundown relics that were converted to apartments have seen their better days. Think of the clientele pregnant girls would attract. What hotel would want a view of scraggly brooms and mops on the back stoop? The houses should be torn down."

Izzie shot from her seat. "And destroy our history?" Mr. Rutherford scurried to her with the microphone.

"Please. Wait for Mr. Rutherford and state your name."

"But Mayor, I just spoke, and everyone here knows—"

Mayor peered over his glasses, his eyes stern. "For the record."

"Sorry. Izzie Ketterling." Izzie fired her next words directly at Mr. Blackburn, "You don't cut down an heirloom rose bush to stick in a pansy."

Blackburn retorted. "You make a mistake equating those shacks to roses, they are more like weeds. And weeds you pluck up and get rid of."

Mayor Brimstead stood and wrapped his gavel. "I remind you. We are here for discussion. That means one at a time, in an orderly manner."

No wonder Padgett had instructed Reed to be prepared

with answers for likely questions and concerns. He and Dan had worked on a solution for the touchy subject of the square. Reed spoke up at the speaker's podium.

"Mayor, if I may?"

The mayor nodded and sat back down.

"Our plan seeks to blend the old and new. We have a hotel franchise interested in the bay front property bordering Feldman Square. Here is one thought you might consider to help give the square prominence and fit into the scheme of things. Our engineer determined that the old warehouse facing Main Street and backed by Feldman Park has no unusual architectural features. Its interior stairwells are in poor condition and would be of considerable expense to replace. If this building were removed, it would create an open space." Reed pulled up a sketch he had drawn on his PowerPoint.

"Utilizing the old brick salvaged from the warehouse, a bricked walk-through with a fountain and benches could lead to the park and show off the houses. In city restorations across the country, the interesting architectural features of old buildings, such as the homes on Feldman Square, attract people with their warmth and hominess. Whatever the use of the houses in question, our engineer ruled their foundations and basic structure to be sound."

A thread of murmuring wove around the room.

Izzie stood and motioned to Mr. Rutherford for the microphone. "Izzie Ketterling. I wanted to add that the clientele Mr. Blackburn refers to would be people in need of help and hope. Like the young woman who works at our church. She was pregnant, abandoned by the father and her family, and had no place to go. She thought abortion was her only answer. But the taking of life has left her scarred in more ways than one. You don't get a do-over on an abortion."

"We're not here to debate abortion," someone yelled from the crowd.

Disruptive chatter spread. The mayor pounded his gavel.

A hush captured the crowd. Marigold Hamilton stood slowly, pushing herself up using her cane. Mr. Rutherford hurried to her and held the mic for her to speak.

"I understand Mr. Blackburn's concerns, but let me fill everyone in on the full vision. The Gardner home would become a restaurant serving home-style meals downstairs, with living quarters upstairs for women in need. The old garden club will be a consignment and craft shop featuring baby items. This concept was tremendously successful in the Atlanta center where Petunia and I have worked for many years. The restaurant makes the maternity home self-supporting and gives young women a place to work and earn credits for the purchase of baby clothes and equipment in the consignment shop. We see the enterprise as a positive means of service to our community and for the next generation."

Silence hovered in the room a moment as Marigold returned to her seat.

"Other comments?" Mayor Brimstead said.

"Yes. Yes. I would like to speak."

"Name for the record."

"Walter Creighton. I am pastor of the church on Main Street in the old Ritz Theater building. I can attest this maternity home would be a vital addition to provide a home environment for expectant women. I'd also like to comment on the advantages of re-purposing a building. The theater our church uses is a classic. Built in the 1920s, it has intricate details that are left out of modern buildings and contains craftsmanship that should not be lost. A higher quality of construction was used pre-World War II, which adds intrinsic value. Old-fashioned facades give a sense of heritage and warmth, which is just the kind of feeling I love to offer church goers. I want to encourage you to promote the use of buildings on Main Street as much as possible."

Harper Billings moved to the speaker's podium. "What the Emerson firm and others are proposing is interesting but think of the overall look and the economics. This approach would leave you with a spotty mismatch of old and new that I'm not sure you would be pleased with in the end."

"Our design team considered the square and believe it could be a perfect small family neighborhood. Keep the city park and trails but put in new homes that carry the same styling used in Oceanside with the cool Caribbean watercolors that have become our trademark. The old homes, including the one proposed as a maternity home, can be moved to a more suitable location. We relocated an old house that was in the way at Oceanside and it worked out well."

Rumblings in the room seemed to receive Billings's suggestions positively. Sympathy for Blackburn and those leaning toward the new look spread throughout the room.

What now? Reed wished Padgett had never pressed for him to present this project. He unplugged his computer and returned to his seat, where Izzie offered a conciliatory smile.

"If there is no further discussion, we will vote on which company will handle our redevelopment. Please hold down reaction until the vote is complete."

"Commissioner Brinkman?"

"Emerson."

Reed looked up. Thankful to foster at least one vote.

"Commissioner Kilgore?"

"Emerson."

Two votes?

"Commissioner Tibbs?"

"I have to say, I like much of what Hargrave presented—the idea of economics and new. I have to go for Hargrave."

Applause started from the newbies.

"We are not finished," the Mayor said. "Commissioner Wills, your vote?"

"I'm going with Hargrave."

A tie? It would be up to the mayor. It was obvious he supported the square, but would that sway his project vote?

"The Hargrave plan has much to like and could bring a proven clientele, but we offer more than just waterfront and pristine bay property. I think our history should be highlighted as well. The pass-through idea from Main to Feldman Park has great possibilities and re-purposing historical buildings will be good for Hamilton Harbor as our city grows. My vote goes to Emerson."

A combination of handclapping and grumbling ensued.

Izzie grabbed Reed's hand and squeezed. "You did it. You won."

The commission room burst to life after the vote. Billings gave Reed a congratulatory handshake. Mr. Blackburn and some of his followers crowded around Reed.

"Good job, Izzie. This feels like a political campaign victory," Emme said.

"Well, it pretty much is. Lots of politics went into this decision. We may have won this battle but not the war, yet." She nodded at the newbie group surrounding Reed. "He'll be working with a split community."

"The commission's choice will bring new life to the

square." Jeff gave Izzie a pat on the back.

The Hamilton sisters approached her. Marigold tapped her cane. "Thank you so much for taking a stand to save the houses on the square." And Petunia added, "Especially for your support of our maternity home."

A lightness touched Izzie's chest. "It is more than my pleasure. I was fortunate to live in that home growing up after you made it into apartments. Those houses are like old cherished friends. I want to help you extend that feeling to others."

When the appreciations and congratulations calmed down, Izzie pulled out her phone and followed Emme into the hall.

"I'm headed back to the shop. You going to call your mom?" Emme asked.

"Right now, I'm calling Cecelia to tell her to sign up for the Feldman design contest."

"You're soliciting competitors?"

"Sure. If we expect people to pay to see the designs, I'd best get the word out. Cecelia will bring credibility to the contest." Izzie pressed her index finger to her chest. "Unlike me, she passed the NCIDQ."

"Hey, national exams don't make a good interior designer. You are a good designer and don't forget that."

"Yes, ma'am." Izzie straightened. "I appreciate every little prejudiced word you send my way. But seriously, we need the interest and support of as many area professionals as possible. The more involved, the more who will come to see their work. The contest will be a great opportunity for the square and designers to receive recognition."

"Understood. I'll see you at the shop tomorrow."

Cecelia, intrigued by the contest, promised to recruit other designers to submit plans. Chatter and footsteps echoed on the tile floor as the crowd dispersed. Reed was on his phone across the atrium—probably reporting the good news to his firm.

Izzie waved. He pocketed his phone and hurried over.

"You are due a Hamilton Harbor congratulations dinner," Izzie said.

"And what would that be?"

"One of our many treasures."

"You know I have you to thank for the treasure theme idea."

"And I am honored."

"Captain Jack's for dinner? He was my pirate inspiration."

"Not Capt. Jack's. It's a surprise."

"Good surprises are always welcome. I'll gather my materials and speak to the mayor, then join you."

Izzie let her eyes follow him.

"Liking what you see?"

Izzie's hand went to her chest. "Claudia. I thought you left already. My heart's banging like crazy."

"That may have nothing to do with me." She pointed to Reed.

Izzie didn't argue. "He's a nice guy. And we'd best keep him happy."

"Doesn't hurt that he is tall with dark hair and nice eyes."

"Maybe." Izzie offered a demure look.

"Uh-huh." Claudia rolled her eyes. "I arrived late, but you did a bang-up job on rebuttal remarks."

"I hope so."

Claudia wiggled her brows and nodded her head toward the commission room door. "And it's promising that the Emerson proposal won out?"

"You can cool it on your not-so-subtle boy-girl nudges, but I am treating him to a victory dinner at Tally-Ho."

"He's in for a treat. I'd suggest Pete and I join you if I hadn't put on a crockpot dinner and just finished a combout with a feisty terrier." She winked at Izzie. "Besides, you probably want him all to yourself."

"What I really want is for him to believe the historic section of town is a hidden treasure. He talks the talk, but I'm not sure he has internalized it yet—being from New York and all."

"With you in his sights, he's sure to succumb to the town's charms. Since we moved into the old Hamilton house, I've found more than ever that the houses on Feldman Square each have a personality of their own. Like ours, with the secret room hidden under the staircase. The allure of the houses is something you have to experience and feel, not just know about."

Izzie felt a touch to her arm and startled.

Ms. Huggins said, "You did very well presenting the preservation case. You have a gift for making people see things, whether with words—or artistry."

Was she treating her as a peer? "Thank you. That means a lot." Even with the dig about Izzie's "artistry," Ms. Huggins's affirmation gave Izzie's credibility a boost.

🏠 🏠 🏠 🏠

Izzie unwrapped her sandwich while Reed eyed the toasted flat bread and peeked inside. The sandwich was filled with sliced meats and cheese—the spicy aroma heaven to her hungry stomach.

"What is it?" Reed asked.

"A Cuban sandwich. Wash it down with a Tally-Ho chocolate shake and you've eaten a Hamilton Harbor victory meal."

Reed tried to drink his shake using a straw.

Izzie held up a spoon. "Use this. You have to stir it a bit before the shake will go through a straw."

Reed tasted the drink. "Creamy, just the right accent to this sandwich."

"Spoken like a true interior designer."

His dark brown eyes sparked in the light of Tally-Ho's neon sign. Izzie had suggested they sit at an outdoor picnic table, rather than eating in the car.

"You don't mind risking another seagull casualty?"

"You thought I was making up how these seagulls dive for food when we first met, didn't you?"

"Sorry, but guilty as charged."

"The seagulls around here mean business when it comes to getting what they want."

"Kind of like the townspeople?"

"I guess so. We do like to have our way, and I'm glad your firm won the job."

"Us too. The team broke out the champagne in New York."

"Well, let's toast Hamilton Harbor style." Izzie held up her milkshake cup. "Here's to a bright future for Hamilton Harbor's regeneration under the Emerson firm's leadership."

Reed sent her a lopsided grin. The sight of that cute dimple penetrated like a laser. He raised his cup. "Cheers. The team in New York is missing out."

"What will Emerson do next?"

"I'm just learning the procedure myself. Finances and target completion dates to meet will be worked out with the city. Then we'll set intermediate goals."

"I'd like to see the pass-through from Main Street to the park as one of the first things you do. That will open up interest and access for those who don't know it's hidden back there."

"A hidden treasure?"

Izzie smiled. "Exactly. Your theme is a Godsend."

Reed raised his brows. "You think God cares?"

"Sure. He's interested in what we do."

"Even everyday mundane activities? I thought he just dealt in the big stuff. Like wars and climate change."

"That too. Look at your project proposal. You have an over-all plan and target date you're working toward. So does God. But while getting to that goal, there are individual steps, people to involve, and tasks to complete along the way to meet the big goal. God has to be interested in the little stuff to accomplish the big stuff."

"Ah." Reed stirred his shake. "Interesting view."

"Don't you ever wonder why you are here at this particular time and place in history? Think of it. Of all the times you could have entered this world, God picked the twenty-first century for us. And we have a purpose in this world, at this time."

"So, you believe Emerson's contract is part of God's plan?"

"If we tap into his direction and pray. Don't you think?"

Reed could almost feel the hardwood floor beneath his five-year-old knees at his bedside as he prayed for his parents to want him. "To be honest, no. I believe in God. But in my experience, he gives us a brain and expects us to handle things and deal with the consequences. For him to care about designing a waterfront, I think is a stretch."

"I look at it this way. He made us with mind, body, and soul. When we are in tune to him, he will spark interest in us to act on things he wants us to do. My passion right now is to help save the square."

Reed swallowed a bite of his sandwich, then asked, "And why the passion? Is it all due to the girl you mentioned at the commission meeting? What's in it for you?"

Izzie held up her straw and let the chocolate liquid drip back into her cup. "It's like this. The cook inside Tally-Ho took various ingredients and blended them to make a creamy drink. I could describe that to you all day long, but until you taste and experience it yourself, you'll never really understand what it's like to drink a Tally-Ho milkshake."

"Your point is?"

"My point is, you are an official part of the community now as a partaker of our victory meal, and thereby eligible to understand my passion. Grab what's left of your celebration dinner. You are going to experience the abandoned houses on Feldman Square."

"I'm not sure this is a good idea." Reed sat in Izzie's car parked between the abandoned houses on Feldman Square, clearly posted with no trespassing signs.

While Izzie busied herself peering in the windows of the rundown Victorian, Reed stared at the restored look-alike Feldman house sitting on the opposite corner.

Reed had reported the interior design fundraiser to Padgett.

"Enter that contest, Reed." Mr. Padgett had said.

"But I thought you wanted me to be working on the interiors for the yacht club and information center."

"That too, but right now I'm more concerned about Fairland Hotels. Their proposed site backs up to Feldman Park and Greg says those vacant houses may need to go."

"The whole reason for the contest is to refurbish those houses. This is a touchy subject."

"Precisely. And you have to learn to deal with these issues firsthand."

"Can't I learn without entering their contest?"

"Dan filled us in on the tensions between the old and new groups. Most likely, it will be the old group that we have to placate. I want you to be a part of the community to get on their good side. Then if the houses have to go, they'll understand and appreciate our efforts to help them. Schmooze. Make friends."

Reed put his attention back on Izzie who was motioning to him. He wondered if Mr. Padgett would include snooping and trespassing in the "schmoozing" and "making friends" category.

"Come on, before it's too dark to see anything."

"What about all the No Trespassing signs?"

"Those are meant for strangers." She flung out expressive hands. "Would you get out of the car? This is important."

"Important, how?"

"I want you to see the potential of these houses."

"I'd see more potential in daylight."

Izzie took a stance, hands on hips. Her head bobbed like a bobblehead toy. Her metallic, autumn leaf earrings captured the late afternoon sun and shot laser beams of light into his face.

Reed frowned and glanced around him before stepping out of the car. He half expected searchlights and sirens.

"This house was one of my favorite places to visit." Izzie pointed to the steep-roofed copy of the restored Feldman house. "Violet Feldman evidently wanted a house like her parents', but love sent her next door when she married Gardner Hamilton."

"So, this neighborhood was all one big family when these homes were first built?"

"Love on the square." Izzie drew a heart in the air with her fingers. "Starting with Albert Feldman arriving with Edith, his mail-order bride."

"I thought mail-order brides were only a part of the wild west."

"When Edith's father died, her family had no means of support. Albert was single and needed help caring for his ailing father. Their union was a marriage of convenience that blossomed into this." Izzie twirled about. "The Feldmans had two children, Edgar and Violet. Their neighbors, the Hamiltons, had Gardner and Regina. When the children turned twenty-one, they were each given a house."

"These four houses?" Reed cast his gaze from the vacant houses to the florist shop and historical society across the park.

"Right. The Flower Cottage was Regina Hamilton's house. She fell in love with Edgar Feldman and moved into his house, now the historical society. But it was originally built as a private school after World War I. Violet Feldman fell in love with Gardner Hamilton, and her house became the garden club. Isn't that the sweetest story ever?"

"I see why you're enchanted with these houses."

Izzie grabbed Reed's hand, pulling him to the rear of the old garden club house.

"When I lived in the Gardner home, I loved to visit Ms. Abernathy who lived in an upstairs apartment overlooking her garden filled with flowers, herbs, and vegetables." Izzie pointed to a weedy plot of ground behind the house. "She treated me to mint tea and tiny squares of carrot cake and gave me pointers on gardening."

"Is that where your florist skills came from?"

"Uh-huh. She had a lot to do with my appreciation for plants and color. Marigold hired me to keep up the gardens at the Gardner house."

"You lived with Marigold and Petunia?"

"Oh, no. After family members on the square died,

Marigold and Petunia turned the homes into rentals, and moved away. My mother handled the cleaning and upkeep for them."

Reed puzzled over her optimistic attitude as she made her way to the Gardner house. Its no trespassing sign stood out like a beacon.

Izzie disappeared behind the rear of the house, while Reed studied the exterior of the modified Victorian. A section of the two-story house had a mansard roof with a decorative widow's walk. Some spindles were missing. The edges of the roof shingles curled with age. A climbing jasmine vine overran the front porch railing, wrapped around the posts and grabbed the porch overhang. The overgrowth could be hiding all kinds of disrepair. From his experience living in Grandma's aging house in New York, something always required mending.

"Back here," Izzie called. "We're in."

"What do you mean we're in? Did you break in?"

"Sort of," Izzie dusted her hands together, "but not really."

Reed eyed her and then her car sitting out front in plain view." I don't know about your town, but in New York it's called breaking and entering, and worthy of a trip to jail."

"Lighten up. I lived here eighteen years and learned a trick on how to enter when I came home late. Besides, Marigold and Petunia won't care."

"Why not wait for a key?"

"Gee whiz. Time's a-wastin'. Where's your sense of adventure? I just want you to see these houses as the hidden treasures you talked about in your presentation."

"Can't you just tell me?"

"No." She gave him an incredulous look. "You have to experience it. Remember the milkshake?"

Izzie reached for his hand and gave it a tug. So much

for resolve and firm resistance. He followed.

The back door was standing open, and they stepped into a musty kitchen with a black and gray speckled linoleum floor. Izzie opened a cabinet door next to the porcelain sink. The aroma of various spices spilled out. She thrust her head back, closed her eyes, and inhaled deeply.

"Smell the cinnamon?"

Reed nodded, checking behind him for blue lights. "I smell trouble too."

"Ms. Finlaw's cinnamon rolls were the best. We looked forward to her night to cook."

"You cooked for each other?"

"We did. It's a group effort living in a boarding house, at least for us it was. As a little kid, I never knew there was such a thing as single-family homes."

She seemed pleased and privileged. Maybe she was.

"In the kitchen, everyone pooled resources and cooking responsibilities. There was a specialty every night. Monday was beef hash night, left over from the pot roast on Sunday. Tuesday, spaghetti; Wednesday, chicken and dumplings; Thursday, pizza; Friday, fish; and Saturday potluck, made from leftovers and veggies from my little garden. It was fun with everyone contributing."

Izzie stepped into the next room, joined by a walk-through pantry. "This was my mom's and my room."

The room had a fireplace, built-in bookshelves, a tiny bathroom that looked like the afterthought add-on that it was, and a window view of the dilapidated house next door.

His own mother's bedroom, next to his bedroom at his grandparents' house was bigger than this one. But Izzie had a mother who cared enough to keep her with her.

"What about your father?"

"I never knew him. My mom was pregnant with me

when she was in high school, and my father, if you could call him that, took off. She never heard from him nor tried to find him."

Izzie stared out the window. The silence awkward. But Reed understood the haunting vacancy of parental abandonment. One can cover the effects on the outside, but inside the scar remains.

"If it weren't for a maternity home in Atlanta where Marigold and Petunia worked, I might never have been born."

"The reason you support the maternity home?"

She nodded. "My mother's family disowned her, and there was no program like that around here."

Was that a tear? She brushed at her face and turned away. "I've always envied those with dads."

He could relate. "I grew up without my mother and father."

Izzie turned. "You said your grandparents raised you after your parents divorced?"

Reed walked to the mantle and ran his fingers through the dust. "My parents were just teenagers when I came along, and having a baby put a crimp in their career plans. Before my grandparents died, I lived with them." A few tears from Izzie, and he's sharing the background he'd rather forget? He brushed his hands together, shaking off the dust. "If you were born in Atlanta, how did you end up back here?"

"When the Hamilton sisters worked at the pregnancy center in Atlanta, they offered my mother the job as the rental manager. She handled the renting and kept the common areas inside the houses cleaned in exchange for free rent. I am proud of her. She runs her own cleaning business in Tallahassee now."

"Commendable—all while raising a child. My father

became a preacher, of all things, and my mother, a designer, but they had no room in their life for me." There he went, sharing again. This optimistic girl had that effect on him.

"Your design talent must be genetic."

Reed shrugged. "I don't know about the talent, but by entering the profession, I can at least appreciate not wanting a kid around smearing peanut butter and jelly on design plans."

"It's only you on holidays and such, now?"

"Just me. But I'm good with it. It's the way life is." Reed turned back to the fireplace. "Didn't you hate these cramped quarters?"

"It was cozy. Look at this." She walked to the bookshelves, pushed on the edge, and the shelves swung open revealing a tiny room. "This was my study space. Marigold said it was built as storage or a hiding space in case of war." She turned and nodded toward the window. "Many an evening, I stood looking outside and pretending my Prince Charming would materialize from Ms. Abernathy's rows of roses. We'd fall in love, and he'd make an over-the-top proposal."

"Did any of that pretending come true?"

She giggled. "No. But the dreaming was still fun. Living here was like having a huge blended family in five houses with a park in the middle. I had all kinds of company and room to ramble."

Izzie led him to another room with built-in, glass-leaded cabinets. "This is the dining room." She pointed to the front of the house. "Up there was the living room, or what they called the parlor when the house was first built in 1935."

She opened double hung solid wood doors leading to the entry hall.

"Is this cypress?"

"It is. See what I mean about treasure? They don't make 'em like this anymore. I'll show you the upstairs."

The staircase leading from a foyer appeared to be of oak, simple style and sturdy. Their footsteps echoed in the empty house, but he could envision Izzie skipping up them in years past, as enthusiastic as she was now. The house did have possibilities.

She pointed to the four rooms from left to right and named the renters. "John Parilla, the bank teller who helped me with my math homework. Rhodie Finlaw, the good cook who listened to all my problems. Arnie Blauser, the Elvis impersonator, and Sylvia Easton, the artist who inspired me with her creativity."

"Is Sylvia the one who shouted at the sunrise?"

"Yes." Her eyes sparkled. "You remembered."

Amazing. This girl found exhilaration in the tiniest things.

Reed walked to the end of the hall that looked out over the bay. "This is a spectacular view. Too bad the main living areas didn't face this way."

"Oh, but we still enjoyed the view. We had no air conditioning, only fans. On especially hot summer nights, Sylvia and I wrapped ourselves in sheets, laid outside on the cool grass, and fell asleep under the black sky with hundreds of stars winking at us and the moon shimmering on the bay waters."

Izzie stood so close to him, the joy of her remembering radiated like a heat wave.

"You make having no air conditioning sound exotic."

She cradled herself with her arms. "I'd awaken on those nights, not from discomfort, but snuggled in a sense of well-being with the dew settling on our sheets."

She looked up at Reed. Her countenance glowed. "You know, the Bible talks about the freshening dew. God provides that free for the taking. God is so good."

She grew up in a rooming house confined to one room with her mother, who did the cleaning, and she saw it as a blessing? And him? If he were honest, he often sulked in his room plagued by the tragedy of a mother who didn't want him, and a preacher father who'd left him behind.

He could be grateful for his grandmother's care but never saw his lot in life as a blessing. He wanted out of the old, stuffy, American four-square with the enclosed front porch and cluttered interior. Simple, plain, and new. That's what refreshed him.

"What made you happy when you were a little boy? Did you ever camp out under the stars?"

"Are you kidding? My grandma would have had a fit. First, for messing up her sheets with grass stains. And then, she'd complain that I'd catch a cold in the night air or fall prey to a kidnapper. Besides, I can't say I ever wanted to lie outside on the ground even with a tent. Sometimes, on hot evenings, we'd sit on our porch and play what we called The Game."

"What was The Game?"

She looked up at him with those eyes, a smoky shade of bluish gray. A genuine interest emanated from her, making his heart long to touch hers and share his innermost thoughts.

"Well, we …" He cleared his throat and started over, focusing on a copper earring instead of her disconcerting eyes. "When Grandma or I spotted a car with out-of-town plates, we'd make up a story about where they were going. I'd imagine some faraway place and wish I could jump on the back bumper."

"Sounds fun. I'll try The Game out on Richie, Emme's little boy. Where did your imagination take you?"

"Hawaii, Jamaica, Iceland, Australia, and the list goes

on. Your childhood experience made you want to return to your roots, mine left me wanting to leave and never revisit the row houses of Brooklyn."

"Did you ever imagine coming to Florida?"

"I always thought of Florida as the mysterious place that snatched my parents from me."

"Maybe there is a reunion in your future?" She paused a few seconds.

Reed could only offer silence to that idea.

"Speaking of sitting on your grandma's porch, you need to see the front porch on this house."

She led the way to the foot of the stairs. "I used to sit right here and wait for Arnie after clean-up on pizza night. He'd get his pipe—I can almost make out the sweet scent—and come out on the porch and sing, while we all gathered around.

"Sounds like something straight out of the Andy Griffith Show."

"You know, you're right. Let's go out on the porch."

The main house was sturdy, but the porch was a different story. The weathered floorboards creaked under their weight. "That's where we gathered. Arnie sat on the swing." Izzie tugged at the vine wrapped around one arm. "These vines are taking over. I remember when I helped Ms. Abernathy plant them."

"Looks like you did a good job."

The evening air was cool, and the setting sun painted the sky the color of orange sherbet. The darkening shadows of evening embraced them. He grasped her attachment to these houses. He helped pull stubborn vines from the swing, enjoying the closeness as his hand brushed against hers.

A spotlight glared onto the porch, hitting his face. Shielding his eyes, Reed saw a black and white police car stopped in front of the house.

He took a step back. A board cracked and collapsed under his weight. His leg crashed through the porch floor, and pain shot through his ankle.

CHAPTER TWELVE

The sweet smells of roses and carnations filled the Flower Cottage. Izzie sat at the worktable and finished tying a pew bow for a wedding.

"It's been two weeks, and I still can't erase the effects of Tony's harsh reprimand for trespassing and Reed's pained expression."

"How is Reed's leg?" Emme asked and lifted a vase of roses from the cooler.

"He assured me, okay, but I'm afraid his trip to the ER and four stitches will make him more of a skeptic than a believer where saving the houses are concerned."

"Accidents happen, and when he sees the interest in the square, he'll realize the value in saving the houses." The midday sun streamed through the rear window of the shop and lit up Emme's blond hair in an angelic halo.

"I don't know. He didn't exactly bubble with enthusiasm."

"Few bubble like you. Speaking of," Emme touched one of Izzie's blue earrings, "these look like bubble-blowing wands."

"They are. I found them in the trash at the furniture store. Cute, huh?"

"Richie will probably try to use them."

"Olivia blew on them."

"Sounds like her."

"Her dog, Fritz, chewed up one of the fabric swatches I was going to use on my display board for the contest entry."

"Maybe it was for the best. You ended up with a fantastic look on your entry." Emme glanced at the wall clock. "Ten minutes 'til noon. The winners will be announced shortly. Excited?"

"As a long-tailed cat in a room full of rocking chairs." A piece of floral wire popped loose, poking Izzie's finger as she wrapped floral tape on a boutonniere. "Oh, fine. A blood-stained boutonniere won't be appreciated at the Wilson wedding."

"I put a new box of Band-Aids and ointment by the sink for hazards of floral work and Richie's boo-boos."

"I can't relax until the Spencers choose the designers for the Feldman house."

"Finish the boutonnieres later. Fix your finger."

Izzie ran cool water on her pricked finger and checked the clock on the wall. 11:53. It was almost time for the noon show, featuring news and local happenings, when Lake and Mallory were to announce their top five choices in the design contest. The diversion of a pricked finger did little to stop the turmoil inside. She diverted her attention to the rear parking lot.

Emme had lined the wooden walk leading to the back deck with a sea of festive pink, red, and white poinsettias. She had a knack for creating a mood with her floral designs. Izzie had strived for an elegant, yet livable, and comfortable feeling in her design submission. Had she been successful? In minutes, she'd find out.

She had pored over fabrics and furniture styles, considered lighting, and stewed over the best colors and textures. And then arranged and rearranged the design board a dozen times. She was happy with her final submission. But now, looking at the rich colors in the poinsettias, she thought maybe she should have leaned more toward the true reds instead of muted tints and shades. The show was about to start.

Blending, combining, making do with what you have—attributes she had learned on the square—had become her style. But that style wasn't always received well. The high school principal didn't appreciate her paint designs, and Ms. Huggins didn't accept the drawings she put in her term paper.

"Can't you write words like a normal student?" she'd asked.

"Sketches instead of words should break up the monotony of reading words all the time." Ms. Huggins wasn't keen on her response.

Did acceptance have to mean conformity? Maybe she had picked the wrong profession. Or should she go with the flow to fit in? Too late now. At some point you settle for what you decide is best. It may or may not work for someone else. Like the NCIDQ exam judges.

"Time for 'Hamilton Harbor Today.'" Emme turned up the volume on the small television in the work area. "I've crossed my fingers. Probably unnecessary. You're a cinch to be in the top five."

"I'm over here second guessing everything I put on that board."

"I love the colors you selected. It's some of your best work."

"I may have outdone myself publicizing the contest." She took a deep breath. "I heard there were fifteen entries at last count."

"Good. More reasons for yours to stand out."

"At this point, my stomach is pleading to get this over with."

A picture of the Feldman house flashed on the television. "Here we go." Emme turned up the sound another notch.

DESIGNED FOR *Love*

Mattie Mason, anchor for the noon show, tapped her mini mic then beamed into the camera. "Lake and Mallory Spencer are the new owners of the restored Feldman house and a part of the Save the Square group. They are here with Mayor Brimstead to explain about a unique fundraising project. Mayor, first tell us some history of the square."

"No, Mayor." Izzie grasped prayerful hands. "Tell us later."

"Glad to, Mattie. Feldman Square is a park surrounded by six homes. Truman Hamilton and Albert Feldman, our city's founding fathers, built the first two in 1912. Hamilton operated a shipping business out of the harbor, and Albert Feldman ran a sawmill and lumber company. Hamilton's granddaughters donated the center park to the city, and through other generous donations, it has become a beautiful asset to the community. Four of the houses have been restored or rejuvenated, leaving two to be saved. One built for Gardner Hamilton stands on the corner of Second and Hamilton, and next to it is the house that became the first garden club in town."

"The square brings a rich history to our downtown area," Mattie said. "Mr. Spencer, you and your wife have offered the Feldman home that you're purchasing to be used as a fundraiser. Tell us about it."

Izzie shook her head; the bubble blower earrings whacked her cheeks. "Can't they explain after announcing the designers? The suspense is driving me buggy."

Emme held up her hand. "Patience. They have to explain how it works for the public to participate."

Izzie crossed her arms over her queasy stomach and tried to listen to Spencer. "… adapted their contest rules for our community. Five interior designers that we select today will compete to decorate the home. A panel of experts will judge the work, and for an admission fee, the public can view the design ideas and vote on their favorites."

"Sounds like national television talent competitions," Mattie said.

"It is. We hope the contest will generate interest in the square and the philanthropic efforts of the Hamilton sisters."

"Indeed. And after this commercial break, Ms. Spencer will explain the contest rules."

"Good grief." Izzie touched her head to the worktable, her earrings clunking against the hard surface. "I'm too jittery to watch this."

Emme patted Izzie's shoulder. "That's okay. I could use baby's breath in this bridal bouquet." Emme held up white roses she was arranging into a tight cluster. "Go out front and snip some by the garden gate. I'll call you in when Mattie's ready to broadcast the winners."

"I'd be glad to." Izzie grabbed the clippers and stepped out on the deep front porch of the Craftsman cottage. Bounding down the front steps to the stone pathway, she stopped by the rose-covered arbor that framed Feldman Park.

Across the street, Claudia walked a Pampered Pooch client. Behind her were the rundown houses, once filled with laughter. She pictured them during the Christmas season, lined with multi-colored lights. But now they stood dismal and sad, like abandoned dogs in a shelter, waiting for some attention.

Was she weird to have such an attachment to these houses? This square? Activity needed to return to them before she could feel whole.

She stooped down and picked up a blossom that had fallen to the ground. Once vibrant, now brown and dry, it crumbled between her fingers to mere dusty fragments.

DESIGNED FOR *Love*

No hope for restoration. But not the houses. There was hope for them. She cast her gaze to the other houses on the square and settled on the Feldman house. Would she get the chance to help decorate it? Would Reed wonder which designers they selected to compete in the contest. Would he care? She snipped some choice stems of baby's breath.

"Izzie, come on."

Her heart pounded in her throat and temples. *Calm down, girl. It is what it is. They've made their selections.* She'd have to live with the results.

She stepped back in the cottage, jumped over the mat to keep from setting the buzzer off, handed Emme the flowers, and sat at the worktable.

The Spencers, the mayor, and news anchor stood behind seventeen design board entries.

"These were all fantastic submissions, and we are so thankful for the interest. But we had to select five," Mallory said. "Only numbers were on the submissions, not names. So, we join the audience in learning who the selected designers are. Here goes."

Izzie's display was third on the left in the lineup. Mallory stepped to the first one on the left.

"We selected number one. We like the color scheme."

Mayor Brimstead pulled the card from the envelope labeled with a one. "Cecelia's Designs."

Mallory's hand hesitated over Izzie's entry. A surge of hope flooded her but stopped with the abruptness of a plumber's wrench tightening a gushing waterpipe. Mallory moved on.

"This one, entry number five had nice use of texture."

The mayor read from the envelope, "Oceanside Design Studios."

"Great," Izzie said. "Who can compete with Oceanside?"

Pick three was Four Seasons Interiors from nearby Peyton Beach.

"For our fourth pick, we appreciated this submission's clean lines," Lake said. The mayor flipped open the envelope, pulled the card and read: "Reed Harrison of Emerson, Emerson and Padgett."

Izzie's scalp prickled. "Reed?"

"Did you know he entered?" Emme asked.

She shook her head. Why would he enter? To show he could win on his own, that he didn't need her to manipulate a win for him? He mentioned nothing about entering. His talent might help save the houses. After all, that was the point of the contest. Izzie could feel the pulse throbbing under her Band-Aid. She should be happy for the winners, shouldn't she?

"They still have one more to choose." Emme held up fingers crossed so tight the knuckles were white.

"And fifth pick is … wait, I missed one," Mallory said.

"Come on." Emme pointed to Izzie's board on the television. "Turn back."

Mallory did turn. She walked back and reached out. "Here it is. Our fifth pick."

The mayor opened the envelope and announced, "Izzie Ketterling of Izzie's Creative Designs."

Reed stood on a step ladder, securing a leafy garland entwined with cranberries and popcorn around the front door of the Feldman house. The newly formed decorating team had gathered the night before to string the fragrant strands.

Izzie held a section up for him while she talked to Cecelia.

"In the spirit of Christmas, I'm glad Mallory asked the contestants to decorate outside in a joint effort. It's been fun getting to know everyone. What do you think of including a nativity scene on the front lawn? The whole reason for the season is the birth of Jesus," Izzie said.

"Sounds good to me. What do you think ladies, uh … and gentleman?" Cecelia asked.

Brandi and Candy, working to secure a matching garland to the porch railing, enthusiastically agreed.

Izzie tilted her head, "Reed?"

It didn't matter to him. "I'll help you put together whatever you ladies decide."

Wiping away the moisture trickling down his cheek, Reed stepped down from the ladder. It had to be nearly eighty degrees. What in the world had attracted his parents to this state? Hot, humid Florida, they could have it.

He preferred the holiday season chilly. He'd left a daytime of forty degrees in New York with freezing temperatures at night. The way it should be. It was December, for heaven's sake. Time for office parties, festive food, and decorations. Leave it at that. Nativity scenes and church had slid by the wayside for him—not without reason. But if a manger scene was on the agenda, he'd help. He was here to make everybody happy.

"Good." Izzie said. "Should we put it on the right side of the lawn?"

Cecelia walked out to the street, "As people turn onto Second Street from Bay Drive, the nativity would be the featured view."

"And the first thing that would come in sight if approaching on Hamilton Avenue." Candy pulled out her phone and swiped the screen. "I have some pictures I've been taking of different nativities in the area. This one is really nice."

Reed shoved his hands in his pockets and turned to view the garland. His reflection in the etched oval on the beveled glass in the door stared back. He'd rather think door wreath than Mary, Joseph, and a baby who was supposed to bring peace to the world. That was not his worldly experience.

Yesterday evening when the group met each other, all agreed to use nature and natural materials as much as possible in keeping with the turn of the century Christmas decorations when the house was built.

Listening to a holiday radio station, the ladies sang Christmas classics while they strung the berries and popcorn and wired Ligustrum clippings to make the garland. The Spencers hadn't moved in, but the kitchen appliances had been installed.

Mallory had provided dinner and kept popcorn in supply, making it the way his grandmother did—on the stove in a pan with a little oil. When the decorators met, everyone hugged. The greeting was not a New York tradition, but he was swept into the neck-hugging. They apparently gave no thought to personal space invasion. He was more comfortable with a handshake. Was this what family was supposed to feel like?

The Feldman home decorators consisted of youngish Candy, on-task Brandi, adept Cecelia, festive Izzie, and him—the token male. As a team, they made an interesting study in shapes, colors, and textures. Appropriate for interior designers.

He ran his fingers through his hair, already slicked back, and contemplated the expanse of railing yet to be draped with the remaining garland. Never would he have imagined a marina redevelopment project could turn into cranberries, popcorn, and a nativity scene.

Izzie looked at the photos on Candy's phone. "We could

make this scene with a minimal amount of wood. I'll check with Pete and see if he has some scraps."

Candy said, "I have a friend who lives on a farm and could supply us with a bale of hay."

"We can use my utility trailer to pick it up," Brandi said.

"I need to check things at the office," Cecelia said. "There's plenty of palmetto bushes out there. I'll clip some for the roof and be back shortly."

"Reed," Izzie said, "hold down the fort."

He stood holding a strip of garland, stunned.

Izzie turned to leave, then turned back. She placed her hands on her hips, sending her golden earring angels to flight and said, "Hold down the fort means to keep an eye on things until we return." The others giggled.

"Ah." Reed reared his head back. "Will do." Everyone departed, and he returned to the railing project. He checked the way Brandi and Candy had wrapped the railing on the left side of the porch, so he could replicate the spacing on the right. He marveled at how women, jabbering all the time, still managed to get things done—and done well. He did better with peace and quiet and being alone with his thoughts.

He draped the garland while mulling over the design for the door wreath he'd volunteered to make. Creating a wreath had always been his task at his grandparents' house, probably the only part of Christmas that was joyous for him. At least his grandparents and their friends appreciated his work. They said he had design talent like his mother. Their remarks were meant as a compliment but stung him as a hurtful reminder that his mother had never been around to direct him, encourage him, or even see one of his door decorations.

This would be his first Christmas without his grandmother. Making a wreath would help fill a void he had refused to acknowledge.

"Wow."

Reed jumped and turned around. Mallory stood on the front sidewalk, McDonald's bags in hand.

"It is really shaping up." She held up the bags. "Where is everybody? I brought lunch."

"Do I smell food?" Izzie appeared from around the corner of the house.

"You do. Burgers or chicken nuggets, your choice. I'll keep them warm in the kitchen." Mallory made her way to the front door, stepping over bits of discarded pieces of greenery.

"Reed, I need your assessment. Pete has some ideas for us to look at."

"What about holding down the fort?"

"Mallory's here. Come on."

"The last time you told me that, I ended up with four stitches in my leg."

"Forgive and forget the Good Book says … at least I think it does. Anyhow, just … come on."

She intrigued him. He followed. Her bubbly enthusiasm lightened his dull spirit.

Behind the Hamilton house, Pete greeted him with a handshake. So, neck-hugging was just a woman thing in the South? "We could use another opinion. From the sketch Izzie showed me, these posts can make a frame with supports behind it."

"Would those plywood scraps work for a back?" Izzie asked.

Pete searched through wood pieces. "There isn't a piece big enough to fit across the back."

"Turn the strips horizontally." Reed picked up a strip about two feet wide by eight feet. He held it at an angle. Attach it to the frame and you'll have a rough stable appearance.

"I like it," Pete said. "You must have done this before."

"I have. My grandmother recruited me for all kinds of church projects."

"You went to church?" Izzie asked.

"An old church in Brooklyn with my grandmother until my teens. Then I didn't go nearly as much as Grandma wished. Church projects were her sneaky way of getting me there."

"Take these pieces to start the frame," Pete said. "I'll be by later to help. Use my tools." Pete pointed to his toolbox.

Izzie and Reed carried the wood scraps to the Feldman house in two trips and laid the lumber on the lawn.

"Teamwork." Izzie slapped his hand like they had achieved some grand feat. Her spirit and energy moved him with warm feelings that went beyond the Florida weather.

Candy and Brandi arrived with a big bale of hay.

Cecelia pulled in behind them in her SUV, the rear stacked with palm fronds.

Candy sprung from the car. "We had a great idea. Since we agreed to limit our decorations to natural things, we should have a live nativity scene."

"We can all play parts," Brandi said.

"I'll be a shepherd coming to see the baby," Cecelia said, joining the group.

"Shepherds, that's what Brandi and I want to be too."

"My dad has a perfect faded, striped bathrobe I can use. That leaves Reed for Joseph, and Izzie, you will make a great Mary. All you need is a shawl to cover your spiky hair," Cecelia said.

"Mary's hair could have been spiked underneath her head cover." Izzie wiggled her brows and the motion set the Christmas angels dangling from her ears twirling.

"You'll make a great Joseph," Candy said.

Was this some cruel joke? Him? Play Joseph? If he agreed, wasn't he like the church hypocrites? But if he turned them down, he'd jeopardize the mission. If he was to gain community trust, he had to go along.

Was a New York office with a window worth it?

🏠 🏠 🏠 🏠

"Joseph," Izzie whispered to Reed. "What time is it?"

A carload of onlookers had just loaded and pulled away from the curb.

"Fifteen minutes to go."

"Thank goodness. I almost whacked the little kid that kept pulling my robe. He was looking for trouble." Brandi said.

"I can appreciate the torment those Buckingham Palace guards must endure when tourists try to rattle them." Izzie rubbed her hands together. The evening air was chilly.

Cecelia spoke up. "While there's a lull, I'd like to say that I've enjoyed working with you this week. And although one of us won't be moving on in the competition, it doesn't mean we can't stay in touch."

"And doesn't mean we can't remain friends." Izzie added. "It's been fun working with everybody."

The five designers had become a team. Izzie looked at each one. Tonight, the group would be whittled down to four. This was hard. She didn't want anyone to be cut. She enjoyed the communal energy and wished they could continue to work together. Being with fellow designers gave her a sense of acceptance—a good feeling. At the same time, she felt guilty that she wanted to win.

But like the poor houses on the square, life wasn't static. It moved. Sometimes up and sometimes down, but always forging ahead. Participating in the contest would stir interest and gain finances for the worthy goal of the Hamilton sisters. If she went no further in the design competition, she could relish coming this far.

And if she lost, she could be there to cheer and remind the others of their whole purpose for competing. They might have more talent in their big toe than she did, but they couldn't touch her in enthusiasm for saving the Gardner house and old garden club.

"Ladies, this whole be-in-competition-and-friends-at-the-same-time concept," Reed made finger quotes, "is a new phenomenon for me. I've never seen this kind of camaraderie in the business world ... or among other competitors."

"Life is too short to get caught up in squabbles," Candy said. "If I go no further, the experience still puts me in the success column.

"I've enjoyed the opportunity to watch the bedrooms come to life with everyone's ideas." Brandi said. "Cecelia, I confess, I thought that burnt orange was ghastly looking in the can. But when you put it on the wall and added Mallory's photos with the white frames, it really popped."

"Thanks. A favorite idea of mine was Izzie's window curtain overhang with a simple cushion bench below that created the illusion of a window seat. And Reed, your stenciled trim at the ceiling in monochromatic colors. Understated yet tasteful."

"Enough with the accolades. Back in character, ladies. There are a couple of cars pulling up. Deep breath, everyone."

Izzie placed her hand on the manger holding a lifelike baby doll. Brandi, Candy, and Cecelia held poses outside the homemade stable. Reed's fingers rested close to hers, sending a magnetic warmth that ignited her spirit.

When the last of the visitors voted and left the house, Reed announced, "Time's up."

"Hallelujah." Brandi said.

Candy scratched her back with her staff. "Ahh."

Cecelia slouched out of her old bathrobe. "I certainly wouldn't have let my kids pinch shepherds."

"An adventure in patience for sure." Izzie pulled off the band that anchored her pillowcase head cover. "Especially when Olivia brought her dogs. How many live nativities feature Mary holding a bichon in her lap?"

Brandi said, "When Fritz lifted his leg on a corner post—"

Reed burst out with a belly laugh, and everyone joined in.

"Hi, all." Claudia crossed the lawn from her house next door. "I brought hot mulled cider to warm you after your stint in the cold." She removed the lid, and the sweet and tangy aroma filled the air. "I have instructions from Mallory to deliver it to the kitchen."

"Mmm. The shepherds will lead the way to make sure you get there safely," Brandi said.

The shepherds departed, while Izzie tucked the doll she'd rescued from a child back into the manger.

"Apple-cinnamon. A snap in the air. It smells and feels like Christmas." Izzie halted and pointed. "Would you look at that?"

Reed bumped into her.

His presence added to the magic of the moment. The night was clear, and the crescent moon shone bright against the evening sky. "Don't you just love the season?"

He placed his hands on her shoulders. "I'm beginning to love watching you love the season." His touch was light. Every inch of her skin tingled.

"If I could package this view and the night air, it would

convince Fairland Hotels to be a part of Hamilton Harbor's redevelopment project."

She stiffened. "I'd hate for a hotel to block the view from the square."

"It's a big sky."

"Hmm, I guess."

Reed moved to her side. His shoulder touched hers.

She breathed in his aftershave. What had she wanted to say? Oh, yes, Cecelia's comment. "I've considered what Cecelia said earlier about one of us being voted off yet hoping the alliance will continue."

"It was a nice sentiment, but it's not the response you'd get where I come from."

"No?" Izzie turned to face him.

"Don't you believe it's unusual for competitors to feel kindly toward each other?"

His lips were close to hers. The hint of a five-o'clock shadow gave her the urge to touch his face. "Well ... I'd say it was ... you know, the Christian thing to do."

"Why Christian?"

She looked back at the moon to keep her mind off his lips and her head on topic. "Christians are supposed to love one another. Competitors can care about each other."

"Also, not my experience."

"Maybe you haven't found the right fellowship." She looked up at him. The moon sparking his eyes.

"Maybe." He leaned in to her ever so slightly.

"There you are," Claudia said. "You're holding up chow time."

Izzie wrapped her arms around her waist and strode to the back steps leading to the kitchen. Their first kiss ended in disaster. Maybe it was for the best to shy away from a second ... at least for now.

The team shared a Christmas buffet with the Spencers. Mallory stood to address the small group. "We want to thank all of you for the indelible mark you've made on this home. I will cherish your spirit and hard work each time I step into the upstairs rooms."

Lake stood, and Mallory stepped aside. "But it's time to move on with the contest, which requires we narrow participants. Those who will continue will be announced on Mattie's noon show Monday, but we will inform you of the partnerships for the next tier, so the new teams can be ready to start work on Monday."

Mallory touched her husband's shoulder. "You are all winners, because the contest has caught the attention of Eugenia's Designs in Orlando. Eugenia judged the contest we patterned ours after, and she has agreed to judge our final round."

Cecelia whistled. "That will lend credibility to this competition."

Reed's jawline went visibly taut.

"You are all very talented," Mallory said. "After tallying the points from our local professional judges and votes from the visitors, those selected to move on are Brandi, Cecelia, Izzie and Reed. Candy, you made the choice difficult."

Izzie waited her turn to embrace Candy.

Reed left room without saying a word.

CHAPTER THIRTEEN

Reed sat on the cold concrete bench by the boat landing behind Pirates' Cove Motel. Black bayou waters lapped against the barnacle-crusted posts of the boat slip. The moonlight tumbled over the restless water.

Was this what it meant to be between a rock and a hard place, or how about the devil and the deep blue sea?

He'd entered the contest under Padgett's orders. But now his mother, Eugenia, would be judging the finals. He shouldn't stay in the contest, but pulling out now would not only mess up the fundraiser. This was his opportunity to make his mark as one of the youngest to move up to management in his firm. Padgett had warned Reed that he would have drawbacks and made it clear that Reed would be evaluated by how he handled them. Could he really bring value to Emerson, Emerson, & Padgett?

His grandmother sold his brown plaid suitcase in a garage sale for a dollar—the one he'd kept packed for months in case either parent came for him. But they didn't come. On his seventh birthday, he unpacked. The clothes had been pressed flat so long that the fold lines didn't want to loosen when he wore them. He shoved the empty suitcase under his bed and never used it again. A suitcase of little value that belonged to a boy that felt the same.

But the boy became a man.

He kicked at a pebble and watched it sail over the water, making a clean dive entry.

He was an accomplished, employed designer. He would act the part, like Joseph in the nativity scene, even if he didn't feel worthy. He was drawn to Izzie, but he had to keep in mind that ultimately their goals could be at odds. One of them would be hurt. His part to prove himself to Padgett was to take the risk.

Reed heard the jingle of bells and footsteps on the walkway behind him.

"You're upset about Candy?" Izzie plunked herself on the bench beside him. She wore a red and green striped tasseled cap with bells attached and had changed into jeans and a jacket.

"No." Being close to her again was more upsetting. "She'll be fine. She told me earlier that a condo owner saw her room and contracted her to redecorate his master bedroom suite."

"So …"

"Why did I leave? My mother is Eugenia."

"Oh … Ooh," Bells jingled as she turned to face him. "Eugenia of Eugenia's Interiors? Your mother? You said she was a designer. But she's a prominent designer. I mean, I've heard of her. Is Harrison her last name?"

"Maiden. Married name was Roberts. I don't know what last name she uses."

"You never see your mother?"

"The last time I saw her, I was six years old. She wouldn't recognize me if she fell over me, but she knows my name. My parents not only left me behind …" Reed let out a chuckle with no humor behind it. "… they signed on the dotted line to let my grandparents adopt me. Harrison became my official name, which was confusing and embarrassing for me as a youngster."

"I understand last name hurts. Like yours, my mom was a pregnant teen, but my father skipped out. She never married. I was in first grade when I found out that made a difference to some people."

"What happened?"

Izzie leaned forward, pressed her elbows to her legs and rested her chin on her clasped hands. The bells on her cap fell mute.

"During recess at school, I overheard my best friend, Madison, talking to a group of girls at the swings. They had their backs to me. Madison said, 'My mom is having Izzie moved to the front of the class away from me, because she is illegitimate. I'm not to associate with her anymore, and you shouldn't either.' Ms. Finlaw, who lived upstairs, explained what illegitimate meant."

Reed let out a low whistle. "Sounds archaic in this day and age."

"Small town living sometimes has its drawbacks. Everybody knows you, faults and all. That's why I champion the underdog. I detest unfair labels, and I guess that's why I feel compelled to prove myself."

"Prove what?"

She shrugged. "I don't know. That I'm trustworthy, reliable, professional, a contributing member of society—something like that. Enough about me. Where you're concerned, you'll just be a number to the professional judges. Your mother won't know the names of the designers she's judging."

"Just the same, I don't want to discredit the contest. Lake and Mallory need to know."

"Sure. And you need to know that after you left, Mallory announced the teams for the next stage."

Reed lifted his head. Sparkles from the Christmas lights on Captain Jack's pirate ship shone in Izzie's eyes.

"It's the sheep herders against Mary and Joseph."

In the time he'd spent playing Joseph the past two days, eyes fixed on Izzie's profile, he'd hoped they might get to work together. That thought in itself was a new experience for him. He was a loner and had been for all the years he could remember. Grandma did a good job of preaching no attachments and getting serious too young. He seldom dated the same person twice—even in college. He had trained himself to be content in his singular state.

"Earth to Reed. Are you okay with us working together?"

"Oh … no … I mean, yes. Sure." He held up his hands. "I think … maybe."

Izzie's bells jangled. She turned to face him with her face scrunched.

"Sorry. Working with you is fine. It's just … I worry about the integrity of the contest."

"Look." She wagged a finger at him. "Save your worry until you need it."

The little gesture, accompanied by jingling bells, didn't quite ring true. Worry was not something Reed wanted to save.

Monday afternoon arrived with a sense of hope and energy flowing from Izzie straight into Reed's spirit.

"See? Outside judges are shielded with double-blind protection. No need to have worried about your mother's judging."

Izzie stood, arms crossed, in the Feldman Victorian sitting room she and Reed were to decorate as a result of a coin toss. Slated to be the Lake's study, the room carried the fresh scents of lemon oil, glass cleaner and refinished floors. Izzie, herself, was decorated in a white pullover and jeans, both adorned with shimmery appliques. Her silver beaded hoop earrings caught the sun streaming in the window, sending spots of light prancing about the room.

"Easy to say, don't worry."

"True. But my mom said worry is energy wasted, and I should shift that vitality into creativity."

"If that's where your ideas come from, you must have shifted a lot of worry."

"I'll take that as a compliment. Besides, when all is said and done, I'll bet your mother will be proud of your design success. Like Candy said, being picked to work on this project is an honor."

Make his mother proud? He snickered inside. "To be proud of something predisposes caring."

"She might surprise you." Izzie tapped her lower lip while taking in the room. "You ready to start work?"

"Very much. Now I know Mallory is confident the judging system will keep contestants' and judges' names secret."

"Good."

"What do you think of the room your 'heads' call got us in the coin toss?" Reed asked.

"You say that like we're in your least favorite room."

"Well … I'd formulated some special ideas for the dining room, so I need to redirect my thoughts."

"Funny. Our thoughts were running in the same direction. I pictured wall sconce lighting for the dining room …" She wrinkled her nose. "… but not in here."

Reed looked over the list Lake and Mallory had furnished with their objectives and budget for the study.

"Okay, Lake requires a place to relax, read his paper, watch TV, listen to music, read a good book, study a case file, enjoy a cup of coffee. Mallory is looking for rich colors, plenty of room for books with access to the high shelves, a calm ambiance, and good lighting for reading, knitting, and watching old movies. The television should not be the focal point."

He folded the paper and stuck it in his jacket pocket. "There goes my vision of a man cave with a 70-inch TV."

Izzie grinned. "This has to be a co-ed cave." She examined the built-in book shelving. "You don't see this quality of wood and craftsmanship in homes anymore."

Reed ran his hand over the reddish-brown shelving. "Mahogany. Wonderful cornice trim at the top. The window will help with the lighting."

"What can we use so Mallory can access the shelves near the ceiling?" Izzie was thinking aloud. "We should spend part of the budget on comfortable reading chairs. Maybe we can find a large basket for Mallory's knitting to put by her chair." She stepped back. "It would be nice if we could find a pull-up lap desk for Lake and a side table for his books and papers."

Reed envisioned wheels whirring into action inside Izzie's head.

"I like to start with a focal point. Any ideas?"

Izzie clapped her hands under her chin. "I know just the thing. Come on."

"Uh-oh. Those are scary words." He rubbed his leg.

She jutted out her cute chin. "Accidents happen."

"I probably shouldn't ask, but where do you have in mind?"

She grabbed his arm," We are going junkin'."

An hour later, Izzie, donned in coveralls she kept in her car for such occasions, had accumulated a discarded banister finial and four wooden spindles from a construction dumpster behind a downtown music store.

And why not? The store was undergoing a redo. Reed freed a wooden-framed picture of a stylized pointing finger inscribed with "Pay Here" from the rubble. The glass was broken. "How about this?"

"Love it. You're getting the hang of treasure hunting."

"Think so?" Reed held the picture, coated in sheet rock dust away from him, and stifled a sneeze. "What are you going to do with this stuff?" Reed added his find to the others in the back of Izzie's Suburban.

"I don't know ... yet. Interesting pieces, don't you think?"

"For junk, I guess."

"Therein lies the term, junkin'. Sylvia Easton, the art teacher at the boarding house, trained me. She could look at a piece of junk and imagine all sorts of interesting possibilities for it. I used to have such fun letting my imagination run wild with hers. I helped her design a fabulous light from beer bottles and driftwood."

Reed pressed his lips together hard. He saw the ghastly lady's leg lamp from the movie, *A Christmas Story*. He stifled a laugh in case she was serious.

"It sold for a hundred-fifty dollars."

Reed couldn't hold back. He guffawed. "Please tell me you're kidding. Someone paid money for a lamp made of beer bottles?"

"And driftwood." Izzie's frown turned into a glare. "I'll have you know the lamp was unique. And a lot of work. *And* a lady bought it for her lake house in ... THE HAMPTONS."

"And she could have been pulling your leg."

"For a hundred and fifty dollars?"

"You've got a point." Reed slammed the rear door of Izzie's car shut. "Where to next?"

"Uncle Bob's Trash and Treasures."

"Is this how you usually start planning your interiors?"

"I do. I listen for what the client wants and then start mulling over ideas to make their living space unique to them. Not just a cookie cutter room you would see in a furniture ad. That's what interior designers are for. Right? How do you begin a plan?"

"With pencil and scale paper."

They drove past the old theater on Main Street. The marquee read Hope Community Church, Revival Celebrating the Twelve Days of Christmas begins Dec. 26. Maybe he needed a revival of his individual versus conventional energy he'd boxed up and hidden long ago to please his grandmother. He'd always loved going into his mother's old bedroom. As a teen, she'd decorated her room with splashy colors and wispy puffs of iridescent fabric that resembled clouds hanging from the ceiling. Eventually, Grandma took down the clouds and painted the room off-white.

"I suppose it's good to scale the room first, because I have had to change things around when an item was a poor fit. But when a vision hits, I need to move on it, or I might lose the inspiration. I try things out, looking for that 'this is it' moment."

"I guess my 'this is it' moment happens on paper. Then it's just a matter of putting it together."

"Okay then. You do your thing. I'll do mine. Combine our expertise and see how it comes out."

At Uncle Bob's, Reed set aside a pile of dusty boxes, moved a mannequin wearing nothing but a New Orleans Mardi Gras hat and a smile, and pushed a broken ladderback kitchen chair aside until Izzie could examine a metal gate she'd spotted propped against the wall. Reed lifted it out, propped it against the wall and dusted his hands together. "Am I becoming an expert in junking all in one day?"

"Just scratching the surface." Izzie scrutinized the find. "Oh, my. This is fabulous."

Reed looked at the dull brown metal and shrugged. "Not the way I'd describe it."

Izzie ran her finger over the ornate curvature of the grill work as if it were fine china. "Reed," she said in a hoarse whisper, "it's an old teller cage … and it's brass. Can't you just see this in the Spencer's study? It's amazing."

More amazing was watching Izzie. She was breathless. He studied her discovery. "Lake might see it as part of his work. Like jail bars, maybe?"

"No. The library wall. Mallory wanted a way to access the floor to ceiling shelves. Polished, this would make a magnificent ladder."

"For starters, it's not long enough and second, it's not made for climbing. Ladders have to meet certain tests and weight capacity requirements."

Izzie sighed. "Now you sound like the explanations of analysis on the NCIDQ exam I failed."

Reed shrugged. "That test is all about health and safety, not creativity."

"Yeah, well, I still think this piece is screaming, 'I belong in Lake and Mallory's study.'" She made air quotes with her fingers.

"I'm willing to consider what your mind conjures up."

Did he really say that? The dust must have worked his nose and coated his brain.

CHAPTER FOURTEEN

Izzie rushed into the Feldman study, the door slammed behind her. She raised her hands above her shoulders and used them to emphasize each word.

"You. Will. Not. Believe. This."

She paused as the paint fumes hit her. Reed stared down at her, edger in hand.

"It will blow you away."

"Well, let me return to ground level before that happens." Reed's rubber-soled shoes squeaked against the metal of the ladder steps. "What won't I believe?"

"My mom's cleaning business is a franchise. The CEO of the company has pledged ... are you ready? ..."

Reed nodded.

"... to match the funds we make from the decorating competition."

"Good."

"Good?" Izzie flung her hands outward. "Doesn't that just knock your socks off?"

Reed looked down at the socks peeking out of his work shoes. "Still on."

Izzie gave his arm a poke. "Come on, show me your I'm-surprised-and-impressed look."

"Like this?" He lifted his brows and opened his eyes wide.

"That looks more like you saw mommy kissing Santa Claus. There should be a genuine thrill of emotion, jump-up-and-down excitement. Mallory screamed when I called to tell her."

"You're asking way too much of this New York boy."

"I guess, but isn't that great?"

"It is." Reed smiled at least. "What franchise does your mother run?"

"Spic & Span Cleaning Services. She has contracts in the Tallahassee area—a big business for someone who never finished high school." Izzie's eyes stung with tears. Her mom had sacrificed a lot but kept her never-quit attitude. "I'm proud of her."

Reed's expression softened. "Your mom must be quite a lady."

"She's amazing. And she got her break here on Feldman Square. Now that Marigold and Petunia have offered the last two vacant houses as a service to young women like my mother …" She blinked back waterworks trying to take over. "We must preserve the houses."

Izzie swiped at her eyes and faced Reed with what she hoped was a cheerful face. The look in his eyes startled her. Was it pity? Compassion? Understanding? A mix of all three? He stood somber and motionless a moment.

"Therefore … we need to work hard to prepare this room so people will pay to see the competition?"

Izzie blew air from puffed out cheeks and reeled in her emotions. "You've got a point." Izzie pushed up the sleeves of her old sweatshirt, already paint-spattered from other design projects. "Have Brandi and Cecelia been working in the dining room?"

"They finished their painting and were leaving when I arrived."

Was that a hint? "You edge and I'll roll?"

"That'll work." Reed climbed back up the ladder.

Izzie positioned a second ladder to work behind him. "I had a difficult time today making a client see that the overstuffed furniture she selected was the wrong scale for her room. But my mom's call made every little irritation I was choking down go away. How was your day?"

"I spent most of the day on a conference call with the team in New York."

"How is that working?"

"Okay. We are feeling our way through the process. It's experimental, having one of the team on location to check out and answer questions. The other team members are able to be more productive in their usual workspace."

"Is it hard on you to work in poor lighting in the old motel?"

"Actually, it's been pleasant. The weather is clear and cool, with great lighting on the back patio. Capt. Jack's pirate ship docked behind the motel gives me inspiration."

"Chalk one up for Florida. New York isn't the only happening place."

Reed went silent, then finally said, "Maybe so."

Izzie stepped down from the ladder to reload her roller with the burgundy paint they had selected for the walls. Her mind traveled to the teller cage fence from Uncle Bob's, still in the back of her car.

"Reed, those bookshelves require a ladder, and the teller cage keeps telling me it is the solution."

Reed climbed down. "The teller cage speaks to you?"

"Haven't you experienced something jumping out at you and you're sure it's the right thing?"

"You mean like when we found the color for these walls?"

"Exactly. And that's how it is for this teller cage. It belongs over there. I know it."

"But how can we conform it to the safety code?"

"Where there's a will, there's a way. Will you help me bring it in?"

"I'd rather finish this painting and not let it dry on the pad."

"It won't dry that fast. Let's bring our find in, so it can acclimate to the room and show us where to put it."

Reed gave her a curious look.

"All right. Work with me here."

Reed shook his head and sighed. "I can see I might as well bring it in, or the walls won't get painted."

Izzie followed Reed, their footsteps echoing down the long hallway. She liked this guy and the challenge of working with him. He was no "yes" man. He said what he felt. He might not agree with her, but he did try to work with her. Or was his cooperation really exasperation?

After Reed removed the grill, Izzie slammed the rear door of her car shut and ran ahead of Reed onto the porch to open the front door.

"Where would you like this to reside while you listen to what it has to say?"

"Lean it by the bookshelves."

Reed set the teller guard base on the floor, leaning it carefully against the shelving. "Talking yet?"

"Too early. It's not used to the room yet." Izzie backed up and studied the junk store find.

"While you wait for revelation, let's paint."

"Oh. Sure. Sure." Izzie grabbed her roller.

After an hour, they'd worked their way to the wall next to the bookshelves. Izzie put her brush in the tray and massaged her shoulders. Through the window, she could see the array of mini lights that outlined the giant oaks in Feldman Park. She stretched her neck and looked at the teller cage. So out of place in the corner. Hands on hips, she pulled her shoulders together. A car drove by, drawing her attention to the window again—the best view in the house during the daytime.

Reed let out a long sigh "Only one side of this door left to edge."

"The window."

"What?"

"The window is the first thing you see walking into the room. That's where the teller fence belongs, on the window."

Reed didn't scoff at the suggestion. He stopped his painting, moved the piece and propped it on the windowsill. The width fit perfectly. The height filled about two-thirds of the window.

"You may have something here. The natural light behind it will show off its unique scroll motif. Unique, yet simple."

"Straight masculine lines blended with the more feminine wrought iron grill work. She clapped her hands. A perfect blend for Lake and Mallory, don't you think?"

Reed examined the window frame. "A welder needs to hinge one side so it can be opened to raise the window. We can't block a means of escape in case of fire."

"Oh. I forgot about the safety issue ... again."

"I like this idea better than trying to climb on it," Reed said and propped the metal treasure underneath the window.

"The teller fence is happy there." Izzie gave a nod of satisfaction, turned and picked up the roller to finish painting.

Her phone sounded. She juggled the roller, trying to retrieve the phone from her back pocket.

Reed grabbed the roller. "I'll finish before you paint more than intended."

"Mallory, hi." Izzie punched the speaker button with her knuckle. "I'm putting you on speaker, trying to keep from getting paint on my phone. Reed's here."

"Good. Will you two play Mary and Joseph again this weekend? Our admissions sales took a big jump with the live nativity. The shepherds have other commitments, but I was hoping you two..."

Izzie tilted her head and looked at Reed. He stopped painting. Please say, yes. "What do you think?"

He shrugged his assent and went on painting.

Woohoo. Had he acquiesced to please her or to increase sales? It would be nice if he considered both.

"Okay. We'll do it."

"Wonderful. I was hoping you would. I contacted the Hamilton Harbor News and even Lyman at *Talk of the Town*. They will run a special feature on the matching funds offer."

"Great. Let's just hope Lyman manages a positive spin."

"I know what you mean. But it's worth taking a chance to advertise the fundraiser."

After ending the call, Izzie said, "You are a good sport."

"More like a hypocrite."

"Why would you say that?"

"Posing as Joseph when I haven't crossed the doors of a church in years."

"Really? You mentioned getting recruited to work on church projects."

"To please my grandmother."

He clipped his words. A darkness covered his countenance. Best she didn't pursue this subject right now. Maybe later. "Ah. Well, I still say you're a trooper."

Reed stepped from the ladder and set the roller on the paint tray. "Isn't a trooper like a policeman?"

"No. Not that kind of trooper. It's like someone who is reliable, uncomplaining, and hard-working. Honestly," Izzie gave him a curt nod, "it's a good thing you came to the South to expand your vocabulary."

"Sho nuff?"

"Oh, fine. Now you're making fun."

"Nope. Using my new vocabulary expansion. I guess I'll have to use another Pirates' Cove bath towel for my Joseph head cover again."

"The towel turned you into a perfect Joseph."

Reed poured unused paint from the tray into the paint can. Izzie erased a few paint spatters from the floor with a paper towel dabbed in mineral spirits.

"To me it's ironic that a vocabulary-challenged, non-church attending Yankee comes South and is pressed into service in a Christmas nativity scene."

Sounded like a nudge from God to her, but she said, "Maybe it's broadening your horizons." She flashed him a smile, and he allowed his dimple to show up.

"Who is this Lyman you were talking to Mallory about?"

"Have you ever seen The Enquirer?"

"Sho nuff." He gave her a full-dimpled grin.

"Hey." Izzie gave him a punch to his upper arm.

"Hey yourself." He rubbed his arm.

"Lyman is a reporter for the *Talk of the Town* weekly newspaper that keeps up with all the local gossip. He loves to twist and sensationalize whenever and wherever possible. Never trust him with a secret."

"I take it you know from experience?"

"Yep. In high school, I had this great prank all planned out. The idea came from Ruth Abernathy. Her hometown garden club planted winter rye in the shape of the town's name. When you entered their town during the cold months, they had a natural bright green sign contrasted against the brown grass."

"I envisioned the words Hamilton Harbor High sprouting up pretty and green on our rival, Melrose Beach High School's front lawn. I planted the letters late at night using a flashlight. When the words began to green up, I gave Lyman a secret tip to keep an eye on the grass. He blabbed, and I ended up having to plant the whole lawn with rye grass. Took me a while, but I found time to let the air out of all of Lyman's tires."

"Wow. I guess I better not cross you. What about Christian attitude and turning the other cheek?"

"Here's how I see it. Sometimes you need to forgive, because people may be wrong but sincerely wrong. You should put yourself in their shoes and give them benefit of doubt. However, if they intentionally hurt you, that's another story. Don't worry, unless you earn it like he did."

"Point taken."

🏠 🏠 🏠 🏠

Reed knelt beside the trough of hay holding the baby doll representing baby Jesus.

"Swing," a little boy begged his parents.

The swing set at Feldman Park had to be more interesting than staring at a couple of motionless adults for a little boy. Reed wanted to whine too. His knee, pressed into a clump of hay, throbbed. His bent position strained his back. He'd gladly take the youngster to swing in the park, for the chance to stand up.

"Shh. That's the baby Jesus with his mother and daddy. You should be quiet while he's sleeping."

"Swing," the child continued to plead.

"We might as well let him go," a man's voice said.

"Well, okay. Tell the baby good-bye."

"Bye, bye."

The voices faded. "Thank goodness. My back aches and my leg is cramping."

"My nose has itched for thirty minutes," Izzie said,

rubbing her nose. "Boy, it makes you appreciate the freedom to move."

Reed stood slowly, arching his back. "Oh, wow, standing has never felt so good. Kneeling is not easy."

"Freeze alert. A car is pulling up."

Reed rested his hand on the staff Pete fashioned for him from a tree limb and fastened his gaze on the baby.

Car doors closed and footsteps sounded on the sidewalk.

"Look, Mom. Remember the time our youth group participated in a live nativity?"

"I ... I think I do. You played Mary, and I was so proud."

The weak voice trembled, reminding him of his grandmother's speech, so fragile, during her last days.

"That's right. You remember, Mom. That's right."

The excitement in the daughter's voice was hard to mistake. This must be a mom who struggled with memory—Alzheimer's perhaps.

He'd been in a youth group once. But his involvement ended when his grandfather died. How could he embrace a religion where Christian parents abandoned their children and each other and trusted church members bilk the elderly?

The reminiscing people left, and another car door slammed. Reed shifted his gaze to Izzie this time. Studying her was far superior to staring at the red and black flecked wallpaper in his motel room, which might have been his plight if he weren't playing Joseph.

Working with Izzie had been a surprising bright spot to his whole "win over the townspeople" mandate given him by Vance Padgett.

He enjoyed her bold creativity, though her bent toward dropping everything to follow her instincts was disruptive.

"Toss me that throw pillow," she had said when she walked into the study yesterday. Izzie held a picture with wiggly streaks of dark green paint on a spattered cream and burgundy background. Nothing he would take a second look at. But the plaid chair cushion with shades of the same colors blended well with it.

"Makes the colors pop, doesn't it? I saw this in the hobby shop. It was a canvas being used by customers to view sample colors. They gave it to me."

"What in the world will you do with it?"

Izzie pressed her hands together, her eyes sparkled. "I'm crazy about your idea to have a fold-down library table for puzzles, board games, and such. So, look at this." She folded the table designed and built by Reed on a frame attached to the wall. They stained the table bottom to match the mahogany trim and shelving in the room. "Attach the canvas to the bottom of the table. Then when it's folded against the wall," she pushed it up to demonstrate, "Voilà. It becomes a framed painting."

Her find really was an ingenuous addition to the room. His practice of designing, then executing the plan in an orderly manner, got the job done, but Izzie's added touches gave their project flair.

Several groups of nativity spectators continued to come, and most went from the nativity to view the house.

When there was a lull, Reed said, "Can I ask you a personal question?"

"I guess. I may not answer, but you can always ask."

"Fair enough. You said you used to envy people with fathers. Yet, you came to see growing up in a rooming house with only your mother as a blessing. How did you come to that point?"

She didn't even hesitate with her answer.

"I came in from school after a few of my friends had endured teasing chants on the playground. Kid stuff. Mary, Mary messy Mary. Janie, Janie talkative Janie. Izzie,

Izzie no dad Izzie. The things the others were teased for, they could control. I couldn't control the fact that I had no father. I held in the hurt until I talked to Ms. Finlaw."

"What did she tell you?"

"She shared something that I never forgot. She explained that I wasn't without a dad. None of us are. She read a scripture from her Bible that states Jesus's Father is our Father and will not leave us as orphans. I took comfort in the fact that I had a heavenly Father even though I never knew my earthly dad."

Sounds like you benefited from having a host of people playing parenting roles.

"That's how I came to see it. You said your parents live in Florida? Do you know where?"

"Not exactly. Mother is somewhere in the Orlando area. The last I heard, my father was going to school in north Florida. I'm not sure where he is now."

"You should look him up while you're here."

Reed snickered. "I doubt he'd care to see me. Why should I bother?"

"Sometimes childhood hurts look different when we grow up."

Grown up. Reed's grandmother said he was born grown up. Reed looked at the polished shoes peeking out from under his brown tunic. Neat, orderly, simple—that was his way. His grandmother had always praised his reliable, balanced way of handling issues, comparing him to his mother's oddball, unpredictable ways. Maybe he'd never have developed the skills he had without growing up as he did. But he wished he could learn to be thankful for his circumstances like Izzie.

Reed pressed against the staff. Who would think it could be so hard to stand still? This was even more challenging than his lengthy conference call today with the team.

Dan shared that the Fairland Hotel chain was showing more interest in the project. Their representative had sent specific questions, and the team conferred on how to respond. Among the points discussed were the vacant houses that would border the hotel property.

"Reed," Dan had said, "your job of gaining trust will be even more critical now. The proposed hotel location adjoins those rundown houses. You need to sell the Save the Square people on getting rid of those houses. We'll design some nice transitional landscaping between the properties."

"But if the houses are restored, they could make a nice backdrop for the hotel," Reed had said.

"You seriously don't think the hotel will agree to go in there with a bunch of unmarried, pregnant girls in their backyard," Dan said.

"I'm stuck in the middle of this fundraiser. If there is talk of tearing down those houses, you can kiss any good will I've built good-bye."

"Greg, could the houses be kept intact and moved?" Mandeville had asked.

"They are strong structures, but for the cost of moving, set up, and refurbishing plus property expense to put them on, you could build a completely new facility."

"How about that? Use the funds raised to build a new home in a more suitable location? Maybe Emerson would agree to spring for the property. I could draw the plans," Mandeville said.

"Hopefully, we are arguing a moot point ..."

Izzie's whispered, "Reed. Lyman is here," interrupted his thoughts.

Reed remained frozen in character but could feel scrutiny run over him.

"Well, well. Could that really be the famous conniving

Izzie Ketterling, playing the role of Mary? What a hoot."

Izzie growled a response with minimal lip movement and eyes still on the baby. "A hoot is you being considered a real reporter."

Reed moved his head slightly to get a look at the man. He was shorter than Reed, had a ruddy complexion accented by a red suit jacket and a black felt hat with a press card stuck in the hatband.

"Hey, I'm looking to make a nice story about this decorating contest and fundraiser. Remember the power of the press." He tilted his head and chuckled. "This is great. Izzie Ketterling , a captive audience."

Should Reed intervene? Defend Mary's honor as Joseph? Probably not.

A little girl ran up. "Look mommy, a baby."

"That's the baby Jesus. The whole reason we celebrate Christmas."

More people crowded in. Lyman disappeared.

An hour later, Mallory declared the evening the best yet.

Izzie and Reed strolled to the waterfront to unwind. The water's sluggish lapping against the bay front seawall was soothing. Reed breathed in the salty scented air, cold but refreshing. "It feels so good to move again."

"The cold was getting to me," Izzie said. "How about you?"

"I guess I'm more used to the cold. It's actually pleasant without the snow, slippery ice, and mess when it melts." Reed rested his arms against the railing. "So that was the infamous Lyman giving you a hard time?"

"Yep. And there is no telling what kind of article he'll write." Izzie stretched her arms and arched her back, then tugged her jacket closed and leaned against the railing.

The movement brought her close. He was drawn to her

not only because of the nearness but her deep concerns over her cause. Reed encircled her shoulder. A warm energy radiated from her into him. "If the word gets out about the fundraiser. Surely it will be a good thing."

"My lips probably look like they agree only because they are frozen into a smile and numb after gazing at the baby Jesus for two hours."

Reed rubbed his hands together vigorously, creating a warming friction. He grazed her cheeks with his hands and ran his fingers down, lightly touching her lips. "Better?"

The moonlight reflected in her eyes and hair, giving her skin a radiant glow. She pressed her lips together. "Not much feeling yet. They need help."

Reed lifted her chin and his lips met hers ever so lightly. "Izzie," he breathed her name.

"Try that aga—"

Reed drew her close and kissed her again. Her lips awakening under his. The brisk wind swirled, encasing them in a world of their own. A magical world where Izzie's precious houses wouldn't be torn down and his job wouldn't be to manipulate the people who trusted him.

CHAPTER FIFTEEN

"How does Lyman come up with this stuff?" Izzie lifted her latte from the bistro counter. "Ye-ow, this is plenty hot, Elaine."

"Sorry, new cups. They need these little cardboard jackets." Elaine slipped one on Izzie's cup and handed it back to her.

"What did Lyman write this time?" Mellie asked.

Present for the hens were Francine, Loretta, Mellie, and Margaret. The rooster side was light. So far, only Lake and Dave had arrived.

Izzie read loud enough for all to hear.

"Mary and Joseph Used to Lure Visitors into Voting on Interior Design Contest."

Elaine shook her head. "You can count on Lyman to find the dark side of any news piece."

"But to question the motives of the nativity? It's Christmas, for goodness' sake. You'd think he could write one decent human-interest story," Francine said.

Lake spoke up. "He'll tell you, sweet stories don't sell newspapers."

"His stories don't sell me," Mellie said. "I don't subscribe to *Talk of the Town*. Look at the *Hamilton Harbor News* headline." Mellie held up her paper and read, "Live Nativity Graces Feldman Square."

"That sounds much better." Margaret sniffed. "The stuff you read in that weekly paper is shocking."

"It doesn't shock me coming from Lyman," Loretta

said. I had to deal with that boy's shenanigans throughout high school."

"Ladies, you're forgetting, it's the bad stuff that grabs people's attention, and we live in a depraved world," Dave said.

"But Lyman goes above and beyond." Izzie slid off the stool. "Listen to this. Reviving the relics on Feldman square has stooped to a new low. The Save the Square people are using Mary, Joseph, and the baby Jesus to generate traffic into the Feldman house as a fundraiser. The designers are trying to cover its age like a woman resorting to a face-lift and …" Izzie smacked the paper and spit out the next word, "…liposuction." She paced. "Sometimes it's better and less costly to move on with the new, rather than revive the old. As Ed Blackburn put it in the last commission meeting: 'To really attract new clientele to our area we need to press forward. Looking to reclaim the old, only slows progress.'"

Izzie stopped reading and huffed. "Do you believe this guy? And he doesn't stop there." She read on with increased pitch, "If our community is to ever move forward, groups like Save the Square should not tie the hands of developers and shackle them with restraints from the past. Let them do their job as they see fit. That's what they're paid for. We should grab hold of the future before it passes us by."

Izzie slapped the *Talk of the Town* paper onto the counter. "I'd like to grab hold of Lyman right around his scrawny—"

"Press card?" Elaine offered.

Izzie turned to Elaine, who held the "tone-it-down" expression she used when they were roommates in college.

Izzie frowned. "Yeah. Sure. His press card," she said and plunked down on her stool. "Among other things."

"Don't worry. We understand your frustration," Lake

said. "Hopefully, the article won't affect Reed's appreciation of the square and its potential."

"Yes, but drivel like this, I'm afraid, will push the redevelopment team to bulldoze our efforts on the square."

"Why give Lyman's reporting that much credence," Elaine said as she arranged a new batch of blueberry bagels in the showcase.

"It's just ... I was beginning to kind of like Reed, and I don't want this gunk to push him into Blackburn's court."

"Tell me more."

"About Blackburn?"

"No, silly. About 'kind of liking' the guy." Elaine looked at the bistro entrance. "And said guy has just arrived."

"Here's the fellow you think can be swayed by yellow journalism," Dave spouted out to Reed from the men's table.

"Oh, stop." Francine said."

"Just a little friendly ribbing."

Reed looked behind him. "Were you talking to me?"

Lake stood and held out his hand to Reed. "You and your firm just happened to be the topic of conversation, which should come as no surprise when you're around this bunch."

"You and Izzie made a sweet Mary and Joseph," Francine said from the ladies' table and the others tittered in agreement.

A pink flush hit Reed's face.

Lake gave Reed a pat on the back. "I'm impressed with what you and Izzie did with the study."

"Thanks."

Izzie held up the front page of the *Talk of the Town* and motioned Reed to join her.

"Read the headlines to Lyman's story."

Reed glanced at the headline and merely nodded.

Izzie wrinkled her forehead. "You're not upset?"

"Captain Jack showed the paper to me this morning at the motel. I read it to the team in New York along with the article in the *Hamilton Harbor News*. Sort of balanced perspectives."

"Your boss knows what Lyman wrote?"

He nodded. "It's okay," then spoke to Elaine. "I'll take a double espresso to keep me fueled for another cold evening in that manger scene."

"You still want to participate?"

"Of course. With both these stories out, we should expect an even bigger crowd. Or should I say lure more people in? Dan thought the publicity was ingenious."

Izzie thumped the paper. "Well, I didn't like his reference to the houses as old relics."

Reed accepted the insulated jacket for his cup from Elaine and took a sip of coffee. "Perfect Elaine."

Elaine dimpled up.

"Face it." Reed swiveled on his stool. "There are two factions in town, and my firm's job is to work with both."

"And Izzie thought you'd be thin-skinned and all ruffled," Dave said. "I figured a New Yorker could handle Lyman's penny-ante stuff."

Reed smiled. "Oh, some things bother me."

He turned to Izzie, his black-brown eyes trained on hers.

Izzie cleared her throat and stared back at him. She'd ruffled him scratching his car, awarding him the pumpkin-carving prize, and putting him in harm's way when he ended up with four stitches.

Izzie lowered her voice. "You don't cease to amaze. What I think will rile you doesn't, and vice versa."

"How so?"

"You were upset receiving the pumpkin carving award,

which was meant to be a nice gesture, then when you are accused of luring people to spend their money, you're okay with it. I don't get it."

Reed shrugged. "One's business, one's personal." Reed picked up a church flier from the stack on the counter.

"There's twelve days of Christmas down here? We only have one in New York."

"It's a special revival celebration at the church," Izzie said. "You should come."

Reed's shoulders drooped like a man sentenced to die.

A lurid headline affected him less than an invitation to church? He'd shared his hurts. Maybe visiting her church could change his mind about the Christian community. "If for no other reason, come to see the inside of the church. It's a historical building, once the only theater in town. Chalk it up to research. Your boss would want you to, don't you think?"

"I probably won't be working down here that long."

"What if you and I win the team competition?"

"The decorating will be completed before Christmas, and this event starts December the twenty-sixth." He placed the flier back on the pile. "I should be back in my office by then."

"Will you come if you're still in town?"

"Sure."

But his sure, sounded more like shoving a door shut.

Izzie parked behind Reed's car in front of the Feldman house. She stepped out and breathed in the clear, crisp air. Cool enough to wear her "Christmas Should Be Felt, Not Bought" sweatshirt. She opened the rear door of her Suburban and selected supplies to take inside for the final decorating challenge.

Mallory had been kind in her remarks the day before.

"For their outstanding, ingenious, and creative work, the team members to move on to the final competition will be Izzie Ketterling and Reed Harrison."

The announcement had drawn a crowd of a hundred or so at Feldman Park, and Mattie Mason was there with her television film crew. "You two come up here for your battling assignments."

Mattie held up two envelopes. "Ladies first."

Izzie drew the receiving room, which would be Lake's office, and Reed would decorate the old parlor to be the living room. She and Reed had five days to complete their assignments.

Mattie had told the onlookers, "The rooms will be open for viewing and judging after Christmas. So, plan to return and see how the designers bring these rooms to life."

"I'd like to see how these rooms are brought to life myself." Izzie chatted to herself. She reached for the doorknob at the front door adorned with the wreath Reed had fashioned, using magnolia leaves from Feldman Park. The garland created by the original design team still gave the front porch a pleasing fragrance. She clutched two heavy wallpaper books topped with a ring of paint sample chips in one arm. A bag of fabric swatches and her purse dangled from her other arm as she tried to open the door.

Thud ... plunk.

"Ouch."

The door swung open. Reed widened his eyes, then glanced at the overturned wallpaper books. "Here, let me help you." He picked up the bulky books.

"Thanks. I didn't want to have to make two trips."

"My grandmother called that a lazy man's load."

Izzie laughed. "The description fits." She stepped

into the room and set down the bag and her purse on the windowsill.

"Well. Would you ever have thought two months ago, in the Tally-Ho parking lot, we'd be competitive comrades?"

Reed shook his head, "Not even remotely."

"So—not asking for any design secrets, mind you—do you have the plan of attack for your room yet?"

"Working on it," he propped an elbow on his wrist and pinched his chin. "How about you?"

Izzie took a moment to scan the room. "Lake wants an ergonomic space for computer work, a place to interview clients and conduct lie detection tests along with a place for case files and office supply storage. He'll require task lighting to support the natural light." She opened her arms and slowly rotated. "Lots to accomplish in a ten by ten room." Her clunky earrings swayed and whapped her on the neck.

Reed leaned in and tapped her earring. "Are those boxes?"

He smelled fresh, like a pine forest after a rain. The memory of his kiss beside the bay waters flowed over her. "They're supposed to be storage cubicles. I cut up a green plastic strawberry basket and used a glue gun to make miniature crates."

"Amazing. Whatever sparked that idea?"

She raised her shoulders. "Sometimes I dress for the season, my mood, or in this case for my design project. I'll be moving stuff into this room, so I'm wearing moving crates."

He showed off his dimple. Her heart skipped. Room. Focus on the room.

"Don't you love working with an empty space and plotting the possibilities?"

"I prefer to work on a new interior from building plans.

It's a different challenge, working on this old house with preexisting architectural features that need revival."

"Speaking of revival, you are coming, aren't you?" She would use the don't-give-him-a-chance-to-say-no approach. "The revival lasts twelve days and kicks off the day after Christmas. You'll be back in town on the twenty-sixth. Don't worry about bringing food, I'm taking rolls and a salad."

"I don't—"

"I know you don't understand the twelve days. But in theory, Christmas officially doesn't end until January 6, with the celebration of the arrival of the wise men."

"Ah. The twelve days of Christmas, December 26th through January 6th?"

"Right. By then, nights won't be tied up with this decorating challenge. So, plan on coming. But for now, I am closing this door to do my room. I have to acclimate."

She leaned against the closed door and sucked in a breath. The little dangling crates tapped against her cheeks like a pat on the back. He hadn't said no. She didn't give him a chance.

What just happened? He felt like he'd been on a wild New York taxi ride and shoved out onto the sidewalk.

The door Izzie closed looked like the one between the kitchen and dining room at his grandmother's house. The door had been pushed closed to shield him from hearing his mother's argument with his grandmother. But he still heard.

"Mom, it's for Reed that I have to leave to learn a decent trade."

"You should learn to be a decent mother."

Then the back door slammed.

That was the beginning of the end of seeing his mother. A week that summer, she took him to the lake to sail a little boat she'd bought him. She smelled sweet, like lilacs.

The boat sunk.

Visits from his mom became short holiday visits. His dad's visits were mostly empty promises. Then contact with both his parents stopped.

Grandma said it was for the best.

Her definition of best wasn't the same as his. He had to accept that his parents didn't want him and never made room for him in their lives. The hurt had overwhelmed him then. It still clung to him. That's just how things were.

And now, this new decorating challenge with his mother being in on the final judging had weighted him with mixed feelings of anger and heartache—a hefty backpack.

The mother who gave him life, then gave him up to pursue her career, would judge his work. Did she have any idea he had become a designer? Would she be pleased or not care? She'd never suspect her son would be working in this little coastal town in Florida. What if she declared his room the winner of the competition? Would she accept that the son she gave up had some worth? He smirked at the thought.

And that wasn't all that nagged him. The objective of this competitive effort was to save the derelict houses on the square. But that goal was spiraling toward a likely head-on collision with the Fairland Hotel chain contract that could mean advancement for him.

Reed ran his fingers through his slicked-back hair. For now, he'd go to Izzie's church revival for one day to appease her. That was a week away. He wouldn't dwell on it anymore today. This room had to be ready for public viewing. Then he had to return to New York for a team meeting and Christmas party, which would be his only Christmas celebration. Since his grandmother died, this was his first Christmas with no family. None. He just wanted to get it behind him. It was not a happy thought to have the holiday stretch out twelve additional days.

Reed picked up the pad of graph paper he left on the mantle and began jotting down his initial thoughts for the focal point and room arrangement.

Clunk. Clunk.

Izzie's boots sounded on the wood floor in the next room. He could picture her pacing, while her creative wheels turned. Izzie was acclimating to her room. He missed her warmth and cheerful enthusiasm.

He unclipped his tape measure from his belt and measured the width and height of the fireplace mantle and drew the fireplace to scale on his paper.

Clunkity. Clunkity.

Izzie's hurried footsteps sounded. The muse must have struck.

Could he receive vibes from this room the way she did?

Reed smiled and set down his pad. Why not?

He stepped into the center of the room as he had seen her do. Closed his eyes, and breathed in. He smelled the fresh varnish of newly refinished oak floors and breathed in the chalky scent of re-mudded sheet rock, ready for a new coat of paint.

Reed couldn't bring himself to ask the room to talk to him the way she did. He stood there a moment.

Nothing.

He opened his eyes.

No great revelation.

He stared at the fireplace. Nothing spoke to him.

He pulled Mallory and Lake's list of objectives for the room from his shirt pocket.

Mallory wanted a pleasant place to welcome guests, converse, relax and watch TV or cozy up to the fire on a winter's evening. Lake's requests were simple—comfort, a wide-screen TV and a good remote.

There was his first order of business—television placement would go above the fireplace. He might not be as creative as Izzie, but he was practical.

He considered the three sash windows that looked out on the front yard and the nativity scene. He closed his eyes again. All he could see was Izzie's profile as she played Mary. He could smell her sweet scent when he held her close. He opened his eyes. What was he doing? Rooms didn't talk to him.

Focus, man. He was a professional, trained in looking at a room's dimensions and features, combing over the room's purpose, and coming up with a plan. He retrieved his pencil and pad from the mantle and began measuring the rest of the room.

He heard the tug and rumble of Izzie opening a window in the next room. He wanted to open the door and benefit from her ideas, her enthusiasm, warmth and funny expressions. He'd always preferred working alone, but now ... now, decorating this old home was not the same without Izzie.

🏠 🏠 🏠 🏠

Izzie stood in the middle of what would be Lake's office. "Room, you are not talking to me at all."

She looked at the paper poking out of her purse. Maybe she should try Reed's technique. Wouldn't measured and methodical suit an office?

Her boot heels clunked against the wood floor as she strode across the room with purpose. She pulled out a flier for Hope Community's Twelve Days of Christmas and flipped it over.

Pen poised, she sat on the wide windowsill. Now what?

She sketched an outline of the room. She approximated the shape of the room and noted the doors and windows and then waited.

Nothing.

What would Reed suggest?

A focal point. The desk? Not a very creative focal point, but it would be the largest item in the room. She drew a rectangle to represent the desk, but the scale wasn't meaningful without graph paper. Besides, she usually measured by stepping off items to place the furniture.

Face it. Reed was the gifted planner. She admired his exacting skills, but without him there to comment on her ideas as they pinged in her mind, she was at a loss.

Think, girl. Get your act together. Fresh air. Maybe that would free her mind. The window rattled as she pushed it up and let in the chilly breeze from the bay. That only reminded her of Reed's arms holding her and his tempting lips taking over hers.

Who would have ever thought her creative spirit would depend on having the input of a New Yorker? Decorating the Feldman house was not the same without Reed.

CHAPTER SIXTEEN

Reed stood outside the old theater and read the marquee:

Hope Community Church
Join us to celebrate the Twelve Days of Christmas
December 26-January 6

Could making it this far count without going in? He'd returned to New York. Seen everyone. Talked business at the obligatory Christmas party. Munched salty nuts. Tasted tangy meatballs. Drank sweet punch. Now he had returned to the red and black velvet wallpaper in his home away from home, ready for work.

If he didn't go in, he wouldn't see Izzie. His heart skipped. He'd missed her … a lot. But under these circumstances, his willing heart was being held back by his unwilling feet.

Izzie had nudged him to come to church since he first read the flier about the Twelve Days of Christmas. "Church fellowship can be uplifting, accepting and forgiving. It's not deceptive or hypocritical all the time, like you think," she had said.

A glass door swung open. "Reed, you came. How's the team? How was Christmas in New York? I heard you had snow."

Seeing her, his heart swelled with joy that he fought to tamp down.

Izzie was her bubbly self and looked striking, dressed

in a white blouse and skirt, with large glass ball ornament earrings that would hang just as comfortably on a Christmas tree.

Stay calm, Harrison. Reign in that smile. "The team is fine. Christmas in New York, fine. The snow turned to ice, not so fine."

"Well, it still sounds exciting to have snow for Christmas. Come in. I was afraid you'd forget."

"Forget? With you around? Not hardly."

She grinned and ushered him into the mezzanine of the old theater. The recessed ceiling held a spectacular chandelier with long strands of crystal beads attached to gilded cherubs perched all around the ceiling. The light gave warmth to the entry and highlighted Izzie with a golden glow.

"Ms. Huggins was right. The architectural features in buildings prior to WWII were unique. This ceiling is magnificent and could compete with any of those you'd find on Broadway."

"Are you saying, New York City has nothing on Hamilton Harbor?"

"I wouldn't go that far."

"Hold on. 'Cause when it comes to food, you may be singing a different tune."

"Hold on to what?" He was always up for a lesson in southern lingo.

She stopped an instant. "I don't know. How about me?"

She grabbed his hand. The warm glow of the room moved straight into his heart.

"You have got to try Francine's melt-in-your-mouth pot roast. Ms. Mazie's yeast rolls are to die for, and I made a no-bake fruit cake that is delish."

"Sounds like I'm going to have my socks knocked off?"

"Yes." Izzie turned and squeezed his hand. "You're

catching on."

In the fellowship hall, they gathered around not only pot roast, yeast rolls, and fruit cake, but black-eyed peas with hog jowls, baked macaroni and cheese, and dark greens called collards.

"This room is an addition to the original theater. The glassed-in area gives a nice open greenhouse effect."

"I agree. Add-ons are required to be different for historical preservation. So how long has this been a church?"

"Let me think. They started refurbishing the building right before I graduated from Florida State. I was in Atlanta a couple of years for design school, then moved back when Emme took over the Flower Cottage. I guess Hope has been operating about five years. Yesterday, they had to open up the balcony to seat everyone, so the church is growing."

"Those stats should help your Save the Square cause."

"Yes. And I hope more of downtown reopens."

"I have to say, the preservation and re-purposing of this building is a good prototype."

"I hope, after tonight, you give church another chance." Izzie gave him a look that sweetened his heart. Did she have him thinking southern now?

Inside, the sanctuary used the old theater seating. Reed followed Izzie down the dim-lit center aisle where they found seats only three rows back from the stage—a bit too close to the front for his liking. Izzie saved seats for Elaine and Jeff.

From the orchestra pit came the traditional strands of "Joy to the World." With lights low and the nontraditional surroundings, maybe this church visit wouldn't be so bad.

Seats around them gradually filled. Elaine arrived with Jeff, who offered a hearty handshake. "Good to see you here."

"You must tell us how our renditions of Christmas music match up to New York's with Radio City, Rockefeller Center and all," Elaine said.

"If you love Christmas, New York is a magical place to be for the season, but from what I hear coming from your orchestra, they could give New York Pops some serious competition."

"And with no long lines and high dollar ticket expense." Izzie gifted him with a grin and a nudge.

Snapshot memories flashed in his head. A five-year-old being lifted over the curb in front of Carnegie Hall, the press of the crowd where his only view was the backside of suits and fancy dresses, the music swelling up to thrill the soul from performers that looked like midgets from his seat in the balcony. A rare remembrance of time spent with both parents.

The sound of the church's performers coming from the tiny orchestra pit was impressive.

A man dressed for the occasion in green slacks and a red shirt came on stage with two women dressed in black slacks and red tops with silvery trim that sparkled in the stage lights.

"Merry Christmas, everyone," he called to the crowd.

Voices rang out in the auditorium, sending the greeting back to him. The orchestra began playing the tune of "God Rest Ye Merry Gentlemen." People rose from their seats.

A tinge of discomfort filled Reed as he heard the familiar hymns of his earliest years. A childhood that had changed from warm to bleak in ten months.

Reed closed his eyes and breathed in the fresh scent of pine. He handed his mother cuttings from the base of the tree that she placed on the mantle, and skillfully wove shimmery beads among the branches. His grandma had brought them all hot chocolate, then turned up the volume on the stereo to listen to Jack Jones and Glen Campbell singing about silver bells and dreaming of being home for Christmas. His dad sat on the sofa showing off his skill with a Rubik's Cube. Reed had crawled up next to him to watch. That was his last Christmas memory with his dad.

Now the same tunes only opened the wound of his parents casting him aside. He'd gone through the motions of Christmas with his grandmother, but the best part of the season was getting past December 25th.

Today was no different. He'd box up those hurts and think about work.

Mr. Padgett had rested his arm on Reed's shoulder. His breath smelled of fruit punch that had a touch of extra spirits. "The team says your working remotely is working out fine." He dabbed the splotch of BBQ sauce in the corner of his mouth. "Use as much time as you see fit on that Feldman competition. At this point, we need you to not only gain favor with the locals but also to win. The Fairland Hotels rep has gotten wind of the contest. He's impressed with your coastal pirate interior designs. Winning the competition might give the final push to seal the deal. After this Christmas break, I want you back in Hamilton Harbor."

"If we get a commitment from Fairland, we will have the prototype we need to get our foot in the door of other small, coastal Florida towns that our acquisitions team is looking at. Won't that be a kick in the pants for the Hargrave developers?"

Mr. Padgett's raucous laugh left a bit of spittle on Reed's sleeve, but the impact of the words soaked deep. What would it be like to win and help seal the deal with Fairland? Could this be his ticket to an office with a window? Could he show his mother what she gave up? Gratification in more ways than one stood poised at his fingertips. He'd never get this chance again. Now, it was up to him to produce.

Reed slouched and stretched his feet under the chair in front of him. The knot in his stomach vanished. He could relax. This was just an old theater with people singing. He'd had a pleasant meal with Izzie and the locals and was only doing what Padgett asked. No other commitment or worry. This was just business and an evening out with Izzie.

The music concluded and Pastor Creighton strode on stage. "Welcome everyone to the Twelve Days of Christmas, our gift to the community to commemorate the days between the birth of Jesus and the arrival of the wise men. I am pleased to introduce our speaker and my good friend, Evangelist Randall Roberts, who is ..."

The knot inside Reed's chest gripped him with an intensity that made it difficult to breathe. He jerked his head toward Izzie. She smiled at him.

What had she done? Was this the reason for her push to get him here? An unsuspecting animal lured into a trap? How could she?

His words came out in an angry, hoarse whisper. "Now I know why you were so insistent I come to church. You may think you know what I need, but you don't." Words shot from him before they were fully formed in his mind. "Lay off."

Izzie's mouth gaped.

The guest speaker took the mic handed to him by Pastor Creighton.

Reed had to get out.

The red exit sign loomed to his right. A beacon for his swift escape. With no apology, because he had no more words to offer, he made wide strides to the exit door.

Reed never looked back. The man standing on center stage greeting the congregation was his father.

Izzie pulled into the Pirates' Cove Motel parking lot. The smell of her peace offering, fresh cinnamon bagels and coffee from the bistro, permeated her car.

Would the gesture make amends for the hurt she apparently caused him? After she realized that Evangelist Randall Roberts was Reed's father, she wanted him to know that she never made the connection beforehand. Why had he jumped to the negative conclusion?

She pushed the gearshift into park, set the brake with a snap, and attempted to shed her own negative thinking. The crystal facets on her dangling earrings captured the sunlight and sent reflective lights bouncing about the car interior. She'd just have to make him understand.

Florida's cold snap before Christmas had mellowed to a sunny seventy-two-degree morning. A slight breeze rustled through the palm trees that lined the front of the motel. She stepped out of the car, reached for the drink tray and bag with the bagels, and bumped the car door closed with her hip.

"You adding delivery services to your many talents, Izzie?" Captain Jack had walked up behind her with a stack of white towels in his arms.

"Good morning, Jack. Today, I am. Can you knock on Reed's door for me? My hands are full."

"The weather is so nice he's already set up his office on the patio behind his room. Come on, I'll open the side gate for you. How's the fundraising project going at the Feldman house?"

"The project has been fun. Admissions have really

picked up since we finished the front rooms for the final judging."

"I saw you and our New York visitor playing Mary and Joseph. You make a nice couple, but I guess the design contest makes you competitors." He looked at the bistro takeout. "At least when it comes to the contest." He gave Izzie a wink as he lifted the gate latch and stepped aside to let her through.

"Right." She wished she could wink away the touchy subject she needed to talk over with Reed.

"Good luck to you. I have to deliver these towels and get back to the office."

Izzie was glad Jack had other responsibilities. She wanted to talk to Reed alone. She walked past veteran red and white camellia bushes as tall as she was. Behind the strip of motel rooms with sliding glass doors along the rear, she could see the stone patio table that held Reed's computer and paperwork. But no Reed.

The breeze rippling the umbrella shielding the table, snatched up a paper and blew it under an azalea bush. Izzie set down the coffee tray and bag to retrieve the paper. Just as she reached for it, the sneaky wind puffed, scooting it just out of reach. On hands and knees, she grabbed hold of the corner of the paper and slid it toward her. The words, unoccupied houses on Feldman Square, circled, caught her attention.

She sat on the grass and read the typed communication on Emerson letterhead.

As discussed, Fairland Hotels is coming on board. They still want the unoccupied houses on Feldman Square torn down. They need the space for parking. You can break the news after that design contest is over. Fairland is very interested in the interior design sketches you submitted. Keep up the good work, and keep the natives happy.

Parking? Natives happy? Izzie's vision blurred, the

blood coursing through her veins felt hot.

"Izzie? Is that you?" Reed said. He had returned to the patio.

She stood and brushed the leaves from her dirt-soiled knees—the rumpled paper in hand.

"It's me, all right. A native come to make peace and let you know I had no idea your father was the guest speaker, but it looks like there will be war after all."

She tossed the soiled paper on the table, slammed the coffee and bagel bag on top of it, and stomped off.

Tears ran hot on her burning face. She pulled up in front of the Feldman house and set her brake with a jerk.

As discussed—

He knew the hotel wanted the houses torn down. He'd been playing her ... everyone. Trying to fit in. Acting like he was helping with the fundraiser. It was all a charade.

She needed to vent. Emme wasn't at the Flower Cottage yet. At seven fifteen in the morning, the only activity came from the road department. The clank and whir of the excavator reverberated across the square. The city was cutting a long promised new street between the park and Calico Jack's and beginning to lay drainage pipes. The project required clearing some trees and wooded area.

The Feldman house wouldn't open for tours until 10:00. She took out her key. The newly decorated home would be just the place for her to release her frustrations to the Lord. He, more than anyone, understood betrayal. And that's how she felt. Betrayed. She'd sit inside, commiserate, and pray.

The key rattled in the keyhole of the antique brass doorknob, and she let herself in. The scent of new paint, lemon oil polish, and freshly waxed floors scented the air. Light glinted off something on the floor in the entry hall between the office and the living room.

DESIGNED FOR *LOVE*

The oriental area rug she and Reed recommended to Mallory muffled her footsteps as she went to examine the object. It was a coin. A gold coin. Did a visitor drop it? But Mallory had someone come and clean the floors and dust each evening, so the house was ready for viewing the next day. How could they have missed this?

She bent down and retrieved the coin. When she straightened, her eyes were drawn into the living room that Reed had decorated. Her breath caught. Had a window been left open? In the dim light, it appeared that a strip of iridescent white curtain had blown onto a chair. Fireplace andirons lay scattered on the hearth. She reached for the light switch. The ceiling fan light exposed the mess. Half of the curtains covering the tri-window alcove were torn and streaked with dirt. Slat on the shutters were broken. Magazines and accessories on the large square coffee table in the center of the conversation grouping were in disarray. The fringed area rug looked as if it were the scene of a wrestling match. Two bricks lay on the soot-covered hearth. Burglary? Vandalism? She pulled her phone from her pocket and dialed 911.

"What's your emergency?"

"I think there's been a break-in at the Feldman house."

"Name and location."

"Izzie Ketterling. I've never paid attention to the number. It's on Second Street. Feldman Square.

"Are you alone?"

"Yes."

"I'll send help."

Izzie swiped at the phone screen to find Lake and Mallory's number, but knocked the phone from her hand. It clattered to the floor and slid under the poker, resting next to an overturned vase of wispy accent reeds.

She squatted down, trying to reach the phone without

disturbing any evidence.

"What's going on here?"

Reed's voice behind her boomed and Izzie lurched forward. Her hand hit on the poker as she tried to brace herself and keep from toppling over. Her knee caught the edge of the poker handle and shot it into the fireplace.

"Look what you did coming up behind me like that."

"What I did? What have you done?"

Izzie stood, rubbing her hand that had slammed against the floor. She straightened her pullover, leaving soot fingerprints.

"You don't think that I—"

"It's not what I think, it's what I see."

"Oh?" Izzie's jaw went rigid. "And I've seen what you and your firm are planning to do. I guess your next project is hiring a wrecking ball?"

"From the looks of things, I can just use you."

"What's seems to be the trouble here?" Jeff Robinson, in his black police uniform, stood in the doorway.

Reed turned to Jeff while pointing at Izzie. "The trouble seems to be a vindictive, crazed woman."

"Crazed?" Izzie reached down to pick up her phone but must have looked like she was going for the poker.

Jeff went into precautionary cop mode. "Why don't you calm down. No sudden moves."

Heat prickles crawled over her. "Vindictive woman?" she spat. "No sudden moves? That does it. Jeff take me in." Izzie put out her hands for handcuffs.

Jeff rolled his eyes and pulled his notepad from his pocket. "I need you to calm down. You made the call. I was on the marina and came right over. Tell me what happened."

"I will when you take me in." Izzie marched past Reed and Jeff into the hallway.

Jeff followed. "Take you in where?"

Izzie went out the front door and headed to the police car.

"Jail."

CHAPTER SEVENTEEN

Izzie had planted herself on the back seat of Jeff's patrol car and wouldn't budge. In the meantime, after Jeff advised Lake about the vandalism and notified an investigator to process the scene, Reed followed Jeff's car to the police station on the north end of Main Street. He pulled into a parking space in front while Jeff's car disappeared behind the police station.

Reed took a deep breath and tried to will his pounding heart to slow. He longed for his little gray cubicle where he could retain anonymity. He could work on assigned design projects, go home to his easy chair, make a bullet smoothie, and sleep in front of the TV. No pumpkin awards, live nativity scenes, competitions, and friendships to ruin. Did Padgett ever have to go through something like this to acquire his spacious corner office with windows overlooking Manhattan? Disappointing a town and losing Izzie's trust wasn't worth a special office.

Inside the police station, he approached a desk sergeant, talking on the phone who acknowledged him with a nod.

"Yes ma'am. I've got your house down for extra patrol, December twenty-eighth through January fourth." He scribbled the note on a pad. "No problem."

He looked up at Reed, "Yes, sir. Can I help you?"

Reed started to speak when Jeff opened a side door and motioned to Reed. "Sergeant. I've got this."

The sergeant nodded, and Jeff held the door for Reed. He entered a hallway with a row of offices to the right and a row of open-barred holding cells on the left. Izzie sat on a vinyl-covered bunk with no sheets.

Jeff stepped into the first office across from Izzie's cell and pointed to a seat for Reed. Reed sat down. Jeff took a seat behind his desk with several stacks of paperwork, framed pictures, two ceramic bloodhounds, and three Styrofoam cups with what looked like coffee that he must have never been able to finish.

"I've known Izzie quite a while," Jeff said. "She might retaliate with a simple punishment—like insisting she go to jail to prove a point—but she'd never do something harmful."

"Look, I'm sorry for all the turmoil, but when I saw the mess in that room, I thought ... I just had a knee-jerk reaction."

"Understandable." Jeff leaned forward and propped his elbows on his desk. "So, let me warn you. She is a forgiving person, but her grace is limited. If she feels wronged, she'll dig in her heels and take a while to cool down." He dipped his head toward Izzie's jail cell. "It's not locked. You can go in and speak in relative privacy if you like. However, you'll have to contend with our regular Elvis impersonator who serenades us while he's here."

"Is his name Arnie?"

"Arnie Blauser, the professional? No. This guy morphs into Elvis when he drinks too much and threatens people if they don't listen to him sing."

To warbling strains of "Jail House Rock," Reed pulled open the heavy iron door to the cell where Izzie sat, cross-armed. Large crystalline snowflake earrings seemed to pull her head down. Her feet in brown ankle boots were planted firmly on the floor.

"Izzie. I ... I don't know what to say."

"Oh, I think you've said plenty with your 'what have

you done' accusation."

Reed sunk down beside her, expecting the mattress to give, but it was like sitting on a piece of concrete.

"I'm sorry I accused you of messing up the room. It was just a shock."

"Shock? How about the shock of learning you're here to keep the natives happy? Helping with the fundraiser is an act—a cruel act—to make us think you support saving the square. You may plan to tear down the houses, but you'll have to do it with me in them." Izzie tightened her crossed arms and turned her back to him.

"I didn't know—at least I didn't know for sure—that Fairland Hotels would join the project."

"But you knew *if* they joined, the houses would be demolished?" Izzie's cheeks flushed a bright pink.

He spotted a tear trickling down her cheek and reached to brush it away.

She flinched and stood.

Is handling emotional stuff what it meant to be a property developer? Not worth it. He'd settle for working in his jail-cell-sized cubicle.

"Why don't you just go?" She sniffed.

The Elvis pretender began to croon, "Are you Lonesome Tonight."

He didn't want to hurt her or the town any more than he had already. Impressing his mother wasn't going to happen. And seeing his father had left him with tormenting anguish. It was all too much. He should leave.

Reed slipped out of the jail cell and stepped into Jeff's office. "I see what you mean about digging in. I'd best leave her alone right now or I'll make things worse. Any word on the vandalism at the Feldman house?"

Jeff gave a decisive nod. "The investigator is still on scene. Lake was at Elaine's and is at the house now."

"Good. I need to talk to him. Sure she'll be okay?"

Jeff pushed up from his desk. His gun belt creaked as he adjusted it around his middle. "Don't worry. We stock plenty of bread and water here," his expression sympathetic. "I'll take good care of her."

Reed's head hurt. Jeff, his wife, and all the regulars at the bistro wouldn't be showing him any sympathy once they learned Fairland's intentions. Being a cad was bad enough, but the ache in his heart over losing Izzie's friendship was far worse. He'd tell Lake he had to return to New York.

Pulling away from the police station, Reed traveled down Main Street. He drove past aging buildings that he'd gained a new appreciation for because of Izzie. The structures displayed a pride in their facades with attention to detail.

Sturdy brick with carved scroll stonework graced the front of Appleberry's furniture store. Intricate grillwork surrounded the display window of an antique shop, and an interesting overhang covered the window of The Pampered Pooch.

Each block of the old town carried its own unique look. Many stores were vacant, but those that were restored had brought new life to downtown. Hamilton Harbor was unique and deserved a second chance.

With no particular plan in mind, he parked in the single open space in front of Elaine's bistro and went in.

The early morning hens and roosters had departed.

Elaine was busy wiping the tables and looked up. "Hi there. I guess it's been an unpleasant morning for you to find the room you decorated in shambles."

Reed pushed out a heavy sigh. "What's unpleasant is my big mouth. Izzie was standing in the middle of the mess, and I'm afraid I accused her."

Elaine picked up a coffee stirrer from the floor and

straightened. "Uh oh."

"Uh oh, is right. She made Jeff take her to the police station and lock her up."

"Oh dear." Elaine moved back behind the counter and shifted to barkeep counseling mode. "Izzie doesn't hold up under false accusations so well."

"I found that out. My mouth spoke before my brain kicked in."

"She has good reason."

"Something to do with prom in high school?"

Elaine poured a cup of coffee and pushed it in front of Reed. "Sit down, and I'll fill you in while I'm between my morning and lunch rush hours."

Reed took the coffee jacket she offered and settled on a stool at the counter.

After adding frothed milk to a cup of coffee for herself, Elaine began.

"It was our senior year. A popular cheerleader, Mandie Grassly, resented Izzie. I was in art class when the teacher, Ms. Hixon, reprimanded Mandie for making fun of Izzie's drawings. Ms. Hixon had posted Izzie's work as good examples for students to follow. She told Mandie. 'If you put forth a tenth of the effort Izzie does, you could have a nice portfolio for college.'"

"Mandie dated big deal football player, Darren Michaelson. But when Mandie and another cheerleader were invited to go on a double date to the prom with some college guys, she dumped Darren. He invited Izzie to the prom to irritate Mandie."

"That was cruel if he was using her."

"I told Izzie she shouldn't accept, but she did. When the college dates backed out, I thought it was funny, but the jilted girls cooked up a scheme to get Izzie out of the picture. Izzie had helped decorate for the prom. The cheerleaders sneaked into the hotel ballroom and wrecked the prom decorations with green and white spray paint."

"When the vandalism was discovered, Izzie was accused. She had stopped by the hotel to make sure the special lighting had been delivered. A guy she tutored was with her but hadn't gone in so couldn't vouch for her. Spray cans were found in her car." Elaine squinted her eyes. "A set-up. Izzie insisted that everything was in order when she left."

"The prom was moved to the gym. That louse, Darren, hooked back up with Mandie. People thought Izzie did it as revenge for Darren's dumping her. Izzie spent prom night cleaning the hotel ballroom as ordered by the school principal."

Reed hung his head.

"Refill?" Elaine asked.

"No, thank you." Nausea threatened.

Elaine added more milk to her coffee and stirred. "The truth came out a couple years later, but Izzie's reputation stuck. She may be a renegade, but she'd never be destructive."

"I ..." Reed swallowed hard.

"Being falsely accused hurts her terribly."

"And my reaction at the church service ..."

Elaine presented a pained look. "She had no clue the speaker was your father."

"I appreciate the insight. This explains a lot."

"I hope the police find out who vandalized the Feldman house. Lake and his law men buddies left here to check it out. I can't imagine who in the world would do such a thing."

"There's more. Beyond the false accusations I made, Izzie has every right to be upset with me. I'm taking myself off the project."

"What are you talking about?"

"The hotel recruited to join the redevelopment project wants the vacant houses on the square torn down for a parking lot."

"But ... why have you helped us with the Save the Square project? You didn't know. Did—"

Reed shook his head. "I was aware there was a good possibility that if Fairland signed on, the houses would have to go. I was supposed to gain your confidence and convince you to be okay with it. The office messaged me about their decision, and Izzie saw it."

"Oh."

Disappointment filled Elaine's eyes, sending chills of regret down his spine. He should never have become personally involved. If winning people over was his task for this job, he was not Emerson's man. He had been foolish to attempt impressing his mother. And he let emotion rule when he took one look at his father.

He knew the rule. One thing his parents taught him. Don't care, then you won't get hurt.

He'd violated the rule—big time.

Izzie sat on the hard, holding-cell bunk, shoulders slumped. The image of the words—*they still want the unoccupied houses on Feldman Square torn down*—seared through her. How long had Reed known? From the start? Had he just been keeping the natives happy when he played Joseph? And when he kissed her?

Was it all an act? Part of his developer training? His interest had seemed genuine. But if it wasn't, that meant he didn't really care about the town, the desires of the people, the history of the square, the houses ... or her. She'd always deemed herself a good judge of character. Had she been so wrong about Reed?

Heat tingled under her skin. She ran cool water in the metal sink and splashed a little water on her face. If only water could wash away Reed's accusation. His words carried the same inflection of disbelief and disappointment as Principal Johnson's "What have you done?" when the damaged prom decorations were discovered. She had worked so hard to make the prom magical. Reed's indictment had ripped the wound open again.

Izzie stepped through the open cell into the hallway. Fake Elvis stepped close to the bars humming softly, then he crooned, "I'll have a blue Christmas without you."

The songster wore snug jeans and a bib-style Western shirt. His eyes, a watery blue gray, peered at her under a tangle of black hair. If he combed his hair, he'd bear a striking resemblance to the real Elvis she'd seen in movies.

She knocked softly on Jeff's office door.

Jeff looked up. "Have you calmed down?"

"I'd like my phone call now."

Jeff pulled a file from his desk drawer and shoved it closed with a bang. "You're not under arrest. Call whoever you want."

He pushed the phone on his desk toward her. She was taking up valuable time he could use on real crime. And a real crime had occurred.

"Did you speak to Lake?"

"He's at the house now with the investigator."

"Oh." She planted her feet on the floor to keep from disappearing into her pool of pettiness. "Do they know what happened yet?"

"These things take time. They have to process the room."

"Like with fingerprint dust? Doesn't that make a mess?"

"It does." He leaned back in his chair that screeched. "Look, Izzie, I need a statement from you. Can you handle that?"

Izzie plopped down in the chair opposite Jeff. "Sorry. I made an idiot of myself."

Jeff didn't argue that point. He began filling in the report sheet in front of him. "Give me your address."

After giving her statement, Izzie wound up seated in front of another desk at Hope Community Church. She had called Pastor Creighton, who graciously came to pick her up at the police station.

"I'm sorry to interrupt your day with the revival going on and all."

"It's okay. I'm here for you. Besides, with a visiting preacher I'm not working on sermon prep."

"Visiting preacher. Part of the reason I'm in hot water."

Pastor Creighton's brow wrinkled, "How so?"

Izzie let her story gush. She paced between the walls of his small office. Her boots sounded a rhythmic cadence that helped her get her story out.

"First, I encouraged Reed to come to church even though he was reluctant. Then when he found out the preacher was his dad, he thought I was sticking my nose where I shouldn't, which I wasn't. I didn't know—"

"Slow down, Izzie. Reverend Roberts is Reed Harrison's father? I had no idea."

"See? How would I know? I mean, he mentioned his mother's married name was Roberts, and Reed uses the Harrison name since his grandparents adopted him, but I never made the connection."

"He and his father are estranged?"

"His parents divorced, left him with grandparents, and stopped all contact with him. He feels wronged, especially since they purport to be Christian. He suffers from unforgiveness, but I don't think he knows it."

"That's not uncommon."

"This morning I went to apologize about coaxing him to the service and assure him I hadn't meant to blindside him. That's when I found out about the plans to tear down the houses on Feldman square."

Pastor Creighton's eyes widened. "Tear them down? But he was helping with the cause to have them restored."

"I'm with you on that one. So, I went to the Feldman house to pray about it, and I saw … uh oh, I forgot to tell Jeff." Izzie pulled the coin from her pocket and held it in her open palm. "This coin was on the floor. Then I saw the damage in the living room. I dropped my phone after I called 911. I'm trying to retrieve my phone under the poker when Reed walks in and accuses me …" Izzie pointed at herself with her thumb and shoved the coin back in her pocket. "of something I didn't do … again."

Pastor listened with his hands steepled under his chin. "I heard about the vandalism when I was at the bistro. So, you're the one who discovered the damage?"

"Yes. And Reed walked in afterward. Things went downhill from there."

"Ah. It sounds like misunderstandings and tempers ignited to choke out rational thinking."

Izzie raised her right hand. "Guilty as charged. Reed sent me over the top when he insinuated I trashed his room for revenge. I've been so wrapped up in self, I forgot I found the coin on the floor in the entry hall. Now what do I do?"

He stared at her a long moment then said, "Izzie, I'm not sure I'm following all of this. But it is always best to do the right thing. Take the high road. You make the first step to right any wrongs."

"But I didn't do anything."

Pastor drummed his pen against his desk, set it down,

then pulled his Bible in front of him and flipped some pages. "Do you remember when Jesus was in the garden and soldiers came to arrest him?"

"I sure do. He was falsely accused too."

"Sometimes people need extra grace. Remember when Peter cut off the ear of one of the soldiers?"

"Uh, no."

"Well he did, here in Luke twenty-two verse fifty-one is Jesus's response, "Permit even this." Jesus touched and healed the man's ear."

"And your point is?"

"You were falsely accused about your reasons for inviting Reed to church, and then again when the room was vandalized."

"Right."

"So, my point is, Jesus forgave even those who would harm him. It is within your power to show Reed what forgiveness looks like. Being angry and walking away will do nothing to solve or fix this situation. It may even make you look guilty."

"I'm supposed to say, no problem? Go ahead. Tear down those houses. While you're at it, take our hopes and dreams along with them?"

"At least listen to him. Could you be falsely accusing him?"

"I saw it in black and white."

"But you didn't hear his side?" Pastor pushed back from his desk and reached for his jacket.

A voice inside nudged her to believe Reed wouldn't stand for the houses to be removed. But a rival voice said, "He isn't the person you imagined."

"Clear the air and start by showing the police the coin you found. Come on, I'll take you to the Feldman house."

In minutes, they reached the Feldman house. Parked in

front along with her car was an unmarked police car with a blue light on the dash. The rumbling of heavy machine equipment was louder and closer to the house as city workers continued clearing trees and underbrush behind the house. Izzie followed Pastor Creighton and climbed the stairs to the front porch.

The bistro's roosters and hens were milling around on the wide front porch.

"Why are y'all here?" Izzie asked.

"To give you a vote of confidence if they try to pin something on you." Dave gave a jovial grin.

Izzie wasn't in a grinning mood.

"Dave, cut it out," Francine said. "The investigator asked us to stay out here."

"I'm here to find out what happened and if we should keep an eye out for hooligans," Loretta said. "And Dave is right, we are all here to support you. A lot of water has crossed under the bridge since you were in high school. You pulled a few pranks, but vandalism is something you would never do. Finding the perpetrators will clear your name."

Petunia nodded, and her curls bounced. "Marigold called to say a man from Fairland Hotels offered a very nice price for the property with the vacant houses. They want it for a parking lot. The offer was lucrative, and she was tempted, but I said no dice."

"With the destruction here and that phone call, I wouldn't be surprised if we were witnessing a little dirty dealing going on," Ralph said.

Lake emerged from the house. "We have news to report that may surprise you." He singled Izzie out as he spoke his next words. "We have identified the culprit."

Reed's flight arrived at ten o'clock last night. He couldn't rest on the plane. Even in his apartment, in his own bed, sleep wouldn't come.

He kept replaying the scene with Izzie in the holding cell at the police station and the hurt in her eyes. And telling Lake it would be best if he withdrew from the contest. He assured Lake that he'd order easy-to-install curtains that would be sufficient to reopen the room to patrons after it was cleaned. The damaged shutters could be repaired and reinstalled later.

He gave in to his restlessness and had arrived at the office at 6:00 a.m. He flipped on the study light over his design table and drew. The sketches and notations had never rolled from his brain to his hand as smoothly and efficiently. With the brakes released and the pressure lifted, he designed what his heart encouraged. He set aside the mandate to tear down the houses and played with the idea of what might happen if they were to remain.

The whir of the copy machine coming to life was the only sound in the office that would soon bustle with ringing phones, coffee room chatter, and the rumble of the mail cart on Emerson's tiled traffic lanes. His gray cubicle work area adjoined the executive suite down the hall—the section that held the offices with the elusive windows.

He took the sketches from the copy tray and spread them out on his desk. The drawings included exterior and interior renderings of what he envisioned for a bay front hotel. Instead of a high rise, he proposed the hotel consist of a series of connected sections, each nestled among the ancient oaks on the vacant property that backed up to Feldman Square. Each would have a splendid view of the water. A parking garage would handle parking needs, eliminating the need to remove the vacant houses.

Here in his climate-controlled office cubicle, there were

no breezes to muss his pages and no erratic temperature changes in the weather as he'd experienced in his makeshift office behind the Pirates' Cove Motel.

But there were no Good Samaritan pirate ships. No squealing sea gulls circling overhead or herons gliding gracefully over the bayou during low tide catching fish for breakfast. No pink-streaked sunrises or golden orange and purple sunsets. And no Izzie. Not even a New York City window office could compete on that score.

Truth is, he really had grown to appreciate Hamilton Harbor, its history, and helping to preserve it. Before Christmas, he had met Captain Jack's great-niece Janine and her rambunctious two-year-old Lily, who was excited about riding on the pirate ship.

"I hear you are one of the competitors in the Feldman house contest raising money for the maternity home," Janine said.

"I am." Reed watched as Captain Jack picked up the youngster.

"You have a cute curly-haired girl there."

"She is a blessing."

Jack gave the little girl some bread to toss in the air and she giggled and clapped her hands when a seagull swooped out of the sky to retrieve the morsel.

"Every day I thank God for people like you who care enough to help women like me with an unplanned pregnancy."

Reed met her with a tentative smile, surprised she'd share something that personal.

"If it weren't for a pregnancy center in Tallahassee encouraging me, Lily wouldn't be here."

The letter with Fairland's intentions that nixed the pregnancy center stared back at him from the open folder on his desk. He was trapped in never-never land. He couldn't stay in Hamilton Harbor and face those who'd put their trust in him, and he shouldn't be back here. The team and Mr. Padgett were not aware he'd returned and wouldn't be pleased that he left without consulting them.

Reed, the rule follower. The one chosen to be the Hamilton Harbor placater. He had failed.

The overhead bank of fluorescent lighting came to life. Reed recognized the voices of two of the secretaries, Susan and Rita. Reed stepped out of his office. "I'm back here. Just wanted to let you know so I don't startle you."

"Reed. What are you doing here? Isn't there a phone conference scheduled with you in Florida this morning?" Rita asked.

"I decided I'd better return and confer live."

"Oh. Mr. Padgett didn't mention it."

"He doesn't know."

Susan furrowed her brow. "You didn't tell him you were returning?"

"No, and I'm sure he won't be pleased, but I had my reasons."

"I hope for your sake they're good ones. He expects the meeting with the Fairland executive to run smoothly." Rita said.

"Shall I tell him you're back?" Susan asked.

"Buzz me when he comes in. He needs to hear it from me."

"I'm thinking you're right."

Reed had risen to his position by understanding Mr. Padgett's vision for a project and then delivering. He had no family, no one to go home to or divide his time with. He could devote all his effort and energy, on and off the job, to the company. But who would have believed the mission the company sent him on would turn topsy-turvy? Creating a redevelopment project to please all factions. Was the mission even possible?

If it weren't for people like you, Lily wouldn't be here.

People like him? He snickered at Janine's words a few days ago behind the motel. It would be more accurate to say, *despite* people like him.

He had hurt those who trusted him, especially Izzie. He should have told her the minute he received the word about Fairland's intentions. He'd been an idiot.

His cell phone chimed. He had a message from Dan.

Where are you? Coon hunting? Heard about the hairy vandals.

Hairy vandals? The phone on his desk buzzed. He pushed the cell phone back in his pocket and answered the in-house phone.

"He's here," Susan whispered.

"Thanks." Reed grabbed his folder and swallowed the lump in his throat. His stomach growled, as he walked toward his boss's office.

"Mr. Padgett?" Reed caught his attention before entering his office. Through the open door, he could see a man already seated at the small, round conference table.

"Reed? What—"

"Sorry sir, I didn't realize you had someone in your office."

"Did I miss something? Is the contest over in Florida?"

"Uh, yes sir, more or less. I ... I ... must talk to you in person."

"Well sure. That way we don't have to try and connect on a conference call." Padgett rested his hand on Reed's shoulder and steered him to his office doorway. "Come in and meet Fairland's top executive. Mr. Dursema is here to seal our deal."

The deal closer stood. He was tall, barrel-chested, had a firm grip and a wide toothy grin. Probably very adept at managing deal closures.

"Reed is our man who has been on site in Florida, working on the development design preliminaries."

"Good to meet you."

Dursema sat down. Mr. Padgett motioned Reed to take the seat opposite Dursema.

Padgett sat between them. "Reed specializes in interiors but will also be instrumental in gaining acceptance of the hotel's projected land procurement on the square that backs up to the hotel property."

"Good. There's a lot to learn, isn't there?"

"Yes, sir."

Dursema continued. "To bring everyone up to speed, Fairland's development team came back with a site analysis that recommended additional property be purchased for parking. The properties where the unoccupied houses sit on the south side of the park would provide the extra square footage."

"Renovating those properties is—" Reed interjected, but Padgett stopped him.

"Let him finish."

Dursema raised one bushy brow. "Our property procurement department has been in touch with the property owners, Marigold and Petunia Hamilton." He chuckled, "Interesting names. Marigold told me right off that they were planning to raise money to renovate the houses and create a maternity home and resource center. She said she wasn't interested, but I believe I've made a monetary offer that will be hard for her to turn down in the end."

"And that's where Reed comes in. Tell him about the contest and how you've befriended the folks down there," Padgett said.

Reed's mouth went dry and pasty. "Five …" the words

stuck. He attempted to moisten his lips with his tongue and pressed on. "I was one of five designers selected to compete in an interior decoration contest as a fundraiser to repair the vacant houses on the square. In a series of elimination rounds, we decorated a restored house on the square built in 1912."

"Of course, our man is a finalist." Mr. Padgett gathered three bottles of water from an under-counter refrigerator and set them in the center of the table. Thankful, Reed took a sip to soothe his parched throat.

"Impressive. The credentials that will make us proud to be a part of this development project," Mr. Dursema said.

Reed took another swig of his water. How could he convey how hard the people were willing to work to save the square? "They've raised about five thousand dollars, charging admissions to see the house at each phase of the contest."

"Commendable. But they'll find their fundraising efforts simply won't produce the money required for renovations. They'll have enough to build a brand-new maternity facility elsewhere, if they take our offer. Surely, since you're working with these people, you can make them see that."

Mr. Padgett let out a giddy laugh. "When will the contest winner be announced?"

"New Year's Eve is the final judging. But that's what I flew back to talk to you about, Mr. Padgett, ... uh, before talking to Fairland."

"Please." Padgett waved his hand in a carefree manner. "We are all on the same team. Go ahead."

Reed swallowed back the acid taste of his morning coffee—too strong for the water he drank to dilute. He wasn't a praying man, but right now he'd like to have a higher power on board.

"I don't like the idea of tearing down the houses," he

blurted.

Mr. Dursema lost his toothy grin. "In this business, we sometimes have to do things we don't like for the greater good. If we're to sign on with this project, we must have the right amount of land. Adequate parking is an obligation to our customers. People need a place to put their cars. They don't drop in on foot."

Mr. Padgett let out a nervous laugh. "That's a good one. He understands. Right, Reed?"

Reed glanced at Padgett's office window view that revealed a steely blue sky and more office buildings planted on streets crowded with yellow cabs. Was this view worth hurting people who had gained his trust?

"I was supposed to take part in their community so they'd like me and go along with the firm's wishes. But this section of town is designated as a historical district." Reed reached for his folder. "If I might suggest—"

"I'm not interested in other suggestions." Dursema's bristly brows pressed together. "They can keep the four houses and the park. We'll add decorative fencing and shrubs to create a visual barrier from that property." He crossed his arms on the table and leaned forward. "This is our deal, take it or leave it."

Padgett tittered and held his hands in a white-knuckled grasp. "Just voicing concerns. But we'll make this deal work. Surely they will see a new building in another location as an outstanding idea."

"You may plan to tear down the houses, but you'll have to do it with me in them." Izzie's determined vow pushed Reed forward.

"Mr. Dursema have you ever wanted something and when you got it discovered it wasn't what you wanted at all?"

Padgett sucked in air.

Mr. Dursema studied Reed a long moment then answered, "I have. I purchased my dream truck, a special edition cab truck. But after I brought it home, it ended up in the shop all the time. I regretted the day I bought it."

Standing and facing both men, Reed said, "That's how the townspeople will feel—regret for ever voting on this firm to handle their development. I've sketched out an alternate plan." He shoved the folder to the center of the table, knowing this would be his only and perhaps his last chance to make an appeal for the houses.

"If I had been sitting up here in New York the whole time, I would no doubt see things your way. But I've been in Hamilton Harbor. I've worked with the town's people for weeks. They are sincere, hard-working folks who wish to preserve their history. I can't be a party to snatching those houses from them."

Reed turned to address his red-faced boss. "I withdrew from the contest. I appreciate you giving me this chance, but I'm afraid I'm not cut out for this job."

"That's one thing you have right. I suggest you take a few days off to get your head on straight. For now, consider yourself off this job."

CHAPTER EIGHTEEN

Izzie's mouth went dry and her body rigid. With Pastor Creighton at her side, she followed Lake into the front hall, then entered the living room where the crime scene investigator pulled off white cotton gloves and placed them in a briefcase sitting on a side table. Fine black dust covered several items in the room.

"We have all the evidence and photos we need. I lifted perfect prints from the fireplace and the poker," the investigator said.

"I tried not to touch anything," Izzie said, "but my phone fell and wound up in the fireplace. I was just trying to reach for it."

The investigator's face remained all business. "I have it right here." Her phone lay captive in a clear plastic evidence bag he held up.

"You think I'm the culprit?"

"I didn't say that ma'am."

Lake swiped the screen of his smart phone and held it for Pastor Creighton and Izzie to see a picture of two raccoons huddled in a corner with chicken bones, paper, and Styrofoam boxes scattered about them. "These vandals were discovered in the kitchen examining the contents of our trash can."

"Coons made this mess in the living room?" Pastor Creighton asked.

Izzie's mouth fell open.

"We've got the footprint proof," the investigator said.

"Uh ... you mean I'm off the hook?"

"Izzie, Pastor, meet Lt. Foster, crime scene specialist," Lake said.

Izzie shook hands with the lieutenant, who handed over her bagged phone.

"Mallory's in the kitchen with another detective, keeping an eye on the perpetrators until animal control gets here to pick them up," Lake said.

"First case of raccoon vandalism I've ever worked." Lt. Foster said. "I discovered coons like shiny objects." He pointed to a brass picture frame on the floor and scattered golden balls that were accents Reed had selected for the cocktail table.

"I guess that would explain this." Izzie pulled the gold coin from her pocket. "I found it in the doorway and forgot to mention it in all the excitement."

The investigator lifted the coin from her hand. "Hmm ... 1908. This is old. Not yours?" he asked Lake.

Lake shook his head. "With patrons in and out, it may have been dropped by someone and the coons found it."

"But why come in here and wreck the place?"

"When clearing forested areas, wildlife is uprooted," the officer said. The rumble of heavy machine equipment working on the street behind the square accented his point. "Apparently the raccoons came down the chimney, tried to get back out and wrecked the room in the process."

Izzie looked at the phone picture of the homeless critters again. "They're so cute. What will happen to them?"

"Animal control will move them to another area." He looked out the window with the broken louvered shutters and curtains hanging in tangled shreds. "Here they are now."

"Want me to tell them to go around back?" Pastor asked.

"Please."

Pastor Creighton went outside while Investigator Foster left for the kitchen, leaving Izzie alone with Lake.

"This is a setback to the fundraiser, but we'll deal with it," Lake said.

Surrounded by the wrecked room, Izzie slowly shook her head. She might as well drop the rest of the bad news on Lake. "The need for a fundraiser may be a moot point. The developers want the vacant houses on the square torn down."

"I heard."

"How did you know?"

"Reed told me. He explained the Fairland corporation's intentions."

"Yeah?" Izzie crossed her arms and pressed them to her middle. "Glad to hear he owned up to it."

"That's not all. Before the coons were identified as the culprits, he said that he had made arrangements to either replace or repair the damaged items in this room, and—"

"Oh ...well good. Then we can get back to fundraising." She used the toe of her shoe to straighten the edge of the rumpled accent rug. "He better understand, the fight for the houses is still on."

"Reed's gone. He withdrew from the contest."

Izzie whipped her head around and stared at Lake. "What?"

"He thought it best to withdraw his name and go back to New York under the circumstances. He asked me to tell you he was sorry for everything."

Reed gone? How had everything turned into such a mess? Her lip quivered. Reed and his firm were supposed to be the key to saving the square and renovating the town—whoever won the contest. Izzie had hoped the competition would be an avenue for Reed's mother to take pride in his skill. She even prayed that somehow, even with the misunderstandings, Reed could reconcile with his father.

One memo had changed everything.

The economics of making a deal with Fairland Hotels now meant tearing down the houses she'd wanted so much to save. She had thought Reed was on her side, but she was wrong.

Her dreams had become a nightmare.

Air. He needed air.

Reed sat on a bar stool at his kitchen counter. He had been scolding himself ever since he got out of bed, and the walls of his apartment were closing in on him.

Could he be any more of a sap?

He'd hurt Izzie's feelings, pulled out of the contest, left his team without a word, upset Padgett, fouled up the Fairland Hotel deal and was currently off the job.

He pulled up the photo Lake sent him again. Raccoons had wrecked the living room at the Feldman house. Add that to his list—accusing Izzie of something coons had done.

He tugged at his collar, feeling boxed in.

Box.

A weight in his chest nudged him. He'd asked Carl Anders, the attorney handling his grandmother's estate, to leave the box in his possession at the old homestead. Instructions were to wait until after his grandmother's death to look inside. With nothing but time on his hands, he could no longer make excuses to avoid the box.

Reed donned his coat, hurried downstairs, and hailed a cab. Thirty minutes later, the cab pulled in front of his grandparents' old brick two-story on a narrow lot in

Brooklyn. The house was a replica of the other homes lined up neatly along the old neighborhood street. He hadn't been able to bring himself to return since locking the doors after the funeral. Bob and May Brewster next door had a key and had promised to look after the house. Reed sent a monthly check to their son, Tommy, to maintain the yard.

The house looked the same when the cab pulled in front. Traces of snow still clung to shady spots in the yard, but the walkway to the front porch was neatly edged and swept. He paid the cab driver and climbed the concrete front steps, worn slightly in the center. The porch floorboards still creaked beneath his shoes and held the memory of a boy on his seventh birthday waiting on the sight of a green Datsun truck. Reed's father had promised to bring him a catcher's mitt and play ball at the park down the street.

At that point in his life, Reed hadn't yet lost the hopeful anticipation of seeing his father.

The same went for his mother ever since the back door closed when she and grandma last had words. When things became so quiet and he could only hear the ticking of the clock on the mantle, Reed listened. He'd lay in bed and try to will the doorknob to the back door to rattle and then open to Grandma saying, "Eugenia, you're home."

But that sound and those words never materialized. The only news regarding his parents he had was an overheard conversation Grandma had with someone after Grandpa died. "Reed's father is going to some preacher school in north Florida, and Eugenia is working herself half to death managing her own decorating business in Orlando, Florida."

He had watched each car that pulled onto the street for three hours the day his father promised to bring him a catcher's mitt. Only one car, a black Buick, stopped. A boy, maybe twelve years old, got out.

"Hi, is your grandma home?"

"She is. Just ring the bell. She'll answer the door."

"Thanks. My dad brought me to collect for the paper."

That boy had no way of knowing the hurt he compounded in Reed's heart. He longed for a daddy who would take time with him and keep his promises.

"Son, I don't think your father is coming," his grandmother had said after she paid the newspaper boy. "I've made your favorite lunch, macaroni and cheese with bits of hot dog. Why don't you come in now?" It was obvious she was trying to smooth over his disappointment.

He never saw or heard from his father again. Not until he walked on the stage of Hope Community Church. Was that what propelled him here? The white rocking chair he sat in to wait on the visit that never happened was still beside the front door. He ran his hand across the wooden slats. A fine film of dust coated his fingers.

Reed pulled out his house key, unused since his grandmother's service in August. His mother was in Paris and didn't attend, but why should she? She didn't come around when Grandma was living.

Reed pushed the door open and stepped into the living room. The air was close, but the familiar scent of Grandma's favorite lilac air freshener still lingered. Sheets shrouded the upholstered furniture. Other furnishings were as he remembered, except for the cardboard box sitting on the table that formed a visual wall between the front entry and living area.

His grandmother had always been a planner in life and proved to be in death. She left explicit instructions for Mr. Anders as executor, and Reed had been grateful he handled all the funeral arrangements. To be fair to his mother, the attorney had advised her not to disrupt her work in Paris. His grandmother wanted to be cremated and have a small

Christian memorial service with ladies from her Sunday school class. They were to have tea and fruitcake she had baked and kept in the freezer for the occasion. She'd even attached a note:

> *With each bite you take, I leave with you a part of me giving thanks for you as my dearest friends.*

He wasn't ready to see the contents of the box at the time of her passing. But with all he'd experienced in the past twenty-four hours, the box drew him to this place. His excuses had run out. He pulled the lid off the box and stared at the large gold-colored envelope with his name typed on the label.

He lifted the envelope, ran his finger under the glued edge and pulled it open. Inside were some legal-sized papers—the adoption papers. He had never seen the documents that officially gave him away, and he didn't particularly want to be reminded now. But his eyes caught the *Whereas.* He read on.

> Whereas, the undersigned parents of Reed Harrison Roberts—Randall Hiram Roberts and Eugenia Harrison Roberts—do agree to his adoption by Earl and Marvella Harrison under these agreed conditions:
>
> Visitation and other contact with the child will be allowed only as seen fit by the adopting parents in order to protect the child.
>
> After the death of both adopting parents, the child will be given the enclosed items from his biological parents.

Underneath the legal papers were two sealed envelopes and a blue album with *My First Book* printed on the front. He flipped through the pages of the album filled with pictures of an adolescent boy and girl (his parents) with a child growing from an infant to a kindergartner. Snapshots of forgotten scenes in his past. Strangers smiling back at him.

Reed picked up the enclosed letter-size envelopes. He recognized his mother's handwriting from the bulletin board in her bedroom. She dotted the letter "i" with tiny circles. The other envelope, from his father? He opened it first.

> Dear son,
>
> You are to read this after your grandparents, who will be adopting you, have passed away. So, there is no telling how old you will be, or the circumstances when you read this.
>
> All I can do is share with you my love and caring concern.
>
> Above all, I want you to know that once I laid eyes on you, I had no regrets you were born, only that I was not old enough to be a proper father with the ability to provide for you.
>
> If your grandparents see fit, I hope to visit you at every opportunity. Please know that even if I'm not there in person. I will always be with you in spirit.
>
> I love you.
>
> Your father, who hates signing these papers.

Reed strained against the lump in his throat. With trembling fingers, he flipped over the envelope with his mother's handwriting. Across the seal was written, *Never Forgotten*. Reed worked his finger under the seal, slicing it with a stinging paper cut that cracked the written words apart.

As he unfolded the paper inside, a photo fell out. A picture of two teenagers cradling a baby between them. He flipped the picture over. Written in pencil were the words, *Eugenia, Randall, & Reed-three days old*. Blood from the cut dropped on the photo. He pulled out his handkerchief and dabbed at the blood that smeared and underlined the words, Eugenia and Randall.

They were just two kids with a kid of their own. Two teenagers who gave him the blood coursing through his veins. He wrapped the handkerchief around the cut. His fingers shaking as he unfolded the handwritten letter.

> To my little boy.
>
> There is so much I want to say to you. I worry that one day you're going to hate me or not understand my motives and think I didn't want you or love you.
>
> As your mother, I had to put your needs ahead of my own. You needed a stable home environment that my mother and father could, and were more than willing, to provide. I pray this is the right decision.
>
> It is with deep trepidation I hand over your care to my parents. I don't want to, but deep in my heart I believe it is the right thing to do. I hope there will be a time in the future that our relationship can be rejoined. I have been advised that If I am to ever be in a position to provide for you, I must take advantage of the scholarship opportunities that are only available for me now.
>
> Your father and I tried to make a go of marriage, but we found that still being dependent ourselves made it difficult to help you. The emotions run high and the hurts run deep. It's hard, but I had to admit I had a baby too young and had to learn the grown-up thing was to take responsibility and do what was best for you.
>
> I have your kindergarten photo sitting in front of me as I write this letter. You are so incredibly sweet. And innocent. And handsome. I was blessed to be able to bring you into this world.
>
> My sense of timing was poor, but I'm completely amazed by you. And it isn't just me. Everyone who sees you thinks you are wonderful.
>
> Of course, your grandparents love you dearly. I know they will take the best care of you. I hope you will see your way clear to forgive me for giving you up.

So you never forget our early years together, I made a scrapbook for you enclosed in this box, and a duplicate for me.

You will find other remembrances in the window seat in my room.

Please know that every time I look at my scrapbook, I can't help but smile. I hope one day we will look at these memories etched on my heart and smile together.

All my love,

Your mother, Eugenia

In the window seat? There was a window seat in his mother's room. Did it have storage in it? Reed set down the letters and ascended the stairs two at time. He opened the door to his mother's room that his grandmother had kept closed. She said it was to save on heating and cooling, but he always suspected it helped her to not miss her so much.

The room had been stripped of his mother's teenage décor. He crossed the room to the window seat and pulled the cushion aside. Hinges.

Inside were piles of letters and cards. He lifted a banded stack. The envelopes were addressed to him. All unopened.

He opened one. It was a hand-drawn card from his mother to him for his 25th birthday. Had she sent a card every year? He pulled out another stack. These were from his father. Some for birthday, some for a special holiday or just thinking of you. Amazing.

He flipped on the study light at his mother's desk and read. Waves of heat touched him, making him light-headed as he read sentiments from his parents that spanned over twenty years.

He dug deeper in the storage bench. Underneath the letters and some unopened packages, he felt the touch of soft leather—a catcher's mitt. His pulse quickened as he grabbed the mitt with a note attached and read:

> Son, your grandmother thinks it's best my visits stop. She told me you get upset after I come, and your grades in school suffer. I don't want to ever hurt you, so I'll stay away.
>
> She said she has explained these concerns to your mother also. I hope things change in the future, but for now, I'll abide by your grandmother's wishes. I know she has your best interests at heart.

When he finished reading, the tears came.

He cried for his parents and their vacant yesterdays as a family. He cried for his grandparents, who lost their tomorrows, sacrificing their retirement years to raise him. He cried for the little boy who always believed he was abandoned and forgotten by his parents. And he cried over the stronghold of unforgiveness that had stolen peace from his heart.

He finally understood.

Izzie stood in the middle of Lake's office. The rain that ushered in a cold front had subsided, leaving steady plinking drips coming from the downspout outside. An early morning frosted chill had settled along the bay front where workers geared up heavy equipment machines to continue their clearing and road work behind the house. The sun sent warming rays through the office windows. Louvered shutters, covering the lower half of the windows, filtered the light and cast interesting shadows across the polished oak floors. Izzie wiggled her sore wrist. Harsh stripping solution had sloshed on her while refinishing the oak file cabinet she'd found at Uncle Bob's.

Crossing the hall, Izzie entered the living room. After the in-depth cleaning by the service Reed had hired, the room was ready for viewing. All of Reed's decor had been reassembled except the window treatments. Without the sheers and shutters that had been damaged and removed, the room lacked the softness and comfortable feel Reed had created.

"Shutters. What a fantastic look. Would you think badly of me if I stole your idea for the office?" Izzie had asked Reed.

"I don't hold a corner on the shutter market. Here," Reed handed her a catalog, "this is the company I use. Feel free."

"Thanks. Let me know if I can help you."

"Since you're offering, where did you find the translucent curtain fabric with a thread of texture?"

"I used the last on a bolt of discontinued stock. But I can take you to a place on the beach that has some fabric with a similar look."

Izzie smiled at the remembrance. "How about this one?" she'd said and peered through a golden sheer with splotches of flocking.

"I think I like what's behind it better."

Had he meant her? Izzie let the fabric drop and smiled.

He tugged out the bolt of fabric behind her. Silly her. He meant another fabric. She flushed.

He nudged her shoulder and pointed to the fabric, "And this too."

The Yankee boy was flirting with her, and the southern girl was loving it. That quip, along with those deep brown eyes, like vats of sweet chocolate, had made her feel warm all over.

But their closeness had shut down. She'd had no word

from Reed since he left her in jail. Only the message he'd left with Lake, yielding victory to her in the contest. An award she couldn't accept, unless earned, any more than she could accept being falsely accused.

She desperately wanted to talk to Reed. But Pastor's sweet prayer intervened.

"Lord, help Izzie wait. It's hard, but sometimes waiting is needed for concerns to settle and sort themselves out."

Izzie pushed her shoulders up tight and moved her neck from side to side, then released to relax her tense muscles. Her emotions had run the gamut of hurt to anger to disappointment. Sleep had come in short spurts as she wrestled with the idea that Reed's mother would be judging their rooms in two days.

Pastor's words rang in her ears. "Do the right thing."

What was the right thing? Beyond the contest, beyond Fairland Hotels, this was Reed's chance to impress his mother and Izzie didn't want that opportunity to slip by him. Of all the scenarios she'd played in her mind, showing his mother his talent rose to a higher level than her personal gain.

If she restored his room and he won, would he be pleased or accuse her of sticking her nose where she shouldn't again? But worse, if she did nothing to bring his room up to par for the judging, any accolades she received would be meaningless. It would be as though she was taking advantage of the situation to look good.

However, if Reed's room won, would it ruin her chances to succeed locally? Should she just leave things well enough alone and win by default, as Reed suggested? She couldn't accept that kind of shallow victory. No. She wanted this to be a valid comparison for the judge.

Besides, Lake and Mallory deserved to have just what Reed had designed for the living room and have it judged on that basis.

On this premise, like it or not, she would put his room back the way he had planned it. But that's where she drew the line. He still had a fight on his hands if he bowed to Fairland's proposal and pressed for the houses to be torn down.

She loved the filtered light effect from the shutters in the office, but Reed's room needed it more with the tri-front windows. The subdued lighting gave the room a perfect glow. Without the shutters and curtains, the lighting was too harsh. He'd said he wished he had the curtain fabric she selected. She had three separate windows the same size in the office. Her curtains and shutters would fit. She could replace them in the office when his order came in. For now, she'd install pull-down shades in the office and put the shutters and curtains up in the living room.

Izzie studied the rest of Reed's decor. He had designed an amazing creation over the mantle. At Uncle Bob's, she had commented that the crosscut sections from a big oak tree might make an interesting table base. But it was Reed that had worked with Pete in his workshop to hook them together with wooden pegs to make a striking three-dimensional collage. The clear lacquer coating Reed added brought out the tree ring grain in the crosscut sections. On the mantle, he added a photo of Albert Feldman at his sawmill. She was tickled that he used the rustic-looking, wooden frame he'd questioned spending good money on when they'd gone junking. Over the doorway entry he'd hung the log cutter's saw that Lake had discovered in the detached garage out back. All gave the room a homey character and were fitting tributes to the occupation of the original homeowner.

For a rule-following city slicker, Reed seemed to have fit right in with the heartbeat of the community. She'd even imagined she might have had something to do with it. But had it all been just a front to get on the community's good side? Was his kiss all a part of the act he was to put on for his firm?

She couldn't think about that now. She had a two o'clock deadline to get this room in order for visitors. She'd remove her window treatments and install them. Thankfully, the raccoon-climbing escapade that had ripped the curtains and broken slats on the shutters didn't damage the hardware to hang them.

Izzie flipped on her CD player and put on Elvis's recording of "Amazing Grace." The song gave inspiration and kept her moving. She hummed along as she unscrewed her shutters and installed them in the living room. The half curtains that went above the shutters, an easy move.

The roller shades she purchased for another job, made a good temporary fix in the office and still allowed for adjusting light in the room. With an hour to spare, she finished the job and stepped back to view the results, rubbing her sore wrist. Reed's room was perfect. She felt a sense of pride, yet a dread followed.

Would Reed be pleased with her attempts to help him with his mother? And what about his dad? She was hurt at first by his false accusation that she had tricked him into seeing his father. Although … had she known … he was probably right to suspect her of getting them together. At least he had a dad. And one that seemed to be a nice man.

Would this assistance help or hurt her career? Help or hurt the Save the Square project? Help or hurt her nonexistent relationship with Reed?

How had things become so complicated?

CHAPTER NINETEEN

The afternoon temperature was a mild fifty-eight degrees when he arrived at the airport, compared to the thirties in New York City. Even so, his nerves chilled his insides and sent shivers down his spine. Reed parked his rental car in front of Hope Community Church. He checked his phone messages. Mandeville had asked him to call. He'd call later. For now, Emerson and the development project held a side seat to what sat in front of him. A bridge burned over twenty years ago. Was it possible to go back?

The marquee in front of the church still held the Twelve Days of Christmas message. Children in the community must love prolonging Christmas. Interesting that the father he would have loved spending a Christmas day with as a youngster was offering an extra twelve days here.

Ironically, Reed's world as a youngster—the one Grandma didn't want disrupted—was now turned upside down after reading the letters and notes she had kept from him. Could this be his chance to right it again?

He'd called Pastor Creighton, who graciously offered to have Reed meet with his father in his office.

What should he say? For twenty years, he'd believed his father and mother didn't want him and didn't care enough to acknowledge him on his birthday. Each birthday he met with dread. Grandma tried to make the day special with cake, candles, and gifts. But the day only marked another year his parents didn't remember him.

What would his father think of how he'd turned out? He checked his hair, smoothed it back, straightened his tie, and grabbed the bag he'd brought with him. His father was probably here already.

Inside, the pine scent of the huge Christmas tree in

the foyer of the old theater greeted him along with Pastor Creighton.

"Hello, Reed. Nice to have you back. Come. I have someone who is anxious to see you."

Was his father as nervous as he was?

The pastor led Reed to a group of offices next to the children's wing. The aroma of salty, buttered popcorn lingered around a popcorn wagon.

He entered the pastor's office. The man standing there was his height with the same near-black hair. The resemblance was unmistakable.

"Reed." His name a breath of blessing coming across his father's lips. With a warm smile and glistening eyes, he reached a hand out to him.

Pastor Creighton smiled, stepped out of the office, and closed the door.

Reed put his hand in his grip, warm and firm. The union he'd longed for as a child seemed surreal. He'd buried the hope in a place marked "hurt." But his hurt split open when his father whispered, "Son, I've waited so long."

Reed, unable to choke out words, nodded. From the bag he carried, he pulled out the catcher's mitt. His chin quivered. "I … I found this yesterday."

The touch of the handshake crumbled into an embrace. The warmth and press of his father's arms chipped away at his crusty heart, hardened by his parents giving him up for adoption. He tried to look back at his younger years from his teen parents' point of view. What would he have done had he been in their shoes?

Reed straightened. "Sorry. My head is still reeling." He brushed at tears streaking his cheeks.

"We are in the same boat." His father yanked tissues from a box on the pastor's desk. He handed one to Reed and wiped at his own eyes with another.

Reed studied the man's face before him. Disquieted, he saw a mature reflection of himself—like those age-progression, missing-person sketches.

"I can't tell you how pleased I was to hear you asked Pastor Creighton to arrange a meeting for us," his father said.

Reed sat down next to his father, then pushed to the edge of his chair. He reached into his jacket pocket and pulled out the letter his father had written to him over twenty years ago.

"After Grandma died in August and neither of you came …"

"I wasn't aware she'd died until after the service, and your mother—"

"I know. She was in Paris, and Grandma's attorney told her it was not necessary to return. Grandma wanted a simple memorial service with her church circle, and Attorney Anders promised to carry out her wishes. That's when he told me about the box left for me. I confess, at first I was … bitter … that at this late date I was given some communication and didn't care to see it."

"You didn't see the contents until yesterday?"

Reed nodded. His eyes burned. He unfolded his father's letter. "I read your letters … but—"

"But what?"

The weight of his question pressed on him.

"Please, ask me anything."

"Why didn't you fight for me?" He blurted the question.

His father took in a deep breath and exhaled slowly. "Fair question." He leaned forward, elbows on thighs, and grasped his hands together.

"Eugenia and I were still in high school. I was seventeen, your mother sixteen. When she discovered she was pregnant, we ran off and married out of state. Our marriage was legal, but Eugenia's parents refused to accept it, since they didn't give their consent."

"My parents were divorced, and I alternated visitation with them. Eugenia stayed with her parents. After you were born, your grandmother cared for you so we could finish high school. We had no means of support. I earned only a little money mowing lawns. We tried to parent you, but we were too young to handle the marriage. We divorced, and that's when your grandmother and grandfather pushed to adopt you. We thought it was the best solution for you to receive proper care, as long as we could see you. But your grandmother had your mother and me served with no trespass papers."

"You're kidding."

"We never imagined she would keep us from you, but since you were adopted, the attorney explained she had every right."

"How could she do that to me?" His phone vibrated. It could wait.

"She said more than once she intended to protect you from the hurt of being shuffled between parents and was afraid you wouldn't get the full-time attention she could give. She insisted she would not allow you to feel unwanted."

"But that's exactly how I felt."

"Sometimes what we desire comes out best if we leave it to God's timing. That's a hard lesson."

His father pushed his chair closer. A frown creased his

forehead, "Reed, please believe me. Your mom and I never, ever wanted to throw you away."

His father's jaw went rigid. He stood, shoved his hands in his pockets, paced with his back toward him to the wall, stopped, then turned and faced Reed.

This was just as hard for him as it was for Reed. Reed walked over to his father. His eyes were closed. Was he praying?

"I guess this whole thing is hard for us both," Reed said.

His dad gave his head a quick nod. "I need you to forgive me for hurting you."

Reed raked his fingers through his hair.

"Forgive. That's exactly what the designer I've been working with said. 'If you don't forgive, you risk remaining distorted and ugly, like someone eaten up with leprosy.'"

"She gives very descriptive advice."

Reed lifted his gaze to the familiar face. His father's eyes were full of longing, like his heart. "I'm afraid I was headed to that leprous existence, but not anymore. I need you to forgive my bitterness."

His dad's eyes softened. He held out his hand. "We are on a two-way street. Forgiveness flowing in both directions."

Reed smiled. "Yes." He grabbed his dad's hand. The gesture melted to a hug that warmed his soul.

After a healing moment, his dad spoke. "I've seen your work at the Feldman house. Very impressive. You inherited your mother's gift."

"It would be nice to be as successful as she has been."

"She's worked hard. I'm proud of her."

"You are?"

His father had a kind smile with a hint of an indention on his left cheek. His inheritance? "We've remained friends over the years. She and my wife, Cindy, keep in touch. Eugenia told her she planned to come up here for the contest."

"She doesn't know—"

"No. Judges don't know the designer's names, and we certainly didn't tell her."

"She may not need to come now. I withdrew from the contest."

"Not according to this news story." His dad lifted a newspaper from the desk and handed it to Reed.

The headline read, "Feldman House Contest Reopened to Public," the sub-caption, "Last night to see the live nativity." The article started:

> *Cleanup is complete at the Feldman house after a romp by displaced raccoons. "Everything is back in order and ready for people to cast their vote for their favorite room," homeowner Lake Spencer said, "and the live nativity will be on display one more evening."*
>
> *Final judging and the winner announcement will be a part of the New Year's Eve celebration at Feldman Park. The contest is a fundraiser for the Save the Square group.*

Reed stopped reading and shook his head. "I don't deserve to remain in the contest."

His dad leaned against the desk, crossing his legs at the ankles. "Because of the hotel's plans?"

Reed lifted his brows at the same time his phone received a message. He could check it later. "You know?"

"Pastor Creighton filled me in on the misunderstandings and why you pulled out. Listen, I understand you feel bad about the hotel's plans, but that's not your fault."

"I knew there was the chance they would want the houses torn down, and my mission was to gain the confidence of the people and persuade them to take Fairland's deal."

"The people seem willing to forgive."

"I'm afraid this road to forgiveness is a dead-end street for me." His phone sounded again. "Sorry, I'd better check this."

He had two texts. One from Lake: Pastor C said U R back. Come by house ASAP.

The other from Mandeville: Look at the living room mantle at Feldman house and CALL ME.

Reed stood open-mouthed by the fireplace at the Feldman house. The living room was exactly as he'd left it before the coon damage, except his first choice for curtain fabric now hung in the windows.

"I heard from Mandeville that your boss removed you from the redevelopment assignment. But I thought you might like to see Izzie's handiwork," Lake said.

"Izzie did this?"

"She installed her window treatments when she realized your order wouldn't arrive in time for the judging."

"I withdrew."

"Izzie said no dice."

"If she used her shutters and curtains here … what about the office?"

"She installed roll-up shades, and I actually like them better."

Reed gave an introspective nod. "Good. I would hope that in the end of all the fuss and furor, you are pleased with your home. I'm sorry about the push to remove the houses, after all the effort to raise money to save them."

"Trust me that won't stop the fight."

Reed pictured Izzie, feet planted in the holding cell at the jail. "With Izzie involved, I understand."

"I received a message from Mandeville. Something about the mantle? Everything looks fine to me."

"Ah, the mantle. Let me show you. The architectural design intrigued Mandeville, and the engineering implications amazed Greg."

Reed creased his brow. The fireplace, with its rich brown mahogany mantle, made an interesting focal point. The sturdy stone hearth was tall and wide enough to provide seating that extended to the right and formed a deep woodbox. "It's a nice-looking fireplace, but—"

"But this fireplace has an unusual mantle." Lake pointed to the decorative corbel support underneath the mantle on the right-hand side. "Mandeville leaned against this piece like so." Lake demonstrated. "And …"

Reed heard a sliding noise.

"The back of the woodbox opens."

Reed dropped to his hands and knees and peered into the gaping hole at the back of the woodbox large enough to crawl through.

"Steps lead down to a small room and a tunnel."

"Did you go in?"

"The room but not the tunnel. That is not a place I'd like to get trapped in. It's full of dirt and tree roots. I suspect this roadwork is affecting it."

As if on cue, beeps and clangs rang out from the road machines.

"Is this how the raccoons made it in the house?"

"No. Chimney. The flue is closed now. We found coon prints down there and …" Lake pulled something from his pocket. "… this."

Reed stood and peered at his extended palm.

"A gold coin? Down there?"

Lake nodded. "Izzie found one in the hallway the same day she discovered the vandalism."

"Do you think there's a connection?" Reed rubbed his finger over the indentations on the 1908 coin with an Indian head on one side and an eagle on the back.

"Don't know. But what adds to the intrigue is a similar gold coin was found a year ago in the abandoned well behind this house. There may or may not be a tie between the finds. Ralph Ensley has contacts with the treasury department. He's checking into gold coinage, and Loretta is doing some research."

Reed examined the lintel below the mantle. "This wood piece blends perfectly and hides its secret well. I can see from an architect's point of view why Mandeville was excited."

"Marigold and Petunia said all the houses on the square have some kind of secret hidden place in their design."

"All the houses?"

There was a knock, and the front door creaked open.

"You open yet?"

"Dave," Lake said to Reed. He glanced at his watch. "We are in thirty minutes," he called out.

Dave dressed in a thick robe and slippers padded into the living room. "Those workers behind the house put up some of those high intensity battery operated lights. They must be trying to meet an end of the year deadline—" Dave spotted Reed. "You're back?"

"I am."

Dave frowned. "I'm surprised you're brave enough to return with the hotel debacle."

The exhilaration of the secret find and reconciliation with his father ran headlong into the dismal reality of the development project. "Actually, right now I'm off the job."

Dave sniffed. "Well, on or off the job, there's a certain Joseph job you should fill, not me."

"I'm the last person Izzie would want to see turn up as

Joseph."

"The way she's moping around?"

Lake laughed. "Ever think she might be moping around 'cause she's having to play Mary to your Joseph, Dave? You're just looking for a way to get out of your job." Lake nudged Reed. "We drew straws at the rooster table this morning, and guess who won."

"Lost you mean." Dave began shrugging off the robe. "It's the least you can do for the cause."

Reed dipped his head. "I'm sorry for any hurts I've caused."

"We understand the pressures of business, but that doesn't negate the fact you need to make amends with Izzie."

"I'd like nothing better, but—"

"He's right," Lake said. "You see how Izzie feels." He nodded at the window treatments Izzie gave up for him.

"Go on." Dave shoved the robe into Reed's hands.

Reed, outfitted in Dave's Joseph robe, approached Izzie, who had her back to him. Dusk was settling around the make-shift stable. No visitors were in sight. "How's the baby Jesus?"

"He's here on time, like someone near and dear is not."

"And who is near and dear to you?"

"Dave, have you caught a cold or something? She turned. "Wait, a mi ... Reed?" Izzie pushed her head covering off.

"Guilty as charged."

"You were in New York."

"I was. But there's air service to Hamilton Harbor."

"But ... where's Dave?"

"He sent a repentant guy to play Joseph to your Mary." He stepped in close. "Lake showed me the living room. You sacrificed your window treatments to restore mine."

"I wanted your room to look like you'd planned for the judging." She looked down, avoiding eye contact. "Besides, the shutters were your idea. No way I could accept winning by default. That would be like kissing my brother, no big deal." She pushed out her lower lip in a pout.

Reed studied her lips. The memory of their kiss sent a shiver through his body, unrelated to the chilly evening air.

"That so? But you don't have a brother."

"Doesn't matter. You get the point. Southern 101. I don't want something that is unearned."

"You mean like a pumpkin pie for a jack-o'-lantern?"

Her shoulders drooped. "That may have been my plan, but you know that your creation was the best in its category."

He waited until she made eye contact. "Izzie Ketterling, I appreciate your efforts."

Izzie managed a tight smile. "I did it for Lake, Mallory … the contest … the square. She cranked up the volume on that last word. Eyes defiant.

Reed lowered his head. "Of course. Look, I hate how everything turned out. But—"

Izzie held up her hand, "Hold up." The glint in her eyes softened. "I'm sorry, Reed. Mandeville said you are off the job. What happened?"

"I didn't exactly praise Fairland's plans. Padgett wasn't happy."

"Oh?" She clasped her hands in front of her. "I feel awful. Nothing will stop our fight for the houses, but you shouldn't lose your job. That redevelopment project was a career step for you."

"I haven't been fired, and I can always go back to the lighting store where I worked before this job if I am." And he meant it. An office in the executive wing wasn't worth hurting the townspeople and Izzie. Reed reached down and lifted her chin. "I'm so sorry for being angry with you when I saw my father at the church service." He took a deep breath, then smiled. "It's because of your invitation, we've reconciled."

She blinked.

A car approached and stopped.

"You have?"

"Long story." Reed helped her put her headscarf on, touching her hand and drinking in her fragrance. He took his position beside the manger.

A child exclaimed, "I didn't know we lived so close to Bethlehem." The parent tried to explain the live nativity and was still explaining when they left to see what the child believed must be Mary and Joseph's house.

Izzie shoved the head cover back off. "This is killing me. You and your dad? Reconciled? How—"

There was a sudden loud clang, followed by the roar of an engine and a forceful thud that shook the ground under their feet.

Izzie jerked her head toward the house. "What on earth?"

Reed stood. "Sounds like something happened where those road machines are working."

Shouts rang out behind the house—one louder than the rest. "Cave-in! Call 911. There's been a cave-in!"

Around Izzie, the vendors in Feldman Park offered their wares. The air was thick with New Year's Eve excitement and punctuated with smells of sweet funnel cakes, kettle corn, and yeasty pretzels ready to dip in hot mustard. The church stage band stirred the growing crowd with "Give Me That Old Time Religion."

Everyone was there to have fun. Fun for Izzie tonight was going to come with the announcement of the contest winners to rid her of the swarm of butterflies in her stomach. While she waited to help Francine with her bake sale, she picked up the local newspapers and focused her attention on the gold discovery.

Claudia plunked down a stack of Adopt-a-Pet literature on the table she had readied for the celebration.

"Look at these headlines." Izzie held up the front pages of two newspapers. "One reads 'Gold Discovery,' and the other 'Illegal Gold Hoard Uncovered.' Guess which headline came from the *Talk of the Town*."

Claudia tapped her index finger to her lips. "Let's see …" then rolled her eyes. "That guy never quits, does he? Does either article mention the value of the gold find yet?"

"According to the *Hamilton Harbor News* the value estimate is well over … oh my gosh … a half million dollars." She read from the article, "In a news conference, Horowitz, attorney for Marigold and Petunia Hamilton, stated the gold stash dates back to 1933 when Franklin D. Roosevelt made ownership of over one-hundred dollars in gold coins illegal because of the economic emergency during the Great Depression. The government called in gold and paid in paper money."

"So, the money uncovered in the cave-in was gold that was never turned in?" Claudia asked.

"It seems likely, from the dates on the coins."

"Who owns the gold now?"

"The sisters. Isn't this exciting?" Francine, with a fresh tight perm, plugged herself into the conversation.

"Francine, you're right." Izzie read on, "Though the Feldman property was sold by the Hamilton sisters to Lake and Mallory Spencer, the contract included the typical clause of mineral rights remaining with the original owners. The gold find is believed to fit in the category of minerals found underground, and the Spencers' lawyer won't contest the claim. When asked what the Hamiltons would do with their newfound fortune, one of the heirs, Marigold Hamilton, didn't hesitate, 'Restore the vacant houses on Feldman Square for a maternity home and pregnancy resource center.'"

Claudia laughed. "I heard that Marigold said she might consider building her own hotel on the bay too."

"That would give those Fairland Hotel people a swift kick in the pants." Francine said.

The sun slipped beneath the bay waters, igniting a blazing backdrop of vivid pinks, oranges and purples to the vacant houses soldiering at attention on Feldman Square. Cool breezes coming from the bay peppered those who were setting up for the evening's event. Streetlights popped on, highlighting the vendors and activities set up around the square with circles of light.

Izzie wore an insulated long-sleeved top with her Save the Square T-shirt on top. "I'm reporting for service at your bake sale table, Francine. Do you want me to work the cashbox?"

"Margaret and Mellie have it under control. I'll holler when we're busy."

Mayor Brimstead, using his cane to support the uneven hitch in his step, maneuvered in their direction. Loretta Huggins was at his side.

Not far behind, Lyman Beardsley followed, pen and pad in hand.

"Izzie," the mayor said, his grin lopsided from the skin grafts he'd endured. "I heard you worked hard to restore the living room after the great coon caper."

"Yes, now both rooms are in good shape for the judging."

Lyman nosed in, "I heard you changed things around

in your opponent's room when he was out of town. Were you trying to give yourself an edge in the contest?"

"Lyman." Loretta used her teacher scowl. "Why don't you zip it. Reed Harrison says she sacrificed her own room decor and made his living room entry better."

Ms. Huggins standing up for her? This was an encouraging beginning for the new year.

Lyman took his chastisement in stride. "Sorry, Izzie. A reporter is always looking for the story behind the story."

"Hey, it's okay. You're a guy who needs extra grace, like all of us at times."

"Me? Grace? Not sure what it means, but I like the sound of it."

"Grace is like being treated well even when you don't deserve it," Izzie said.

"In that case, I could use a double load."

"Amen, buster." Francine said. "If only you would make that into a headline. Pastor Creighton said if you give a little grace, you get a little grace."

Lyman's brow furrowed as Mallory approached.

The mayor chuckled. "Mallory, there you are. Is it time for the interior design fundraiser results?"

"The proceeds pale in light of the great gold discovery."

"Nonsense. This contest has it over the gold find, at least in longevity. Mattie and the live TV camera crew have a crowd gathering." He motioned to the section of the park where space had been saved for spectators to assemble to hear the contest results. "Eugenia is here too."

Reed's mother. From Izzie's vantage point, she could see Eugenia was petite, with dark hair like Reed's. How will she react when she realizes her son is the designer she's judging?

Izzie's mind tried to wrap around all the feelings assaulting her. Part of her would like to win, to make her mark as a designer. But this should be Reed's moment to win and make his parents proud. Oh, to be swallowed up in the joy and wonder of that reunion. Whether or not Reed won, this should happen. But how bittersweet to realize the years stolen from them had been shrouded in lies. More grace required, for sure.

"Pete," the mayor continued, "built us a platform for the occasion. We should add a permanent bandstand to the list of improvements."

Mallory and Ms. Huggins left with the mayor who was still talking. Lyman trailed behind them, leaving Izzie with her thoughts. The announcement of the design winner wasn't the only excitement niggling her.

Last night, dressed as Mary and Joseph, they ran along with the other spectators to see what had happened. News had already reached first responders, a police car pulled up to the work site and other emergency sirens could be heard approaching. Five men in hard hats struggled to hold the rear of an excavator balanced on the edge of a gaping hole where the ground had given way.

"Tie a rope to the machine," a man yelled. "Ed, stay seated. We don't want you toppling over."

"You and me both," the operator said, not moving and still grasping the controls. The machine had pitched forward at a steep angle, his seatbelt was the only thing keeping him from sliding out.

A firetruck arrived, and they worked quickly to right the excavator. The driver could finally gain traction and moved the machine out of the way.

A little boy shouted. "Look … gold!"

Spectators pressed in. "Folks stand back for your safety," Police Officer Tony Duncan cautioned the crowd.

"This is the same area where Emme's son fell in an abandoned well and found a gold coin last year." Izzie told

Reed.

As the crowd pulled back, Izzie could see the glint of gold exposed by the bright work lights. "Please, folks, move back." Jeff had arrived and helped Tony move the crowd. "The surrounding ground could be compromised."

Lake conferred with Jeff and spoke up, "Any visitors whose tour was cut short, please check back with us, and we'll offer you a time to complete your tour."

"For now, this area must be cleared." Jeff said. The crowd began to dissipate.

Izzie and Reed made their way to the front of the Feldman house. Patrons walked back to their cars as vehicles with television and radio insignias pulled in.

"Word travels mighty fast," Reed nodded toward the park. "There's your reporter, Lyman."

"My reporter?" Izzie harrumphed. "He's our small-town malady."

"Let's go inside and shed these Mary and Joseph outfits."

"I'm with you."

The Feldman house was quiet and peaceful in contrast to the shouted orders and rumble of machinery.

Izzie shrugged off her robe. "Reed, we're in the midst of a fantastic adventure. The coons, the gold coin finds, the secret passage, the abandoned well, and now a genuine treasure discovered in a cave-in. That's what these old houses offer—intrigue and mystery."

"But that's not the biggest mystery."

"Oh? What is?"

Reed pulled the towel from his head and peeled off the robe. He straightened his thick hair with his fingers. "How a certain interior designer who had every right to let a guy flounder in the misery of his own making, could turn around and help him. I, twice, falsely accused you and walked out on the contest, and you repay by putting my design room back in better order than I left it."

"Yeah. But you ended up losing your job and your mother was coming to judge—"

Reed stepped in close. Now what was he doing? He lowered his lips to hers, hushing her talking with a kiss that melted her sensibilities and left her gasping for air.

In the middle of the carnival atmosphere, she absently touched her lips and could still taste the sweetness of his mouth on hers, the gentle caress of his hand on her neck. The tingle that shot through her still lingered.

But where was Reed? He had come to Hamilton Harbor seeking forgiveness around the hotel situation, but she'd heard from Capt. Jack that the team had returned. Had Reed finally accepted his boss's vision? He had to consider his career. Would he chalk this project up to experience and move on?

Surely, he would come to hear the contest results. If she won, her dream had been to plan successive TV shows with Mattie that showed the progress of restoring the interiors of the Gardner Hamilton house and the old garden club. But those dreams were just that. Dreams. This was reality. Reed would be the winner and his appearances on Mattie's show would likely feature the stages of decorating the hotel.

Since the gold find and the sisters' pledge to restore the houses and not sell the property, what was next? A fight? Her jaw tightened. "Don't go there, Izzie."

"Don't go where?"

Izzie whirled about.

"Reed."

Mandeville, Dan, and Greg were with him.

"Happy New Year, folks. Can I have your attention?" Mayor Brimstead's voice boomed out over the crowd. "Gather around. We have much to announce."

Izzie, Reed and his team allowed themselves to be driven like cattle in a round-up to hear the mayor speak.

"Welcome to our New Year's event sponsored by our friends and downtown partners, Hope Community Church. The design contest has raised a lot of interest and excitement downtown. To report fund-raising results is Mallory Spencer, one of the owners of the Feldman house with the now famous cave-in in their backyard. Mallory?"

The mayor stepped back to allow Mallory to come to the microphone.

"Hi, all. I am astounded at the turnout we have had for the interior design contest. Five fantastic designers have donated their time for the Save the Square project and made this historic house into a home for us. The admission fee to see the house and extra donations totaled $8,975. Adding the matching funds offered by Spic and Span cleaning company and our total is: $17,950."

The mayor let out a booming, "Yeah." Cheers and applause filled the park.

Reed and the rest of the team applauded with Izzie. Their celebration seemed convoluted. How were they happy about money raised to save the houses when they worked for the company courting the hotel that wanted to tear them down? Since the sisters wouldn't sell and vowed to press on with plans for the maternity home, would the hotel pull out? How would all these events affect Emerson's future development plans?

The mayor was back at the mic. "Please put your hands together for Ms. Eugenia Roberts, the lady who sparked the idea for the design contest fundraiser. I'm proud to say we have the lady with us in person. Eugenia, of Eugenia's

Interiors in Orlando, come on up here."

Applause and whistles. Izzie glanced at Reed. His face lacked any expression. All his physical energy must be at work on his insides with nothing to spare for his face.

Mayor Brimstead kept a running commentary going while Eugenia, smartly dressed in a dark navy pantsuit with a red sweater, made her way to the platform.

Lord, be with Reed. I'm all wrapped up in myself and old houses, but he is seeing his mother for the first time after many years.

"Nice to be here. I've been viewing photo postings this past month with great interest, and I'm delighted to judge the final phase of the contest. I looked at originality, meeting the client's needs, safety codes, and over-all aesthetic use of color, texture, and design. I will be just as excited as you are to meet the winners because right now, they are only numbers to me."

"Thank you, Eugenia," Mayor Brimstead said. "And now, let me bring up everyone's favorite noonday host, Ms. Mattie Mason, who will announce our winner."

There was more applause as more of the crowd gathered in to see the local celebrity.

"Happy New Year's Eve!" Mattie greeted. The crowd cheered. "Is everybody happy?" The crowd cheered louder.

The mayor quick-walked with his cane back to the mic and interrupted. "Mattie, excuse me. But before your big announcement, I have this message from Emerson, Emerson, and Padgett Developers. Fairland Hotels has been added to the Hamilton Harbor redevelopment project, and the hotel has signed an agreement that they will work in concert with the proposed maternity home and pregnancy center." The mayor leaned close to the mic and shouted, "Removing the houses is no longer a part of their plan!"

The growing crowd didn't tire of applauding.

Reed grabbed Izzie and swung her around, her mirror ball earrings leaped with them.

"Is this what you've been working on?"

His nod blurred in her vision as moisture filled her eyes, and her voice cracked. Blinking back the tears, she grasped Reed's face, making it a steady target and kissed him good and hard. He wrapped her in his embrace and deepened the kiss. Her heart fluttered to the sound of angels' wings. Already light-headed, the kiss transported her to a place she'd never been before. Filled with the scent of men's cologne in a yummy flavor, it was a forever after place.

Mattie's voice broke through her crazed senses.

"Mayor, after that news, I'm thrilled to announce the winner of the Feldman House decorating contest. I will be working with this person to produce a series of decorating shows that you're going to love. So, with no more chit chat, the envelope, please."

She accepted the envelope and pulled out the card. She stared a moment, then grinned.

Izzie bounced on her toes. Out with it, Mattie.

"Folks, it's a tie. The winners are Izzie Ketterling of Izzie's Creative Designs and Reed Harrison of Emerson, Emerson, and Padgett. Would you join us up here?"

Izzie grinned, giving Reed a thumbs up. Reed squeezed her forearm and nudged her forward. Eugenia remained seated. Her eyes focused on Reed.

Izzie touched Reed's wrist. "Your mom recognizes you. Go to her." Reed approached his mother. She stood, her eyes glistening in the lantern lights strung along the stage.

"Reed. I'm so proud of you." With that, he grabbed his mother in a strong embrace. When he let her go, tears channeled down her face. Izzie swiped at her own waterworks.

CHAPTER TWENTY

Red roses sweetened the air of the private dining room in the newly renovated Gardner house. Reed moved the flower container a few inches to the right and then angled the Queen Anne mahogany chairs slightly to allow extra space for the cameraman.

Izzie poked her head into the room. "What gives? I know you're a stickler for precision, but how many times are you going to rearrange things in here?"

"Just making sure everything is right for the camera." Reed's lips and mouth were dry, and his forehead wet with perspiration. Great. The opposite of what he needed twenty minutes before going live on the "At Home in Hamilton Harbor" show. He might have twelve shows under his belt, one a month since winning the contest with Izzie, but his nerves today topped those of a year ago when they first went on the air.

Not that he didn't have reason—a good reason. He reached in his pocket to check for the velvet box. The box. Where was it? He felt in the other pocket. Not there.

"Mattie said she wanted to start the filming in front of the living room window. Do you think we should adjust the blinds?" Izzie asked.

"Blinds? Uh … good idea," Reed said. "See what Bradley thinks. I need something from my apartment. I'll be right back."

"You'd better hurry."

"Bradley, check the light here, will you?" Izzie called to

the camera photographer as she left the room.

Reed skittered down the rear steps of the Gardner house and took the steps to his apartment over the old garden club two at a time. He'd changed to a gray jacket and forgot the box. The most important prop for the day. What was he thinking? He grabbed the navy jacket. Relief ran through him when he felt the tiny box.

He thumbed the lid open to make sure the ring, specially crafted from the gold coin Izzie found, was secure inside. The ring glittered to life when exposed to the light. Would the token of his love have the same effect on Izzie? He shoved it in his pocket and raced back to the Gardner kitchen, stopping to catch his breath.

"There you are," Bradley said reaching in his camera bag on the kitchen counter and pulling out a lens. "I think we've got the lighting figured out in the front room."

"Where's Mattie?" Reed asked. "Did she bring the cue cards?"

"You asked me that five minutes ago. The answer's the same. She put them in that private dining room." He switched lenses on his video camera. "What's with the nerves? It's usually Izzie flitting about at the last minute with you standing by all stolid and calm."

"Sorry, just a lot on my mind today."

"Reed," Izzie called from the front room, "Mattie says to get in here."

"Your increasing-in-number audience awaits." Bradley said.

"Scary, when you think about it." TV ratings had reflected a greater viewership over the past year, and Izzie and Reed had signed on for another year of shows.

"Not for me. Sounds more like job security, as long as your ratings stay up."

"I hope ratings don't take a nose-dive after this show."

"Not a chance. Why would it?" Bradley hiked the camera to his shoulder and left the kitchen.

Reed pulled out his handkerchief and wiped his brow. "Why would it, indeed," he mumbled. He grabbed a water bottle from the kitchen counter, unscrewed the cap and took a couple of swallows to relieve his dry throat and moisten his lips. He walked through the dining area into the living room that had been converted into more dining space.

Mattie grabbed Reed's arm, gently guiding him to the love seat in front of the window. "Bradley has the stationary camera framing this spot. Sit there beside Izzie. I'll stand by the fireplace. That way the audience can feel the homey atmosphere in here."

Bradley watched his camera feed from the network. "And we're ready in five, four …"

Mattie moistened her red lips with her tongue, straightened her fitted cream suit jacket, and smoothed her platinum blonde, medium length hair … "three, two, you're on the air."

"Good afternoon. Today, *At Home in Hamilton Harbor* is taking us to the newly renovated Gardner house on Feldman Square. It's February. That special time of year to let your Valentine know you care. And what better way than with flowers, food, and romantic surroundings. Back with us today are our decorators, Izzie Ketterling of Izzie's Creative Designs and Reed Harrison of the Emerson firm. Later in the show, we will show how to create an enchanting setting you won't want to miss, but for now—Izzie, tell us a bit of the history of this house and its current mission."

Izzie wore a red, ruffled top, pink skirt with red boots, and red elongated heart-shaped earrings that danced above her shoulders. She could brighten anyone's day.

"Mattie, Marigold and Petunia Hamilton envisioned

turning the Gardner residence into a self-supporting maternity home. The sisters were raised in this home by their parents, Gardner and Violet Hamilton, who were the children of the city's original founders—Truman Hamilton and Albert Feldman. By the time Marigold and Petunia inherited the properties, the financial hub of the city had shifted from the harbor, and the Gardner house was converted into apartments. When I was growing up, I shared an apartment in this house with my mother. We'll be showing that remodeled room shortly."

"Yes, an amazing transformation," Mattie said. "Reed, tell us how you and your development firm collaborated with the Fairland Hotel to include the houses on the square."

"Our firm presented a proposal to include the houses needing renovation and Feldman Park as a part of the hotel complex. When the hotel is completed there will be a tree-lined drive and landscaped walking trail that winds between the properties. Throughout the gardens, there will be markers explaining the history of the area. The hotel will carry literature on the Boarding House Restaurant which will be one of the dining options for guests. Fairland has already donated a sizable sum and has agreed to maintain the landscaping for the houses and park. The girls being helped will have the opportunity to work, not only serving in the restaurant, but to train for jobs at the hotel in housekeeping, business, customer service, and childcare."

"Sounds like a win-win situation. For merchants, tourists, locals, and hotel guests who want a homey place to dine while contributing to a needy cause, the Gardner house will be the place to come."

"Izzie, show us around, won't you?"

Izzie pointed to the fireplace mantle, "The Gardner house was built in 1935, and the mantle is solid cypress cut at the Feldman sawmill. The floors are heart of pine. The windows are all restrung sash windows with the original glass panes. The mill started operations in the late 1800s but was shut down in 1917 during World War I. Albert Feldman was German and falsely accused of espionage. The mill reopened, but sadly, the tarnish on his reputation lingered. Truman Hamilton, who remained close friends with Feldman, built a school and made the square a tight community to help protect the children from hurtful gossip."

Bradley moved the camera back on Mattie. "Amazing history. Reed, tell us about the colors selected. I love the look."

"We chose tints and shades of burgundy, because the colors blend well with the rich reddish-brown woods in the room, and these colors also stimulate the appetite."

"Aha. Good idea for a restaurant. I understand you have rooms for private dining?"

"We enclosed the small sitting room near the entry for private dining." Izzie stepped to the room and stood back for Bradley to go in and video the room. "Next to it, down the hall, is the second private room. Originally the study, this is the room I used to live in with my mom when this was an apartment building."

"And folks, you won't want to miss seeing this special dining room. Stay tuned to see a room designed to touch the heart."

"And cut." Bradley said. "We've got four minutes. I'll set up my small camera on a tripod since maneuvering will be tight."

"I'll retrieve the ice for the ice bucket," Izzie said. "We were afraid it would melt if we put it out too soon."

Reed watched as Izzie left the room, then asked Mattie, "The cue cards?"

"Safely tucked away behind the breakfront. I'll pull them out after you kneel. But I'm telling you, speak from the heart and you won't need cue cards."

"We're live. I'm afraid I'll draw a blank once the camera is rolling."

"Don't worry, I've got your back ... or front in this case. Here she comes. Good luck."

Bradley began his countdown. Izzie stood beside Reed at the table.

Bradley pointed to Mattie and the red light popped on.

"This private dining room is designed for romance with Valentine's Day around the corner. And what an intriguing feel you have produced in the room. Izzie, what elements did you use?"

"Red is the color for love, so we have a lovely bowl of red roses with white candle accents arranged by The Flower Cottage."

Reed lit the candles, his hand shaking as Izzie spoke. "The candles give the room a romantic glow. And remember, don't use a tall vase of flowers, since it obstructs the couple's view of each other. The table is set with a white linen tablecloth and napkins. I fashioned the heart-shaped napkin ring holders by tracing around a small heart cookie cutter on heavy cardboard, then painting the cut-outs with red acrylic."

"This is beautiful. For the folks at home, the roses add a light, sweet fragrance to the room. Why don't you two sit?"

That was his cue.

Reed swallowed hard. *Now or never, chum.*

With the camera rolling, Mattie stepped back from the camera and pulled out the cue cards. Reed slid from his seat and bent on one knee in front of Izzie. He fished in his pocket and pulled out the little black velvet box. He looked up at Izzie's puzzled face.

"Izzie Ketterling, you have been the brightest and most unforgettable spot in my life since the very first moment we met. In every sense of the word, you have made me a new man, changed forever. With you, I've learned that old discards can be made into redeemable treasures, that the morning dew is the touch of nature's grace and loving kindness. That grits stand for God's Real Impressive Treat for the Soul and are tasty. And most amazing, with you, I've found that forgiveness can make the fragrance of spring sweeter."

Izzie's eyes glistened in the flickering candlelight. Reed cupped her face and used his thumbs to wipe tears that trailed down her cheeks.

"I began falling in love with you from the day you knocked the seagull into my car, and I haven't been able to break the fall …"

Mattie held up a cue card and pointed.

The red light on Bradley's camera reflected from a silver spoon on the table. She wanted him to include the prince charming part. Mattie said it was the clencher.

"But what if Izzie laughs?" he had asked.

"So, she laughs. It's a happy sentiment. And oh, so dreamy."

Reed pressed on. Izzie stared, speechless.

"You said you used to dream of a Prince Charming coming for you in this very room …" He glanced at the cue card. "I'd like to be that prince. Izzie, since you came into my life, I realize I was only half a person. With you, I feel whole. Will you do me the honor of marrying me?"

Mattie fist-bumped the air.

Izzie turned to Mattie who slipped the cue cards behind her back. "Did we mix up holidays? This isn't April Fool's, is it? I mean, this wasn't in the script."

"You don't script a surprise proposal," Mattie said.

Izzie turned back to Reed. Another tear escaped and trickled down her cheek. "This is real?"

"Real as a guy stuck on the floor waiting for an answer. I know you wanted a special over the top proposal, and this is the best I could come up with."

"I'd say you came up with a doozy." Izzie lifted the ring from the box. "Oh, Reed. Is this made from the gold coin I found?"

He nodded.

Her eyes glittered. She looked at Bradley, who nodded and pointed to the red light on his camera. "Uh ... let's see now." She reached down and cradled Reed's face in her hands. "Mr. Reed Harrison, when I used to dream of a prince coming to me in this very room, I never imagined it would be a city slicker from New York. Sometimes life throws us unexpected curves. My answer to you, my Yankee friend who has learned to love grits, is ... YES."

Reed's knees went weak but somehow, he managed to stand. He slipped the ring on her finger, pulled her from the chair and folded her in his arms.

As their lips met, Reed's heart drummed in his ears, and Mattie's voice faded into the background.

"Folks, there you have it. The perfect setting for romance, and a couple designed for love."

"Cut!"

Mattie dabbed her tears. "That was romantic as all get out."

Reed pulled back, still suffering an adrenaline spike, and looked at Izzie. "All get out?"

Izzie slipped her fingers into his. "That's southern for your proposal was intensely over the top."

And with that, Izzie delivered a southern kiss that knocked his socks off.

Enjoy an Everything Pumpkin recipe from the fall festival at Feldman Park.

Power Cooker Pumpkin Chili

INGREDIENTS:

1 lb. ground pork, beef or chicken (optional)

¼ large yellow onion, chopped

½ large green pepper, seeded and chopped (or small red and yellow peppers)

2 cloves garlic, minced

1 15oz can pumpkin puree

1 c. chicken broth

1 15.5 oz can pinto beans

1 15.5 oz. can kidney beans

1 14.5 oz diced tomatoes

1 ½ Tbsp. chili powder

½ tsp. salt

¼ tsp. black pepper

1/8 tsp. cumin seed

¼ tsp. turmeric

1/8 tsp. allspice

1 bay leaf

INSTRUCTIONS:

1. Brown the meat, peppers, onion, and garlic in a drizzle of olive oil until the onions are soft.
2. Add the remaining ingredients. Stir well.
3. Cook under pressure for twenty minutes. (4 servings)

DEAR READER:

I've enjoyed returning to Hamilton Harbor, visiting with the characters, and crafting the houses on Feldman Square with their long-held secrets.

In art and interior design classes, I've learned that colors opposite each other on the color wheel are considered to be complementary, like red and green. When paired, the effect is a vibrant look that can sometimes be jarring if overdone. So, putting together perfectionist, by-the-book Reed with the unconventional, free-spirit Izzie gave me vivid opposites that were fun to contrast from the moment they met.

When I first began writing the storyline of fictional Hamilton Harbor's deliberations at their city commission meeting, the topic became a reality. My own hometown is built on the Florida coast with a downtown and marina in need of rejuvenation. As I wrote scenes, headlines in local media often related or mirrored my characters' problems. Hamilton Harbor's citizens were able to come to an agreement for their marina project. But in real life, the local marina project came to a halt after the ravages of Hurricane Michael … and then came COVID-19 so the fate of the marina is still unfolding.

I'm going to miss Izzie. She has taught me a lot, not the least of which is her statement "God has to be interested in the little stuff to accomplish the big stuff."

And if you haven't read the short story, *The Winter*

DESIGNED FOR *LOVE*

Solstice Bride, about the marriage of the couple who built the Feldman house, stop by my website at www.sallyjoppitts.com and pick up a copy.

Blessings,

Sally Jo Pitts

ABOUT THE AUTHOR

Sally Jo Pitts has had a career in private investigation, lie detection, high school guidance counseling, and has taught in the field of marriage and family living for over twenty years. Now, she brings her experience in affairs of the heart to the fiction page. Writing what she likes to read—faith-based stories—her desire is to inspire and encourage the reader. She is the author of *And Then Blooms Love* and *Stumbling Upon Romance*, books one and two in the Hamilton Harbor Legacy series, available from Elk Lake Publishing, Inc. on Amazon and at your local bookstore.

QUESTIONS FOR DISCUSSION:

1. Deuteronomy 33:13 (AKJV) speaks of the dew as blessing— "Blessed of the Lord be his land, for the precious things of heaven, for the dew..." However, we may take the dew for granted or even as an irritation. What are other things in creation that might be seen as curse but might also be blessing?

2. "Finally, brethren, whatsoever things are true, whatsoever things are honest, whatsoever things are just, whatsoever things are pure, whatsoever things are lovely, whatsoever things are of good report; if there be any virtue and if there be any praise, think on these things" (Philippians 4:8 KJV). Izzie had a way of making negatives into positives. She saw the colorful characters in the rooming house, and her mother's sacrifice for her as a blessing rather than an adversity. Are there things that you've experienced that could be seen either as a positive or a negative? Explain.

3. From Reed's family background, he discovers the truth in Romans 8:28 that "...all things work together for good to them that love God to them who are the called according to his purpose" (KJV). Do you have examples of things that have worked together for good in your own life? Explain.

4. The art teacher Sylvia Easton, who lived in the rooming house with Izzie, became so inspired about God's

wondrous sunrises it led her to shout. Isaiah 26:19b (KJV) tells us "… Awake and sing, ye that dwell in dust: for thy dew is as the dew of herbs …" and Psalm 113: 3 (KJV) says "From the rising of the sun unto the going down of the same, the Lord's name is to be praised." What about you? How do God's wonders inspire you?

5. Izzie was taught by a compassionate neighbor that even though she may not have an earthly father she had a heavenly father. "… his name is the Lord—and rejoice before him. A father to the fatherless, a defender of widows." (Psalm 68: 4b-5 NIV) Do you know those who need this assurance? Share if appropriate.

6. Izzie is reminded by Pastor Creighton of two truths in scripture when she is frustrated by false accusations. "For consider him that endured such contradiction of sinners against himself, lest ye be wearied" (Hebrews 12:3 KJV). "And let us not be weary in well doing: for in due season we shall reap, if we faint not" (Galatians 6:9 KJV). Have you experienced being misunderstood or false accusations? What do Scriptures advise?

MORE STORIES FROM SALLY JO

The Winter Solstice Bride
(ebook short story)

And Then Blooms Love

Stumbling Upon Love

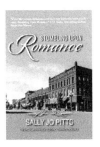

Made in the USA
Columbia, SC
09 July 2021